secrets of my HOLLYWOOD LIFe
FAMILY AFFAIRS

a novel by

Jen Calonita

LITTLE, BROWN AND COMPANY
Books for Young Readers
New York   Boston

Also by Jen Calonita:
SECRETS OF MY HOLLYWOOD LIFE
and
SECRETS OF MY HOLLYWOOD LIFE *on location*

Little, Brown and Company

Hachette Book Group USA
237 Park Avenue, New York, NY 10017
Visit our Web site at www.lb-teens.com

First Edition: May 2008

Library of Congress Cataloging-in-Publication Data
Calonita, Jen.
    Secrets of my Hollywood life : family affairs / by Jen Calonita. — 1st ed.
        p. cm.
    Summary: Sixteen-year-old actress Kaitlin Burke reluctantly joins forces with castmate Sky when a scheming new actress tries to steal the show.
     ISBN 978-0-316-11799-9
    [1. Actors and actresses — Fiction. 2. Interpersonal relations — Fiction.
3. Hollywood (Los Angeles, Calif.) — Fiction.]   I. Title.
    PZ7.C1346Shl   2007
    [Fic] — dc22   2007035302

10 9 8 7 6 5 4 3 2 1

RRD-C

Printed in the United States of America

Book design by Tracy Shaw

For my parents, Nick and Lynn Calonita, with much love

FAMILY AFFAIR—SEASON 15, EPISODE 4
"The Truth is Always the Hardest to Hear"

FADE IN:

1. INT. HAMILTON HOSPITAL, PAIGE'S HOSPITAL ROOM—
AFTERNOON

PAIGE has fallen into a coma after having surgery to repair
the damage she sustained to her vertebrae from the limo crash
on the day of KRYSTAL and LEO's wedding. DENNIS, KRYTAL, LEO,
SAMANTHA and SARA cling to each other as DOCTOR BRADEN
discusses Paige's weakening condition.

                    DR. BRADEN
    I'm not going to lie to you, I thought we lost her. But
    she's stable now and we have high hopes that she'll
    pull through this.

                    DENNIS
    My wife has to make it, Dr. Braden. How can we
    help her?

                    DR. BRADEN
    Talk to her. We've found that sometimes people in
    comas can hear their loved ones. Unfortunately, in
    Paige's case, the coma isn't her greatest obstacle.

                    KRYSTAL
    I know the surgery was rocky, but I thought you said
    it was a success.

DR. BRADEN

It was, but Paige also lost a lot of blood and needs a
transfusion. Paige's blood type is quite rare and no
one in your family is a match.

SAMANTHA

Our mother is a fighter, Dr. Braden. She beat breast
cancer, a drive-by shooting, and survived the
Buchanan Manor fire. I know she'll hold on till we
find someone.

Dr. Braden pulls Dennis, Krystal, and Leo aside to continue
talking. Through her tears, Sara sees COLBY, the tall,
beautiful new girl at Samantha and Sara's school. Colby's
wearing torn jeans and a beat-up hooded sweatshirt. She's
standing at the vending machine, but can't stop staring at
the Buchanans.

SARA

Hey, Sam, isn't that Colby? (Sam looks over.) What's
she doing here? She's been trying to decide on a candy
bar forever.

SAMANTHA

Maybe she's got family in the hospital too.

SARA

I don't think she has family. (whispering) Lila told
me she had to get to school at 6 AM on Tuesday to

get ready for the pep rally and she found Colby
sleeping in a storage closet! Colby begged her not to
tell anyone.

                        SAM
You think Colby's homeless? (Sara nods.) That's awful!

The girls look at Colby. Colby sees them staring and turns
to walk away, but hesitates. Finally she walks over to the
twins.

                       COLBY
Hi, Sam. Hi, Sara. I'm sorry if I'm freaking you guys
out by staring at you.

                     SAMANTHA
(quickly) Not at all! How are you? Do you know
someone in the hospital too?

                       COLBY
(shakes her head) Um, no. I . . .

                       SARA
(sounding suspicious) Then what are you doing here?

                       COLBY
I . . . I . . . I saw the story about your mom in today's
paper. I thought I could . . . help.

SAMANTHA

That's sweet, Colby, but I don't think anyone can help us right now.

COLBY

I think I can.

DENNIS

(appearing at the girls' side) Girls, Dr. Braden said we can go in and see your mom now.

SARA

(voice quivering) Dad, how long does he think she has if we don't find a match?

DENNIS

Sweetie, we'll find someone. I promise. (looking at Colby) Who's your friend?

SARA

This is Colby. We know her from school. (to Colby) I don't mean to be rude, but we're in the middle of a life and death struggle with our mother. You need to leave.

COLBY

But I . . . I overheard the doctor. My blood type is rare too. Maybe I'm a match.

DENNIS

That's very kind, Colby, but it's not that simple. I
appreciate you being here for the girls, but I think
you should go now. (Dennis motions for Dr. Braden.)
Colby fights back tears as she looks at the
Buchanans' distraught faces. Dr. Braden moves to
take Colby away.

DR. BRADEN

Miss, I'm going to have to ask you to leave. This is a
family matter.

COLBY

(starting to cry) I didn't want it to happen this way.
I wanted more time, but now . . . (she pulls Dr. Braden
away from the others.) You don't understand. I am
family. I'm Paige's . . . Paige's . . . (whispers) daughter.

one: *The New Girl in Town*

"EIGHT more lines than me! EIGHT!" My costar, Sky Mackenzie, charges into my dressing room, screaming like a banshee.

I look down at my script for "The Truth Is Always the Hardest to Hear," which is the fourth episode of *Family Affair*'s fifteenth season. Then I look over at my assistant, Nadine, who is ironing my Stitch jeans for my date with Austin. She rolls her eyes.

"What are you talking about?" I ask calmly. You see, as much as I loathe my troublemaking costar, I finally found time to read Nadine's favorite best-selling self-help book (*Unlock the True You*) and I now know it's not a good idea to let Sky's negative behavior get to me. So far the attitude change is working. We've been back on the set of our series *Family Affair* for almost a month and life has been blissfully incident- and tabloid-fodder–free.

"I don't usually count my lines, Sky, but I'm pretty sure I don't have eight more than you do," I say. "I just finished reading through the script and it looks like we're both at Paige's bedside after Colby's blood is used for the transfusion."

Sky stomps over to my well-worn Pottery Barn brown leather chair and begins flipping through the script on my lap, her long hair hitting me in the face. I'm not used to seeing Sky with black hair again. She went blond for the Hutch Adams movie, *Pretty Young Assassins* (*PYA*), which we shot together this summer, but the creators of our show made her dye it back to Sara's black. Sky's hair follicles must have gone into shock from all the chemicals because my *FA* hair stylist, Paul, told me Sky's hair is falling out in chunks. Now she has to wear extensions to cover the damage. I think of Sky going bald and can't help smirking.

"What are you smiling about? This isn't funny, K," Sky snaps, her bony chest rising and falling rapidly. I can see her rib cage through her tight black V-neck tee and sheer cream tunic top. Sky spots Nadine bent over the iron and her eyes narrow.

Personal assistants are a sore subject with Sky. She never seems to be able to keep one on her payroll for more than six months. Sky's last assistant, her cousin Madison, was fired after she was caught leaking information about *PYA* to the press. (We found out Madison was the one feeding the tabs awful stories about me over the summer so I wasn't sorry to see her go.)

"I'm not talking about *your* line count," Sky adds. "Alexis has more lines than me and she's only been in four episodes.

Colby is a throwaway character! Her story arc is only supposed to last a few months. How could she already have more airtime?" Sky pouts. "She's trying to take over the show, K! I can feel it."

"That's what this bonding session is about? Alexis? Does this mean you've found someone new to loathe and I'm off the hook?" I ask hopefully. For once, Sky's hatred is aimed at a costar other than me, which is great because I could sure use the break.

Since we were four, we've been starring on the hit prime-time soap *Family Affair* playing Paige and Dennis's fraternal twin daughters, Sam and Sara — I'm Sam, the Goody Two-shoes, Sara is the bad seed — and Sky has been making my on-set life miserable since day one.

Things got infinitely worse last year, after we started competing for the same movie roles and *TV Tome* named me the hottest young actress on TV. Of course I was excited, but I was preoccupied too. The truth is, around that time, I was getting burned out by the incessant fighting with Sky, both on the set and in the tabloids. The world knows me as "TV star Kaitlin Burke" or "SAM!" or "Teen It Girl" on one of many *Entertainment Weekly* lists. But I thought it was time I learned who the girl behind the camera really was.

So my best pal Liz and I concocted a scheme to give me a few months of anonymity and a much-needed break from Sky. I disguised myself as a British exchange student named Rachel Rogers and enrolled at Liz's high school in Santa

Rosita. The experiment worked. Taking a break from Hollywood made me realize that I have to leave more time in my hectic schedule to just chill. It taught me how to trust people more and to open up to guys. (It's also where I met my boyfriend, Austin Meyers.)

Juggling interviews with Ellen DeGeneres and finding time to do French homework was tricky, but I was doing just fine until Sky butted in. She found out about my double life and blew my cover. As if attempting to destroy my career with lies like "Kaitlin hates Hollywood!" weren't bad enough, Sky continued to torture me by getting a last-minute role in *PYA*. She spent the summer shoot trying to make the director, Hutch Adams, hate me, break up my relationship with Austin, and tarnish the career I had just patched up.

I guess you could say, after all that, I'm not feeling much love toward my costar of almost thirteen years. Sue me.

Sky purses her full lips, which she must have plumped up with Lip Venom again, and scowls at me. "Don't tell me you've fallen for that sickeningly sweet act Alexis is selling everyone from *Access Hollywood* to craft services. I'm not buying it. I can spot a climber when I see one."

"You would know," I murmur. Oops. That's not very *True You* of me. "I mean, cut her some slack. She's only been on set for a month. She doesn't know how things work around here yet. I'm sure she's just overdoing it to try to fit in. It's got to be hard joining a cast that's been together forever."

"K, for once, could you worry about yourself instead of someone else?" Sky rolls her eyes. "We have to contain this girl's popularity before it spirals out of control." I snort. "Only two of her episodes have aired so far and already Alexis is the hottest thing to hit TV since *Grey's Anatomy*! The critics love her, the message boards are all about her, and I heard she's getting invites to all the big parties," Sky whines. "Her smug mug is all over this week's *People*! If we're not careful, Sam and Sara could be history and Colby could be the new, hot teen star of our show."

For a second, I feel a slight pang of jealousy. I mean, I'll admit, initially I was thinking the same thing Sky is now. When I read the first script of the season and saw Colby's storyline, I panicked. Colby is Alexis's character, a new girl at Summerville High that Sam and Sara befriend in the first episode. They don't know Colby's homeless, or that she's got a deep connection to their family. Our creator/executive producer Tom Pullman told the cast the character of Colby was created to cause waves with all the characters on the show for the first half of the season and then the storyline will be wrapped up and the character written off. After I heard that, I calmed down.

Still, I can't help but wonder: If Sky and I are as popular as they say we are, why do they need Colby?

I'm sure I'm just letting Sky's venomous thoughts get to me. Just because Alexis is around doesn't mean we'll be any less popular. That's ridiculous, right? I mean, having Alexis here has its advantages. Like giving the paparazzi a new face to hound. Hee-hee. "Sky, I think you're just being paranoid," I say finally.

"No I'm not!" Sky says. "Don't you remember what happened to Mischa Barton on *The O.C.?* When they needed a ratings boost, they killed her off! Then the show tanked. I don't want Sara's Beamer to flip over the side of a cliff with us in it and then *FA* to be canceled!"

Hmm . . . maybe she's right. No, no. That's silly! Think, Kaitlin. If Sky is venting to you, she must have an ulterior motive. That's what I should really be concentrating on. "Sky, this is crazy talk," I tell her. "Alexis has been nothing but nice. She's not trying to take our roles away. She's just trying to do her own." I pause. "And since when are you and I an 'us'?"

"I'm not thrilled about making you my confidant either," Sky snaps, her dark eyes blazing. "I just wanted to warn you."

I'm only half paying attention now as I reread the script for episode four, which we start shooting tomorrow. We usually shoot an episode over the course of two weeks. The writers pump out a story, two weeks later we film the one-hour drama, and two weeks after that, it airs. That's the one thing you can count on in television — a consistently grueling schedule for all twenty-four episodes of the season (we've learned the viewers hate repeats so we shoot more episodes than most). I look up and smile sweetly at Sky, trying to remain Zen. "Well, you don't have to," I reply. "I can take care of myself just fine. Thanks for your concern."

"Suit yourself." Sky tosses her hair over her shoulder. "But remember: Our contracts are up this year, K. *I'm* not worried about being renewed, of course," she says ominously, "but if I were you, I'd make sure you're seen as valuable around here.

More valuable than the new girl. Don't say I didn't tell you to watch your back." Sky turns on her black open-toed Christian Louboutin heels and slams the door, knocking my newly framed picture of Austin, Liz, and her boyfriend, Josh, off the periwinkle-painted wall.

At the mention of the word "contracts," I freeze. Contract negotiations are not something to joke about. Everyone who works in TV has heard stories about stars whose contracts have not been picked up after a major set squabble or a disagreement about salary increases. Even the most popular star on a hit show isn't guaranteed to be asked back. That's why contract negotiation year is always one I sweat a little. I laugh nervously. "Sky is such a drama queen. I have no reason to worry about my conract," I say to Nadine. I silently pray she will offer me some reassurance.

Nadine eyes me over the ironing board. She's giving me her Yoda-like wise personal assistant face, which means I'm about to get a lecture.

"What?" I say, my voice sounding shrill. "You think she's right about my contract?"

"No, silly," Nadine laughs.

"Then what?" I ask. "Don't tell me you think I was being too mean to Sky!" I groan, feeling a sudden wave of guilt. I'm not very good at being the mean girl.

"That's not what I was thinking either," Nadine says. "I was thinking how glad I am that you got a backbone on that awful movie set this summer. You won't let Sky walk all over you this season."

"Definitely not," I say happily, feeling instantly better. I throw my legs over the side of the armchair and wiggle my freshly painted pink toes. I'm not in this afternoon's scene, so after my four-hour wardrobe fitting, I can leave work at eight to meet Austin, Liz, and Josh for dinner at Les Deux. It's this restaurant/popular night club known for its desserts, like the cupcake tower full of red velvet, lemon, carrot-pecan, and vanilla treats. Yum.

Rhapsodizing about cupcakes makes me think of the other thing I long for: seeing Austin. We haven't hung out since he started school a few days ago. I take out my Sidekick and e-mail him. He and Liz should be in English right now.

PRINCESSLEIA25: Hey U. How's English? Boring w/o me? :)
WOOKIESRULE: U said it. How's work?
PRINCESSLEIA25: Good. School?
WOOKIESRULE: Painful. Already. :(
PRINCESSLEIA25: Sounds like U need cheering up.
WOOKIESRULE: Seeing U cheers me up, Burke. CU tonite.

Aww . . . how cute is my boyfriend? My date is still hours away, but I'm already almost ready to go. I'm wearing an orange Chloé V-neck sweater, tightened at the waist with an oversize brown belt. I'm going to pair the sweater with the jeans Nadine is ironing and have Paul quickly freshen up my hair. (Having a makeup artist and a hair stylist at my disposal is one of my favorite perks!) Paul curled my honey-colored hair, which touches my midback, for this morning's hospital scene, and my makeup artist, Shelly, just touched up my eyeliner, so I should be good. Seeing my boyfriend, watching Sky squirm, wearing my new Gucci brown suede boots — could this day get any better?

"But then again," Nadine frowns and scratches her head as she turns off the iron. Her strawberry red hair almost touches her collarbone now and she's got a green butterfly clip pinning back the bangs she's growing out. Nadine's wearing her standard set attire — a long-sleeved tee, well-worn jeans, and sneakers (today's are pink Pumas). She loves how casual assistants and the crew dress. "Maybe Sky does have a small point."

"What?" I ask, typing out a quick Note to Self memo on my Sidekick. It sounds cheesy, I know, but I've found e-mailing myself is the best way to keep track of my crazy schedule. It also helps to have a Sidekick and a super-organized assistant like Nadine who watches my back.

"I hope all this instant media love doesn't give Alexis a huge ego," Nadine says with a frown. She sidesteps the rack of shoes that wardrobe dropped off for me to try on and squeezes her slim torso around the large sack of fan mail that she's sorting for autograph requests and the occasional craze-o letter that has to be turned over to the police. "Sky is right about one thing. Alexis is in every magazine this week being called the hottest new star on the tube and the best thing to happen to *Family Affair* in years."

"She is?" Jealousy begins to rear its ugly head again and I try to push the thought out of my mind. "Wow."

"It's got to be overwhelming getting so much attention for your first acting job," says Nadine. "I mean, what has she done before? A few commercials in Canada? Her head must be spinning. We've all seen what can happen to a teen star with amazing potential when their flame burns too bright too quickly. They crash and burn," Nadine warns. "But I'm sure Alexis will be fine. The set gossip is probably wrong."

"What gossip?" I'm curious.

"It's stupid, really." Nadine looks uncomfortable. "I shouldn't be spreading rumors."

It goes against *True You* principles, but I don't care. I want to know. "I won't tell anyone," I beg.

Nadine sighs. "I overheard people whispering in wardrobe the other day about how Alexis is trying to butter up the writing staff to get more scenes," she says. "Apparently she's always bringing them cookies during meetings and stopping by to praise the lines they've written her."

"Really?" Huh. I never thought of doing that. I mean, I always thank the writers, but I've never baked them my famous caramel brownies or anything. I frown. "You think she's really trying to get more airtime? She's in plenty of scenes already."

Nadine shakes her head. "I'm sure people are just jealous of all the attention she's getting," she says. Nadine sticks the new issue of *TV Tome* in front of me. "Like this. Take a look at this article."

"Who's that girl?" have been the words on everyone's lips in the *Tome* office, where we can't get enough of gorgeous redhead Alexis Holden, who plays secret-ridden Colby on this season's *Family Affair.* The 17-year-old should spice up Summerville High, where fraternal twins Sam and Sara (eternally dueling costars Kaitlin Burke and Sky Mackenzie) walk the halls. Sure, the ratings are still stellar for this aging nighttime soap, but the addition of Alexis, as Paige's (Melissa Ralton) possible long-lost illegitimate daughter, should add some juice to the stuck-in-a-rut storylines of the past few seasons (Sam and Sara go on a triple-date with their parents? Yawn). Alexis's past seems as secret as Colby's at this point—all the show mouthpieces will say is that she was handpicked by executive producer and creator Tom Pullman for the role and she hails from Vancouver, where she was raised by her single mom—but who cares? As long as the girl can act better than that nitwit who plays Penelope, we'll TiVo in. (*Family Affair* airs Sundays at 9 PM EST.)

• •

I'm quiet for a moment. The article reminds me of a Hollywood Secret that is particularly worrisome. HOLLY-WOOD SECRET NUMBER ONE: There are a few telltale signs that a TV show's days are numbered. One is when a head writer leaves (that hasn't happened yet. Tom has been writing episodes for years). Another is when a show does a ton of stunt-casting. (Um . . . we did have Gwen Stefani drop by *Family Affair* last year. Hey, she's a genuine fan!) The third is when a bunch of new characters are brought on board . . . oh no!

"Do you think our show has gotten stale?" I ask worriedly. "Do you think that's why they hired Alexis?" As much as I sometimes complain about my crazy life on a big TV show, I wouldn't want it to disappear. You hear that, God? I actually love being on *FA!*

"*FA* is the longest running primetime drama on TV and you have top twenty Nielsen ratings," Nadine reassures me. "That's not stale. I'm sure they just hired Alexis to pull off some new plot twists."

"You're right." I tell myself, "I'm sure we've got nothing to worry about with Alexis. She's probably just trying to fit in and maybe extend her story arc for a bit." I grin. "I can't say I blame her. This is a pretty fun place to work — most of the time."

"Yeah, chauffeured rides, a fabulous assistant, a killer time slot — I would have to agree you have it pretty good." Nadine grins.

My stomach rumbles. "Hey, want to go over to crafty and see if they have any of that Oreo ice cream left?" Crafty is our nickname for craft services, which is basically a meal on wheels for the set. No matter what time of day it is you can find food, snacks, and drinks.

"Aren't you meeting Austin for dinner later?" Nadine asks.

"Yeah, but that doesn't mean I can't have a snack now." I race her to the door and fling it open. The long, sparsely decorated dressing room corridor is crowded as usual, with actors in costume racing to their next scene, crew members carrying scenery or equipment, and weary production assistants (we call them P.A.s) on their short lunch break. Nadine and I have barely taken two steps past Sky's door, where loud alternative rock music is playing, when we hear my name, or some variation of it.

"Kate-Kate! Katie-Kins! KAITLIN!" My mom is yelling this as she and my younger brother, Matty, run toward me. Mom's in full work mode in a fitted white pantsuit that offsets her airbrush-tanned body. Her long honey-colored hair, dyed to match my own, is pulled into a ponytail. "There you are! We knew we'd find you hiding out in your dressing room e-mailing Austin for the hundredth time today."

I ignore the dig at my boyfriend. Mom seems to dislike Austin for the very reason I adore him — he's not in the business. "Actually I've been memorizing my new script and now Nadine and I are off to get ice cream. Do you . . ." I stop midsentence at the sight of Matty. His hazel eyes are glazed over and the grin on his face is so wide, it could light up our whole soundstage. "What's with Matt?"

"We've got fantastic news!" Mom gushes. "We didn't want to tell you till it was official, but guess who is a new recurring character on *Family Affair*?" She doesn't wait for my answer. "YOUR BROTHER!"

Wow. After years of Mom begging, fighting, and practically bribing the writers, Matty has finally managed to get on the show. I grab my younger clone — my whole blond, green-eyed family could be an advertisement for the sunny state of California — and give him a fierce hug. "Way to go, Matty! How'd it happen?"

Matt takes a deep breath. "You know how I'm always asking you to get me a job here and Tom always tells you they don't have any parts for a guy my age?" I nod. "Well, Tom called our agent last week and told him they were actually looking for someone this year and he wanted me to audition," Matty says proudly. He's dressed to the nines in gray pants, a burgundy vest, and a white button-down shirt. Very Justin Timberlake. "But Mom called Tom and made him promise not to show me any favoritism just because we're related and hiring me would be a great public relations move. You know, because they'd be able to say they have two Burkes on the same show."

"How professional," Nadine says lightly.

Mom raises her eyebrow at Nadine in that menacing way of hers and Nadine clams up. Mom and Nadine don't always see eye to eye on Mom's showbiz tactics.

"Anyway," Matty says, "Tom and everyone there loved me. They said I was perfect for the part of Dylan, a new junior high student at Summerville High." Our fake high school actually houses students in seventh to twelfth grade.

"That is awesome!" I hug him again and he doesn't fight me. "It will be nice having a built-in ally around here."

"I guess it will be kind of cool to be known as Kaitlin Burke's bro," Matty admits. "As long as it doesn't overshadow my performance."

"Of course." I grin.

"And this means we'll have the same on-set tutor now," Matty adds. "I can't wait to give Donna the heave-ho." Matt's been homeschooled by a private tutor since kindergarten. Our parents said they knew he'd be a big star someday so why not just start with a tutor from day one?

"Tell me more about this Dylan," I prod my brother. "I don't think I've heard of him yet."

"He's this mysterious outsider who wants to hang out with Sam and Sara," Matty explains breathlessly.

"Oh wait," I realize. "I think I heard Trevor talking about this. Is he the guy Ryan's going to be tutoring? The geeky kid from the broken home?" Trevor Wainwright plays my boyfriend, Ryan, on the show.

"I wouldn't call him geeky," Matty scoffs. "But yeah, that's him."

"I probably got that part wrong," I say quickly. "Anyway, this is great news, Matty. How many episodes are you on for?" I smile politely at a crewman passing by who is carrying

Sheetrock and paint cans. Maybe he's heading over to the *FA* wall of fame, in the soundstage entrance hall. That's where there are larger-than-life, hand-painted drawings of the main cast members of our show. Tom swears they're going to redo mine this year. The picture they have of me is from when I'm thirteen and have a mouth full of metal. It's a painful reminder to walk past every day.

"They said I'm on for eight," Matt explains, watching the action swirl around him. "But since I'm only thirteen, child labor laws say I can only work five hours a day. Isn't that ridiculous?"

"How cruel," Nadine agrees. I try to stifle a laugh. Nadine likes Matty, but he tried to get her to do assistant duties for him on the set of *PYA* (he had a small part as my character's brother), and I think it left a sour taste in her mouth.

"I know," Matt complains, oblivious to Nadine's sarcasm. "I mean, I'm sure they'd be willing to give me more lines if they didn't have to write around these restrictions. They can't get the full range of my talent on only five hours of . . . WHOA. Who is *that?*"

We all turn and see Alexis Holden strutting toward us. Her long, flowing red hair (think the hair of a younger, pre-partying Lindsay Lohan) bounces behind her as she struts past us in a formfitting black V-neck tank dress and knee-high stiletto boots. She looks way older than seventeen, as the bio Tom gave us claims she is. Alexis sees me and squeals.

"KATE-KATE!" She gives me a big hug. "How are you

doing? You were awesome in this morning's scene. I wish I could be that cool and calm under the glare of the cameras." She looks at my family and Nadine. "I love this girl."

"Thanks, but I've got a lot of practice. You'll get there." I blush. Gee, Sky has Alexis all wrong. She's so nice! "Guys, this is Alexis, our new guest costar," I add. "Mom, you know Alexis. She's playing Colby. And this is my brother, Matty. He's new this season too."

Alexis turns and squeezes Matty, shoving her chest into his face. The slight come-on can't be helped since Alexis towers over Matt, but either way, Matty doesn't move a muscle. His mouth is practically hitting the floor. "I'm so glad there is someone else new around here!" she gushes. "We have to stick together." Matty nods.

"So this is Alexis," my mother swoons. "I've read so much about you already! You're going to be a huge star just like my Kaitlin. I can feel it. Do you have representation, dear?"

Alexis shakes her head. "The studio says I shouldn't waste the money. They can do it for me." Her voice is always a little raspy, like she just rolled out of bed.

"That's wonderful for now, but eventually you'll want someone to manage you, I'm sure," Mom presses. "Don't hesitate to ask Kaitlin or Matty for my number."

"That's so sweet." Alexis takes my mother's hand and squeezes it firmly. "I'll keep it in mind."

"Nadine and I were just on our way to crafty," I say. "Want to come?"

"Oh, I wish I could, but I was just on my way to the writers' room to bring them some cookies I made," she says, pointing to the bag on her arm.

"So you like to bake?" Nadine asks innocently.

Alexis nods. "I used to love cooking for my friends back home. Baking for everybody here makes me a little less homesick," she says, sounding sad. "What's your favorite cookie? I'll bake you guys something next."

Nadine and I quickly look at each other. I guess that set gossip was wrong. Alexis really is just trying to fit in. "You don't have to do that," I tell her. I don't want to add that I'd probably eat the whole batch in one sitting and not be able to fit into wardrobe.

"Are you sure?" Alexis asks. "The writing staff says I make a mean oatmeal raisin." She laughs.

"I'm positive," I say, but inside, I feel a twinge of jealousy again. She's brand-new and taking the set by storm. It's hard not to feel slightly competitive.

Maybe I will make those caramel brownies to bring in next week.

"Have fun." I smile.

"I will," she says. And with that, Alexis saunters off, leaving the group of us to gape at her model-perfect figure and runway-worthy exit.

FRIDAY, 9/13
NOTE TO SELF:

Dinner w/ A, Liz & Josh @ Les Deux @ 8 PM
*Have Nadine double-check reservation
Mon. call time: on location in Malibu
Hair & makeup @ 5 AM, pickup @ 6 AM
Mon. @ 7 PM: J.T. bash @ Hyde
Tues. call time: 6 AM
Tues. @ 6 PM: Priceless Benefit

TWO: *TGIF*

I've just discovered something about Hollywood hot spots:
Just because you have a reservation doesn't mean you can
get in. Literally.

"Are you sure this is where Les Deux is?" Liz frowns as she
peers through the tinted glass windows of our Lincoln, her
purple satin minidress shimmering in the glow of a nearby
street lamp. Her olive face, dazzling with glitter foundation,
is scrunched up in concentration, and her brown curly
mane is tamed under one of her signature head scarves.

"I think so," I say and bite my lip. The hot Euro-style club
and restaurant is as well known for its hard-to-find entrance
as it is for its dessert. There's a parking lot full of Beamers
and Mercedes, so I know we're close, but the nearby buildings
look too nondescript to be Les Deux. I've only been here
once for a party and the promoters ushered me in so quickly
I didn't get a good look at the outside.

"Aren't big stars like you given the secret code ahead of

time?" teases Austin. He says this as he's massaging my shoulders and it's giving me goose bumps.

"I'll go look for it first," my bodyguard/driver, Rodney, says. "Larry the Liar could be skulking nearby. I don't care if it's against the law to pummel the paparazzi. If that guy gets in Kate's face again, I'm taking him down with one punch."

Rod could, too. Especially after his stunt training on *PYA*. (The film was Rod's first big-screen stuntman credit. Rod's goal is to be the next Arnold Schwarzenegger. Minus the Governor title.) Rodney can be pretty intimidating with his 300-pound frame, bald head, and black sunglasses, but the big guy is a teddy bear when it comes to me.

"It was an accident," I remind him, thinking of the event last week when Larry the Liar tripped over the rope and smashed his Nikon D50 into my right cheek. The bluish-purple bruise has finally gone down; Shelly had a nasty time covering it with concealer.

Suddenly I see someone walk out of a Craftsman-style bungalow at the edge of the parking lot. At first I think they're just leaving their house, but what's a home doing in a parking lot? Then I see two more people, dressed fabulously, exit with take-out bags. That's it! "I remember where we go in," I say excitedly. "It's that building over there!"

"I was beginning to worry we wouldn't get to have any of those lemon cupcakes you rhapsodized about the whole way over," Liz's boyfriend, Josh, jokes. Even in a loose blue silk shirt, you can make out Josh's defined upper body muscles.

He's a kickboxer, just like Liz, and the two met several months ago, around the same time I met Austin. I love that the four of us double-date. It's so adult.

"You shouldn't have worried," Austin says, his mouth twitching. "The Burke name guarantees the presence of the paparazzi and admission to any venue." He winks at me.

I break into a huge grin. Austin loves teasing me about the perks of fame. And okay, I can admit it. Sometimes it really is fun being me.

With the four of us behind him, Rodney walks us to the valet, who is guarding a long line of pretty people. How did we miss this crowd? Rodney whispers my name to the valet who turns and whispers it to a harried guy with a clipboard and the door opens to let us inside. People groan as we walk past them.

"Have fun! Make sure you bring me a cupcake!" Rodney calls after us. "Or two!"

A super-skinny hostess with a cute bob leads us past the gorgeous, modern lounge with rock walls and black leather booths, and onto the patio, where an old French film is being projected on the wall. A fountain bubbles in the middle of several couches and ottomans; trees and bushes dot the serene landscape. The girl seats us at a private set of leather couches and wordlessly hands us each a menu. "I'll be back for your drink order," she says before walking over to the outdoor bar.

Salivating, I quickly scan the eats. The Italian menu looks delish, but I can't help reading about the desserts first. Red velvet, lemon, carrot-pecan, and vanilla cupcakes . . . ahhh. I want to order them all. As I settle into the comfy couch, I feel my achy shoulders start to relax. I happily peek over my menu and stare at my boyfriend.

Austin's blond mop of hair is hanging over his turquoise eyes. As usual, he looks like he just walked out of an American Eagle ad. He's wearing a button-down polo and dark brown khakis.

"What's on your mind, Burke?" he asks without looking up. I blush madly. He's caught me staring at him. Again.

"Nothing," I reply. "I'm just so happy to see all of you. It's been such a loooonnnnnggg week without you guys." After *PYA* wrapped, I had two blissful weeks off and the four of us hung out 24/7. After *FA* started back up, we hung out at night or they'd come by the set (I love showing off my boyfriend!), but now that school has started again, everyone's schedules are all over the map and we're limited to getting together on weekends. It's so depressing.

Liz's smile turns into a yawn. "We missed you too," she mumbles sleepily. "Especially when we were sitting in American history and Mrs. Watson was droning on about our gazillion-page textbook, *The American Nation*."

"We have to read the second chapter on prehistory to the eighteen hundreds and write a short essay by Monday about the most trying time for settlers in the English colonies," complains Austin. "I wish I could rewind three weeks and be back at your house, lying by the pool."

"Me too," Liz chimes in, resting her hands under her chin.

Her eyes look heavy, like she's ready to go to sleep. "I'd even be your assistant again. And that's saying a lot."

"Thanks," I say sarcastically. Liz was my second assistant (Nadine holding the longtime "first" throne, of course) on *PYA* and it wouldn't be a lie to say she hated the job (Tip: Friends shouldn't hire friends). Some good did come out of the experience, though. Liz met Daniella Cook, Hutch's producing partner on *PYA*, and made such a great impression that Daniella gave her an after-school job helping out in the production office. Now Liz is seriously considering a career as a producer someday.

"I am so tired," Liz whines. "But I missed you too much to cancel." She frowns, revealing the dimple in her left cheek. "Between school, kickboxing, and working with Daniella, I could curl up under this table and not wake up till Monday."

Josh laughs, his face turning as red as his strawberry blond hair. "Just wait till your SAT prep class starts next week. You're going to be really wiped." Liz moans.

"Were you able to get into the one you wanted?" I flag down the waitress to take our order before Liz starts snoring.

"Yep. We have it during fifth period," Austin says. "We take that the first half of the year and then second semester we take statistics. Liz and I got into the same class."

"I'm stuck taking it on Saturdays because my school doesn't have a prep during the day," Josh complains. While Liz and Austin go to private Clark High School in Santa

Rosita (which is where I joined them for a few months), Josh goes to the public school across town. "What about you, Kates?" Josh adds. "Are you taking a prep course too?"

I blush. "I don't think so. Monique has been quizzing me, but she says I shouldn't sweat the test too much since I'll probably be on *FA* till I'm fifty." I laugh, but when I think about it, it's not really funny. What if the show is suddenly canceled or I'm slammed in the press about something really awful and I'm fired? If I get a bad score on the SATs, I'll never get into a good college. And if I don't get into a good college, I won't be able to find a new career and new job prospects. And my money will run out. I feel myself start to perspire. An image of Mom, Dad, Matty, and me huddled on a street corner wearing shredded Prada coats flashes through my mind. I shudder.

I guess I could try out for *Dancing with the Stars* as a last resort. Double shudder.

"Are you cold?" Austin asks. I shake my head.

"The SATs are all I can think about," Austin says to us. "Junior year is time to get serious, you know? I don't have lacrosse till spring, so I've got no excuse not to hit the books. Coach wanted me to take track, but I'm not a hundred-meter-dash kind of guy. I'd rather concentrate on getting a killer SAT score so I can get into UCLA or Notre Dame or Boston College."

Wait a minute. Austin is moving to Boston? The realization hits me like a ton of bricks. Liz and Austin are going to college in two years and they're probably going to pick someplace far away. My stomach starts to growl in protest. In the past, I never worried when Liz brought up college because it seemed like such a long way off, but it's really not. Not anymore. I picture myself waving goodbye to Liz and Austin as they drive off to points unknown. Pretty soon we won't get to hang out like this anymore. We'll see each other on breaks and during the summer, but we'll spend most of the year apart. It takes every ounce of energy I have left not to burst into tears right in the middle of the courtyard at Les Deux.

Austin and Liz's futures seem set. So where does that leave me? Do I even want to go to college? I already have a great job. Nadine is always bugging me about college, saying it's really important for my growth. She recites her list of popular stars, like Natalie Portman, who've taken time off to go to class. That's when I say that people like Natalie Portman and Julia Stiles weren't starring on a hit TV show that shoots nine months out of the year when they went to college. But in theory, I guess I could go, if I want to. And if I don't totally fail my SATs. I should talk to Monique about this. She's been my tutor since I started on *FA* and it's her job to prepare me for life by teaching me well, right? My PSAT scores weren't horrible, but they weren't stellar either. I should get SAT help. Just in case.

"So you're thinking of a school on the East Coast?" I ask Austin, trying to sound calm and not at all concerned.

"Maybe," Austin says, looking pensive. "But my top choice is UCLA."

Oh thank God.

"NYU is still my top choice," Liz says. "I've always wanted to go there, but now that I want to be a producer, I'm obsessed with getting in. Their film school rocks. And New York seems like such a great city to live in."

"I will miss you tons, but it really does seem perfect for you," I agree regretfully.

New York really is full of possibilities. Every time I go to New York to do the talk-show circuit, I fall even more in love with that city. In New York, no one even notices celebrities. It's true. There's no paparazzi brigade following you down the street, no cameramen in the bushes waiting to get a picture of your face dripping with Pinkberry yogurt. I wonder what it would be like to live there. It sounds serene, if you forget about the street traffic and constantly honking taxis. But I could probably drown them out with a noise machine from Sharper Image.

I have a fleeting image of Liz and me as roomies at NYU. Eating at Serendipity, flagging a cab with our arms full of shopping bags, Rollerblading in Central Park ... How fun would it be to live 3,000 miles away from home and still be with Lizzie? Sure, I get to go away anytime I shoot a movie on location, but still! If I went to college, I'd be away *all year*. That would mean no parents, no rules, and no publicist. That's kind of cool. Now I'm a little jealous, even if the idea is far-fetched. I push the fantasy out of my head and try to pay attention to what Liz is saying.

"I just hope I can keep up with everything I have on my

plate," Liz says, looking stressed. "I'm on overload already and it's only mid-September. I don't even have an hour a week to watch *Grey's Anatomy*."

"Don't forget driver's ed is starting too," Austin says with a twinkle in his eye.

"That's right," I say, happy to change the subject. "I can't wait for you guys to get your licenses and drive me around. Rodney is going to be so bummed he's not my main chauffeur anymore," I joke. "Austin, your birthday is first, so I guess you're hired." His birthday is October 26, which makes him just shy of two months older than me. My birthday is December 11.

"I can't believe I'm going to be seventeen," Austin marvels.

"Welcome to the club, man," Josh pats Austin on the back. Josh just got his license, but his mom still won't let him take the car at night.

"Any idea what you want, Meyers?" I ask. "Other than a candy apple red Jeep Cherokee?"

Austin shrugs. "Not really — other than you having the day off." He leans over and gives me a kiss. He's so cute.

"I don't turn seventeen till March," Liz laments. "I'm lucky they even let me sign up for the class now."

"Backtrack," Josh says suddenly. "Kates, what did you mean by, 'I can't wait for you guys to drive me around'? Aren't you getting your permit too?"

I bite my lip. "I haven't really thought about it," I reply, feeling small. Wow, this conversation is getting really depressing.

"I think you should get your license." Austin reaches out and tucks a loose strand of hair behind my ear. "You're not going to want Rodney to drive you everywhere for the rest of your life."

Austin has a point. A license is my ticket to freedom. I could actually get in the car and go to Kitson Boutique by myself for once. It would be nice to get one of those cute little convertibles in a deep shade of green. I can see myself driving along Pacific Coast Highway, the wind blowing my hair. "How much fun would it be if we could all take driver's ed together?" I say, feeling wistful. I frown. "But with my luck, I'd show up and *Hollywood Nation* would mob the parking lot with cameras and ruin class." Everyone laughs.

Yes, my life is extraordinary and meeting the President and going on *Oprah* can't be beat. But sometimes I can't help but be frustrated when I realize I'm missing out on normal rites of passage like driver's ed, going to my own prom, or having a dorm room the size of a shoebox. Skipping that stuff makes me feel ancient sometimes. Too ancient for someone who hasn't even turned seventeen.

Austin gives me one of his beyond-perfect smiles that always make me turn to goo. "Private driving lessons are better than driver's ed," Austin says. "At least you won't have to put your life in the hands of three other overexcited teens taking turns at the wheel."

"That's true."

He's trying to make me feel better and it's working.

"Kates, Austin and I are in the same driver's ed car," Liz says. "I promise to spill all the details about Austin's slipups so you don't miss a thing." She giggles.

"As if you're going to be so much better," Austin says to Liz, a smirk spreading across his face. "Picture this, Burke: Liz driving down the 101 with Mr. Thomas, Rob Murray, and me as passengers. That's a horror movie waiting to happen!"

They erupt in laughter. I laugh too, but I feel stupid.

"KAITLIN BURKE! What are you doing here?" My publicist, Laney Peters, interrupts and almost knocks me out of my chair as she hugs me. "How are you, sweetums?"

Sweetums? This can't be Laney even if she does look like her. She's standing in front of me with her latest Gucci bag on her arm, wearing a Dolce & Gabbana tank top and Diesel capri jeans with ballet flats. She could walk the halls at Clark High with Liz and Austin and everyone would assume she was a student. (For all I know, she could be that young. She has never revealed her true age.) Laney's long blond hair is ironed flat.

"I'm great, Laney, couldn't be better," I reply.

"Kaitlin, this is Heidi Caldwell, the West Coast editor of *Men's Matters*," Laney purrs. I look to Laney's right and see a forty-something brunette with long curly hair, smiling at me. She's wearing a fitted black tank and dark denim jeans.

Ohhhh . . . sweetums. Got it. I extend my hand to take Heidi's and shake it politely before introducing Austin, Liz, and Josh.

"We were at Kelly Clarkson's concert at Hyde, but it was so crowded." Laney shudders in horror.

"How'd she sound?" I ask politely. Kelly is one of Laney's other high-profile clients.

"Perfect," says Laney. "And she looks incredible. She may pose for *Men's Matters.*"

"Kelly?" She seems too sweet to slather on some oil and pose in a G-string for millions of guy readers to ogle.

"Everyone wants to do *Men's Matters*," Heidi jumps in and says matter-of-factly. "You should consider it, Kaitlin. Your costar Alexis Holden is on our next cover. We'd have to wait a few months to do another *Family Affairs* star, but I'm sure they'd want you too."

"You shot Alexis?" I'm feeling green with envy even though I've never had the desire to be photographed in a garter.

"Your sales would be through the roof if you did a Kaitlin Burke cover," Laney tells her. "You should have approached us first. Kaitlin is a household name. Alexis will only be on the show for a few episodes, you know." I try to suppress a smile. It's nice to be in Laney's presence when she goes to bat for me.

"Alexis is going to be huge," Heidi counters. "Everyone's talking about her. I mean, the girl came out of nowhere and now she's got a role on *FA*, is hanging with Lindsay and Paris, and every guy in town wants her number. You don't get hotter than that. And we've got her first cover."

I feel my skin begin to blister. Hot? The girl has been on the air twice! Suddenly I can understand what Sky must have felt like last year when *TV Tome* graced me with their "Teen Queen" title. It's not fun listening to people wax on about a competing star's wattage when they're not referring to your own.

"I would like to meet Alexis, Kaitlin." Laney turns to me. "Alexis might not have a publicist. I'll stop by the set next week and we'll have some chai tea. Okay?"

"Sure," I say through gritted teeth.

"Oh, the hostess is waving us over." Laney leans down and gives me a kiss on both cheeks. I'm so surprised, I practically head butt her. She clears her throat.

"Enjoy your night, everyone," says Heidi. "Think about my offer, Kaitlin."

"I will." I smile sweetly until they walk away. Then I rub my temples.

"What was that about?" asks Austin. "Who is Alexis?"

"More importantly," butts in Liz, "promise me you won't do those stupid men's magazines. They're degrading." Austin and Josh blush. They must have subscriptions.

HOLLYWOOD SECRET NUMBER TWO: The reason actresses do men's books is simple: They're great publicity. Hollywood knows the people who buy tickets to a movie's opening weekend, or stand in line all weekend for a concert, are mostly young guys. And the way to get the word out to guys is to do a cover in your underwear for a magazine like *Men's Matters*. Even studios keep tabs on these covers. The dark side of these covers is that they can be demeaning. Have you seen the gymnastic poses some of these girls have to strike? Or the interview questions? Do I really have to talk about being a virgin? I can't even have that conversation with my boyfriend, let alone an entire subscription base!

Laney may have bristled at Heidi about me not getting the cover of *Men's Matters*, but the truth is she wouldn't let me be on their cover anyway. She thinks those men's books are *Playboy*-light and should only be considered if you're a C-level star hoping to bump up to a semi-B. Guess that makes Alexis still a C. Hee-hee.

Wait, that's mean. What's wrong with me?

I tell everyone a little about Alexis and her character before the waitress brings our dinner. My ravioli filled with spinach and ricotta cheese looks amazing, but I have to make sure I leave room for a little dessert. I don't want to overdue it when I have to fit into a size four sample for *FA* Monday morning. "Enough talking," I tell them. "Let's dig in."

"This gnocchi is incredible," Liz mumbles, taking a bite of her pasta. "Doesn't it look *comestible?*"

Austin, Josh, and I look at each other in confusion and then at Liz.

"*Comestible* means 'fit to be eaten.'" Liz sounds so proud of herself. "That's an SAT vocabulary word."

"Show-off," Josh jokes as he takes a spoonful of his linguini with clams. "All right, smarty. What does *demulcent* mean?"

"To de-mulch something?" she asks, sounding unsure.

Austin makes a buzzer sound. "That would be incorrect. Sorry, Miss Mendes, but I'm afraid the correct answer is an application soothing to an irritated surface."

"What's *denizen* mean? An inhabitant. HA!"

"Oh yeah? What about *felicitate*? To wish joy or happiness."

I feel like I'm trapped on some hideous game show hosted by Howie Mandel. I eat my ravioli, staring at another table, secretly wishing I had a list of SAT vocabulary words stashed away so that I could join this bizarre discussion.

I realize I'm staring at Laney and Heidi's table and I notice Heidi hold up a picture to show Laney. It's one of Alexis in a pink bra and panties. I squint menacingly. Even from here I can tell she looks good. I turn to Liz, Josh, and Austin to say something, but they're still busy quizzing each other.

"*Indivisible.* Not separable into parts."

"Please. Who doesn't know the word *indivisible?*"

I flag the waitress over and ask her to put in our order of cupcakes. That's about the only thing that will cheer me up right now.

The SATs, driver's ed, college . . . my biggest problem is whether my call time has been switched or Sky is feeding lies about me to perezhilton.com. I watch the three of them quiz each other and suddenly our worlds seem so far apart.

I've got an SAT question. What's another word for feeling left out?

FRIDAY, 9/13
NOTE TO SELF:

Ask Monique 2 beef up SAT prep Q's.
Have Nadine look in2 permit test requirements &
driver's ed.
Find great b-day present 4 Austin!

THREE: *Dressed for Success*

Please don't tell the press I said this, but I have a confession: I secretly hate weeknight Hollywood events. I'm not anti-social, or totally boring, it's just that I don't like being out late when I know I have long workdays ahead of me. What if I overslept and was late to set? (The last thing I want is for my director or the studio head to write a letter bashing my tardiness and sending it to the press to prove he means business.)

Now that I am over sixteen and no longer fall under the child labor laws, my workdays usually stretch from five AM to eight or nine in the evening and include meetings, interviews, photo shoots, and schoolwork. Some days, it's just too much. That's why I've finally put my size nine Manolos down and told Laney, Mom, and Nadine to run weeknight events by me before RSVPing. Unless it's a major happening, I'd rather go home, watch the latest TiVo'd episode of *Ugly Betty*, and collapse in a large, hot bubble bath.

That doesn't happen that often, mostly because there are

a lot of exceptions to that game plan and tonight's one of them. Hotter-than-hot designer Margo Price (of the famed line Priceless) invited us to her Priceless Waist Exhibit, and even though it's a Wednesday night, even I wouldn't be crazy enough to miss this. Not only do I love Margo's designs, but this party is the talk of the town. Everyone who is anyone will be there. The invite says Margo is celebrating "the skirt's modernization through the last century." Sounds very chic. I think.

"Isn't this exciting?" Mom gushes as Rodney drives my family and Austin to the exhibit at Priceless's flagship store in Beverly Hills. "Margo sent you an invitation personally, Katie-Kat. Did Nadine tell you that? A personal, hand-written invite! From Margo herself!"

"Very cool," I agree, trying to suck in my yawn so that Mom won't think I'm dissing her all-time favorite designer. I'm exhausted. *FA* ratings for the third episode of the season, which aired last weekend, were in the top five again and we delayed filming for an hour today to celebrate our victory. Everyone from my TV mom, Melli, to our executive pro-ducer and cocreator, Tom, toasted the cast and crew for a job well done and then thanked Alexis personally for creat-ing such an attention-grabbing character. I couldn't help be-ing a little ruffled at not being mentioned. (After all, I was the one who gave the tearful meltdown at my mom's bed-side during episode two. When we filmed it, Tom had called it my "Emmy-winning" moment.)

Then, after all the kudos, Alexis tearfully thanked us for

welcoming her and her character with open arms. Sky was standing next to me when Alexis was talking and she stepped on my foot with her stiletto heel. "Fake," she whispered in my ear. Okay, I was a little envious too, but I thought Alexis sounded sincere, even if her ego did seem slightly inflated, like a big star during pilot season.

Sky was even angrier later in the day, when her own scene was delayed longer because of a snafu with one involving Matty and Alexis. I wasn't on set when it happened, but Pete the grip told me in confidence that Alexis wasn't thrilled with the lighting for the scene and begged for it to be re-done. Sky went ape and caused a major commotion. I had such a headache by the time I left work, I told Mom I might have to forget whatever was on my calendar for the evening. That's when she reminded me that tonight was the Priceless party and that she had asked Austin to join us. (Nice move, Mom.) Going to the Priceless bash and seeing Austin is worth the under-eye circles.

"We're so revved up, Katie-Kins," Dad adds. "Margo is the hottest designer and she loves dressing you. Your mom has always wanted to meet her."

"Maybe we'll hit it off," rhapsodizes Mom with a starry look in her green eyes. "And Margo will be calling me to wear her samples a season in advance and begging me to vacation with her on Lake Como." Mom sighs. "Wouldn't that be lovely?"

I'm not used to hearing Mom sound so much like a fan instead of a savvy Hollywood insider. I turn away so she can't see me smirk.

"You guys realize a thousand people are going tonight, right?" Matty points out. Alexis's lighting request delayed production so long that Matty didn't get to finish his scene today. If anyone else had pulled that, Matty would have freaked, but Alexis apologized to Matty personally. He was mush afterward. I teased him that he has a major crush on her and he didn't deny it. "We might not even see Margo," Matty adds.

Mom ignores him. "The point is, Kaitlin, I want you to thank Margo and gush about her brand to the press. Tell them she's your favorite and talk about how you've been striving for that old-world Hollywood glamour feel that Priceless speaks to."

Austin coughs. "Old-world Hollywood feel," I repeat. "Is that the look I'm going for?" I ask, trying not to look amused.

Mom plays with the pearl beading on her silk canary yellow gown — Priceless, of course. Usually when you go to a fashion show, or a designer's event, the unwritten rule is that you wear the designer's clothes as a show of support. Dad and Matty are in Priceless suits, Nadine called in a navy Priceless button-down shirt for Austin, and I got to wear this gorgeous, fitted black sequin Priceless tank cocktail dress. I even pinned my hair back in a tight bun with a Priceless butterfly clip. The look is very Audrey Hepburn, which I'm loving.

"Laney and I discussed it last night," Mom explains with a raise of her right eyebrow, code for *don't get snippy*. "We're going to talk to your stylist about pulling more clothes for you to reflect that feel. Look at stars like Scarlett Johansson. She's styled perfectly these days and she's being taken seriously and snagging Oscar-contending roles. We want that for you too, Katie-Kins. It's never too early to think about your next big career move."

Old-world Hollywood? Next career move? My head starts throbbing again. Thankfully, Austin gives my hand a squeeze and I relax. It's been five days since our dinner at Les Deux and I've really missed being around him. Sometimes I think Austin's psychic. I wonder if he knows what I'm thinking *right now.*

I stare deep into his eyes. Am I crazy to want it all? I will my brain to ask him. Is it ridiculous to worry about being left behind when you guys go to college when I've experienced more than some do in a lifetime? Jennifer Aniston knows my name, I have Brett Ratner on speed dial, and I have enough money in the bank to buy a small desert island. Should I really care that I can't take driver's ed like a normal person? What do you think, Austin?

I wait for a reaction. Austin smiles at me.

Hmph. What does that mean?

"What do you think, Kate-Kate?" Dad is saying. "We'll let you, Austin, and Matty walk the carpet together and your mother and I will head inside to the exhibit. We don't want to cramp your style, you hot rod."

Austin looks confused. I keep forgetting to tell him about my dad's loony car speak, a holdover from his days as a car salesman. I always cringe in meetings with my dad, who is now a Hollywood producer, when he comes out with some crazy phrase like, "That engine's gonna need some fine-tuning before we start filming!"

"Sure, Dad, that's fine," I agree as Rodney pulls up to the store, which is lit up like a Christmas tree from the flash-bulbs of a few dozen paparazzi. There is a packed red carpet and a few hundred curious fans.

Rodney opens the car door and Laney is right there waiting to take over. "Hi," she whispers, looking chic in a white Priceless pantsuit that accents her airbrushed tan. Her long blond hair is combed pin straight and held back by gold Priceless sunglasses. "Make sure you talk about how much you love Priceless," she reminds me as she takes my arm and Austin's and steers us over to the first reporter. Matty runs along behind us. Laney rattles off my topics: Priceless. Check. Say how much I love *FA* and how great the new season is going. Check. *Pretty Young Assassins* is coming out next spring. Check. I make sure I mention all of the above as Austin, Matty, and I move from one reporter to the next. Everyone who is anyone — Reese, Julia, Ashley, Hayden, Eva, my pal Gina — is here tonight to support Margo Price. Suddenly I don't feel tired anymore. I feel like I'm at a Hollywood reunion!

"I still can't get over how you know all these people," says a starstruck Austin after we say goodbye to David and Victoria and Tom and Katie respectively. "Does everyone know everyone in this town?"

"Pretty much," I say with a bright, toothy grin, knowing the cameras are still on us. We make our way to the next reporter. It's Maria Meadow from *Access Hollywood*, looking skinny and gorgeous in a Priceless pencil skirt and a cream silk tank. Matty has moved ahead of us and is talking to *Hollywood Nation*.

"Kaitlin, that dress is beautiful on you," she gushes. "How'd you pick it?"

"I've been a fan of Priceless forever," I recite, "and Margo . . ." I overhear another conversation and stop midspeech.

". . . *Family Affair* has been a dream come true, Gary, but you know, it can be tough being the new girl. People can be very cliquish."

Hmm . . . That sounds like Alexis talking. I didn't know she was here tonight. Did she just call *FA* cliquish? That's weird. Our show is known as the friendliest on the lot.

"I've heard Sky and Kaitlin are pretty friendly," I hear the reporter say. "Aren't you all around the same age?"

"They're quite nice, Gary. But to be perfectly honest, they're very busy with their own schedules, you know? They don't have time to show little old me around town."

What is going on? I gave Alexis a personal tour of the studio on her first day there! And I've invited her to lunch half a dozen times and she's always turned me down! Talk about unappreciative.

"Kaitlin?" Maria questions. Austin jabs me in my side.

"I'm sorry!" I blush. Where was I? "Margo sent this dress over last season and I've been waiting for the right . . ."

"Well, either way, Alexis, all anyone can talk about tonight is you, you, you," I hear Alexis's reporter continue.

"Stop, Gary! You're making me blush!"

"I'm serious. You have made *Family Affair* fun again. You've only been on-screen in three episodes and already we're in love with you. Colby is such a great character and you play her mysteriousness beautifully."

"Thanks, Gary. I really try. I don't have that tough Hollywood exterior like most of these girls or my coworkers. I grew up poor and we only had one TV. No cable. I wasn't groomed on *Family Affair* and all this Hollywood glamour. I'm just trying to learn as I go and I'm so grateful to the press for embracing me. I'm blessed to be playing Colby. I can't believe it's my storyline that has put *FA* back in the top five where it belongs. The network has been so grateful, but they shouldn't be. I'm just grateful they gave a kid like me a job."

"Is she kidding me?" I blurt out. Alexis is taking sole credit for our show and painting herself as Mother Teresa! And shy? She's always been overly friendly with everyone on set, and shy girls don't stop filming and complain about the lighting. What is going on with her? Austin coughs loudly.

"I'm so sorry, Maria!" I remember where I am again.

Maria just stares at me and now I'm very embarrassed. "That's your new costar Alexis Holden over there, isn't it?" she asks.

I cringe at hearing Alexis's name. "Yep, I just was trying to get her attention." I laugh nervously. "But I'll catch her later. Please forgive me for spacing out," I apologize. "I don't know where my head is tonight! Can we start over? Ask me anything." I try to forget about Alexis and concentrate on finishing my one-on-one, and two more identical Q&A's, before entering the store. Matt makes a beeline to the gift bags and leaves Austin and me alone to mingle.

"Are you okay, Burke?" Austin's blue eyes are filled with worry. "You don't look so hot."

"I'm just annoyed about some stupid work thing. It's nothing." I try to shrug it off. Austin gives me a mock stern look. "I'll tell you all about it. Just not here."

Believe me, I've learned my lesson about keeping secrets from my boyfriend. But what am I supposed to say? That part of me is jealous of all the attention Alexis is getting? We're all busting our butt on *FA*, but because Alexis is new, she's taken the spotlight. The other half of me is ticked off that Alexis is painting herself as this martyr who's single-handedly saved our show, which wasn't doing too shabbily to begin with.

But maybe I'm just being paranoid . . . I hate this jealous side of myself. Alexis is new at this whole interview thing. She could just be nervous and not know what to say to reporters. I'm sure that's it.

"Take my mind off work," I press Austin. "How was your day?"

"Good," he yawns. "Liz and I had our second driver's ed class. I got to drive this time. We went down Ventura and I attempted to parallel park. I hit a curb and knocked the back right hubcap off." He blushes.

"I'm sure that happens to everybody." I try to sound upbeat. "What's parallel parking again?"

He groans. "You really need to take your permit test."

"I know," I agree, pulling out my Sidekick to add another Note to Self reminder about permit tests. "What's going on with your SAT study group?"

"We met for forty-five minutes to talk about SAT essay questions and then everyone had to leave. Honestly, I was bored out of my mind. Rob and I were itching to practice sprints. If I see another SAT vocab word, I might hurl."

"You're going to ace that test," I tell him. "Maybe you're just on study overload. I know when I practice my lines too much they all get jumbled in my head."

"You're probably right," he admits, his eyes doing a double-take as George and Brad pass by and wave. "But the test isn't until November. I've got a ways to go with the studying. I'll probably be studying on my birthday!"

"Speaking of birthdays, can you help me figure out a great gift to get my boyfriend?" I smile at Cameron and Drew as they float by. "What do boys like?"

"I don't know." Austin grins. "Maybe you can help me instead. My girlfriend's birthday is coming up soon and I have no idea what to get her either."

"I happen to know your girlfriend and one thing she hates is parties." I'm serious. Austin looks surprised. "Ever since I can remember, Mom and Laney have thrown me these big parties with lots of publicity. They invite all these people I don't know . . ." I trail off. "It's kind of turned me off celebrating."

"But you're turning seventeen this year!" Austin argues. "You've got to have a party."

"I'd rather celebrate *you* turning seventeen." I'm firm. "What do you want for your birthday? Give me a clue. Please? PlayStation 4000?"

He smiles. "Funny. All I really want is you, Burke. You know that."

Now it's my turn to blush. I try to think of something romantic to say back. Something to enhance the moment, like . . .

"K!" Sky suddenly appears, throwing her arms around me and knocking me into a waiter carrying maki rolls. "Smile big, *Celeb Insider* is watching," she whispers in my ear. Three flashbulbs go off simultaneously as Sky kisses me hard on the cheek. I smile tightly till they disappear and then push her off me.

"What was that about?" I ask when they've disappeared.

"I was trying to get us some good press," Sky complains. "All anyone seems to care about tonight is Alexis. She's becoming an overblown diva right before our eyes."

I roll my eyes. "I wouldn't go that far," I say, but I can't stop thinking about what I overheard Alexis say either.

Sky huffs. "Austin, get your girlfriend to wise up a bit, will you? Not everyone is as annoyingly sweet as she is. Tell her to join forces with me to stop Alexis."

"Join forces with you?" I'm incredulous. "I'll never turn to the dark side."

Austin can't help but laugh, causing me to as well, and making Sky so mad she turns her attention to a passing Adrian Grenier.

"Your life is surreal," Austin chuckles.

"Tell me about it." I giggle. "Come on, let's forget about Sky and go get some food. I'm starving." We make our way through the packed Waist exhibit. There are hundreds of people in the modern three-story store, admiring the designer's skirt collection from the past fifteen years. Skirts are displayed everywhere we look — on staircases, in the ground-floor dome, affixed to glass walls, and twirling midair.

"KAITLIN!" Laney yells over the roar of the DJ spinning loud music to drown out all the talking. "There you are!" She smiles at Austin. "How did the interviews go? Did you mention Priceless? The movie? *FA*? What did they say about your dress?"

"It went great, Laney," I reply in a soothing tone.

"Good, good," she says, watching the scene around us rather than my face. "Did you know Alexis is here tonight? I want to meet her. Everyone is talking about her — and you, of course," she adds quickly.

"Thanks," I reply, grabbing Austin's hand and swinging it instead of swinging at something in frustration.

"Someone told me Alexis has been at every event in Hollywood over the past three weeks!" Laney marvels. "She's really trying to make a name for herself, huh?"

I bite hard on my lower lip to keep from screaming. I never thought I would be the It Girl forever, but I can't believe how quickly people have latched onto Alexis. She's only been in three episodes! Despite the fact that anyone could overhear, I remind Laney — and tell Austin — about HOLLYWOOD SECRET NUMBER THREE.

Want to know how hot a star is? Count their monthly red carpet appearances. The hotter the star, the fewer they make, that is, unless they have a movie or album to promote. When they're doing the publicity tour, all bets are off — a star may go to four events in one week just to gush about their incredible new project. I guess you could argue that Alexis is hitting the town to do just that. *But*, if Alexis is still hogging the carpet nightly a month from now, that means her star wattage is going nowhere. True A-list stars don't have to go to an opening of an animal shelter or talk about their favorite lip gloss. They know the real way to keep in the public's good graces is to sit home on their $5,000 couches and be as elusive as Johnny Depp.

Laney looks skeptical. "Some appearances are good appearances, you know," she sniffs. "Like this one. There are a few people I'd like to introduce you to. Can I steal her away for a minute, Austin?"

"Sure." Austin smiles shyly. "I'll get some food for us and meet you back by the table Matty grabbed. He's guarding the gift bags he snagged each of us." I laugh.

Laney takes me around the room, introducing me to two producers, a hot new writer, and the director of the head of a rival TV studio. On my way back to Austin, I bump into Kirsten, Scarlett, and two other stars I haven't seen in ages, and then sign a few autographs on cocktail napkins. It's almost a half hour before I make it back. Poor Austin. He must be so bored.

I'm ten feet from the table when I stop dead. Who is that? A girl with long red hair is holding court with Austin and Matty. They're enthralled by whatever she is saying and every few seconds the group of them erupts in laughter. The girl keeps putting her hand on top of my boyfriend's. Once, I can understand. But I've counted *five* times so far and Austin is doing nothing to stop her! I'm about to storm over to put a stop to this girl's flirting when she turns sideways and I glimpse her face.

Oh. My. God. It's Alexis.

"Austin, you are beyond cute," I overhear her say as I rush up behind them. They don't seem to notice I'm there. "You must be the most real guy at this party. I like that."

"I'm pretty real too," Matty jumps in.

"You both are," Alexis corrects herself. "Thank you for being so nice and talking to the lonely new girl for a few minutes. I should go, but Austin, remember, if you ever want to talk about being new to this scene, you have my number. Call me."

"I'm back," I announce loudly. The guys jump. Austin quickly puts his arm around me, but Matty can barely take his eyes off Alexis's porcelain face.

"Hey, Kaitlin!" Alexis says sweetly.

A little too sweetly, if you ask me.

"I was just talking to your brother and your boyfriend. Have I told you how adorable I think he is?" she whispers in my ear.

"Nope, but I know he is," I say with the biggest grin my face can make. "Aren't I lucky?"

"Yes, hang tight to that one," Alexis says, with a wink. "Remember what I said, boys," she adds loudly. "I'll catch you later. There are still so many people here who have asked to meet me. I'm overwhelmed!"

I smile again. I'm afraid if I open my mouth to say anything, I'll regret it. Once she's out of earshot, I let loose. "Why was she talking to you two?" I demand. I sound so catty, I know, but I can't help it.

"Alexis was just giving Austin and me some pointers about fitting in." Matty looks at me like I should be hauled off in a straitjacket.

"Pointers? Why would she be giving Austin pointers?" I ask them both. "Austin isn't even an actor. No offense."

Austin shrugs. "I tried explaining to her that I went to high school and wasn't in the business, but she just kept talking about me and Matty being new too and all of us being able to understand each other." Austin looks at me curiously. "Why do you look so upset?"

"I'm not." My voice sounds shrill. But I am upset. Alexis was blatantly flirting with my boyfriend! And she knows he's my boyfriend! I've introduced them several times on set. Why would she do that? I can't believe she kept touching him like that. "Why would I be upset?"

"I don't know. You have no reason to be." Austin kisses me and I start to calm down. I tune out as Matty and Austin gab about our gift bags and the twenty percent off Priceless voucher tucked inside. All I can think about is Alexis. Suddenly I feel hot breath in my ear.

"Don't be a fool," the person behind me whispers. "I saw the whole thing. Alexis was totally flirting with Austin. If she has no qualms doing that, what else is she willing to go after that's rightfully yours?"

I don't even have to turn around. This voice I know. It's Sky's. And for once, I have to admit, she could be right.

TUESDAY, 9/17
NOTE TO SELF:

Remind Nadine 2 look in2 driver's permit test.
Wed. call time: 7 AM
Thurs. call time: 6:15 AM
Fri. call time: 8 AM
Sat. – date w/ A
Sun. – CosmoGirl! photo shoot
Finish CosmoGirl! essay. Ask Nadine 2 read it over!
Next Tues. – Interview w/ Access @ 1:15 PM during lunch
Spa day w/ Liz, Mom, Laney, Nadine – Sat. Oct. 5
FIND AUSTIN B-DAY GIFT!!!

CeLeb hot sheet

Chatting with *Family Affair*'s Alexis Holden!
The tube's newest babe tackles our fill-in-the-blanks.

By Lisa Gigli

HN: We've asked Kaitlin Burke and Sky Mackenzie these questions and now it's your turn!

Alexis: (laughs) I'm sure my answers could never be as cool as theirs, but bring them on!

HN: Okay, what's your favorite food?

Alexis: I guess I would say steak, not that I had much of it growing up. That's why it's so important for me to help others. I volunteer at a soup kitchen and I bring Omaha Steaks with me.

HN: What a do-gooder you are.

Alexis: Stop! You're making me blush.

HN: What's your favorite read?

Alexis: *Hollywood Nation*, obviously.

HN: Good answer! Who is your favorite *FA* cast mate?

Alexis: Oh, lordy! I could never choose. They're all so wonderfully amazing. From our wardrobe designer, Renee, to Pete, my favorite grip, to our awesome writers. I could never pick just one.

HN: Favorite TV show — past or present?

Alexis: *Family Affair*, of course! But I do like it better now that I'm on it. Just kidding! (laughs)

HN: So do we! What's your favorite way to spend the day off?

Alexis: Going for a hike in the mountains with my pug or helping others. There's no better high.

HN: Who's the one person you'd like to meet, living or dead?

Alexis: It would have to be Gandhi. He's such an inspiration.

HN: Where do you see yourself in ten years?

Alexis: Hopefully blissfully married and still working, if the public likes me enough. I hope they do!

HN: We do! We do! Okay, who would win in a *FA* catfight: You, Kaitlin or Sky?

Alexis: It wouldn't be me! Those two are tough as nails and I guess I'm not letting the cat out of the bag by saying they don't get along. They love to tear into each other! You should see it! I would just step out of the way and watch the fur fly — as long as neither of them go hurt, of course. I love them both to death.●

FOUR: *Seeing Red*

"No. No. No. NEVER. Not for even twenty seconds. NO WAY . . . Wait. That might work. Okay, that's a maybe."

Sky is talking to herself as she flips through the long rack of pricey red dresses looking for something to wear for our *FA* promotional photo shoot. It's been almost a week since I was rude to her at the Priceless party and she's still snubbing me because of it. It's actually kind of peaceful. Hee-hee.

"What if I like Kaitlin's selection better than my own choices?" Sky whines. "Does she get to wear it if she saw it first?" Renee, our head costume designer, throws up her hands in exasperation. Her mouth is full of tiny pins that she's using to do quick alterations, so she can't yell.

I look through my own packed rack of ruby red numbers for today's last-minute cast shoot. Since *Family Affair*'s ratings are the highest we've had in five years, Tom and the rest of the show's big guns want to rush out new print advertisements of the entire young cast. They're convinced part of the ratings draw is our new teen storyline with Colby (aka Alexis). Just hearing Tom gush about Alexis is a sore subject with me. Sky and I have been TV faves for years and the studio hasn't given us glowing praise the way they have Alexis! Now they're putting her in magazine ads even though she's only sticking around for half a season? It's so unfair!

Ahem. It's wrong of me to think this way, I know. But it's not so bad if I'm not actually saying these things out loud, right?

Because of this week's tight shooting schedule — we're filming beach scenes on location for three days in Malibu — we've got twenty-five minutes to get dressed and retouch our makeup and then half an hour to do the shoot. The guys will be dressed in black and white and the girls in racy red numbers that will pop against a white backdrop. The wardrobe room is in chaos trying to get us all ready in time. Thankfully there are so many gorgeous designer duds to choose from, I'm not having a hard time picking one.

HOLLYWOOD SECRET NUMBER FOUR: As much as I'd like to take my dress pick, this gorgeous Lulu Lame gown (black v-neck top, empire waist, red satin skirt . . . sigh, it's heavenly), out for a night on the town with Austin, it's probably not going to happen. Stars rarely get to leave the set with their wardrobe. Some of our clothes are borrowed from designer lines that haven't even made it to the runway yet. Others are samples that have to be whisked back to the production house to be used by another celeb-in-need. And still other frocks are paid for by the studio, which means they're the property of *FA* and are saved for recycling for a black-tie wedding scene down the road.

If I want this fiery Lulu Lame, I'm going to have to beg Renee to let me buy it. I grab her arm as she bustles past me with an armful of crisp white dress shirts.

"How much is this dress?" I whisper.

Renee scrunches up her face in concentration. "I think it was around one thousand dollars. Why? Did you want to buy it?"

I shake my head vigorously. "Nope," I say quickly. "Just curious."

Well, at least I get to wear it for half an hour.

Sky is getting her dress fitted. Some of the recurring teen stars like Luke, Brayden, Hallie, and Ava (they play Sam and Sara's classmates at Summerville High) have picked out their outfits and are getting their makeup done. I don't see Alexis anywhere. Matty is dressed too — in a black cashmere V-neck sweater and black Ralph Lauren trousers — and is standing in front of a mirror practicing smoldering expressions. But behind him, Trevor Wainright is slumped against a rack of clothes and looking miserable. Trev plays Sam's main man, Ryan, and in real life was Sky's blink-and-you-missed-it boyfriend at the end of last season. When Sky dumped Trevor to go after our egotistical *PYA* costar (and my ex), Drew Thomas, Trevor was so heartbroken he flew home to Idaho to be with his family on their farm.

"Hey, Trev," I say, stepping over a pile of hangers and Armani shirts to reach him. "Are you okay?"

"Sky's barely said two words to me since I got back," he replies, sounding hoarse.

I want to quip "you're lucky," but don't on account of how sad his blue eyes look. Other than that, Trev looks hotter than ever. Two months of driving a tractor have bleached his blond locks white and given his skin a deep golden glow. "I thought we were on a break, but she told me to stop bothering her because we're officially over."

"I'm sorry, Trev," I say. "Sky is tough to pin down, but there are plenty of girls who would kill to be your girlfriend." I turn Trevor around to face his wardrobe rack. "We've just got to find you something killer to wear this morning. This ad will drum up major dating options. Trust me." I flip through white shirts. A small, bony hand stops my own.

"Back to your own clothes," Renee mumbles through the pins in her mouth. Renee has a fanny pack with sewing equipment strapped to her broad waist and her brown hair is pulled back in a ponytail, and she looks like she means business. "You have ten minutes left to pick out your own outfit, remember?"

I sidestep piles of discarded clothes to reach my rack and hold up the Lulu Lame dress. Sky appears out of nowhere and stares at my choice. She's already put on a clingy spaghetti strap Lycra number with a pleated bottom.

"I don't remember seeing the Lulu Lame," Sky complains. "Not that I'd ever be caught dead wearing satin."

"I guess it's good you didn't pick this one then," Renee says with a wink, tightening the back of Sky's dress with her pins before ushering her toward the makeup room door. "Okay, I've sent the other kids out, Matt Burke is getting his foundation touched up, and Trevor is settling into a nice Armani suit. The only one we're missing is . . . Alexis." Renee frowns. "She's probably in some dark corner with one of the writers."

Sky and I look at each other. "What's that supposed to mean?" Sky asks.

Renee suddenly looks like she just swallowed a pin. "Nothing." She says quickly. "A wardrobe room joke. Now go get ready." she sends us away. "Kaitlin, go in the dressing area and put that Lulu Lame gown on so I can fit it. I'm going to see where Alexis is."

Two minutes later, as I'm zipping up the back of my dress, I hear bickering. It starts soft and begins to grow as I slip into my open-toed black Gucci heels. I pull back the dressing area curtain expecting to see Sky in the middle of an argument with Renee and instead I see Alexis stomping her Coach heels. I quickly hide behind the curtain so that she doesn't see me.

"I'm not wearing these atrocious gowns, Renee," Alexis is protesting. "Need I remind you that I'm five foot nine? How could I possibly wear a minidress? It will look like a thong!"

Whoa. Someone hasn't had her morning mocha latte yet.

"Alexis," Renee says patiently, "I picked out almost *thirty* dresses for you. Only two were minidresses. Look at this dazzling Peter Som number. It's one of a kind, you know. Rachel McAdams wanted it to wear to a film premiere but I snagged it for you first. It would look great on your gorgeous statuesque frame."

Nice one, Renee. She's always had a way of making even the plainest sheath dress seem like Cinderella's ball gown.

"It's ugly." Alexis pushes it away. "I don't like anything here! Nothing," she pouts. "I'll need more choices."

"What about Sky and Kaitlin's racks?" Renee offers, striding over to our other dresses.

Alexis coughs. "I'm not wearing their leftovers."

WHAT? She did not just say that! What is up with her? She's never this cranky on set.

"I need something original," Alexis says, walking toward the other side of the long room with Renee close behind her looking nervously at her watch. I can barely hear them now because they're so far away, but I don't miss Alexis's next remark. "I should stand out. I want to wear something that isn't red."

Talk about an ego inflating fast. I've got to get out of here and cool off. Alexis's back is turned so I could probably run for it. I take a step to leave and then get knocked backward by Sky diving into the small dressing area with me. She bangs my right elbow into the wall. Ouch!

"What are you doing here?" I whisper.

"Spying," Sky says. "I was coming back in to change my heels. These don't make my ankles look slim enough." I look down at her cute peekaboo-toe Bally sandals. "I stopped when I heard Alexis whining. I was hiding behind that rack of clothes by the door." She wiggles her arms to nudge me. "Move over."

My fleeting escape moment is gone so I don't argue. Instead, we both listen intently.

Renee walks past the dressing area alone and I hear her mumble, "Just a few short weeks on the show and she's already a diva." Hear, hear! Then out loud, I hear her add: "All the girls are wearing red, Alexis, even Sky, who is usually the one who gives me a hard time. Tom wants the girls in red, guys in black and white. No exceptions."

"I'm not like everyone else," Alexis says. "I'm not like that prima donna Sky Mackenzie." I smirk at Sky, who looks like steam is about to shoot out of her five-carat-diamond–adorned ears. "And I'm not looking like little Miss Goody Two-shoes Burke either." Sky stifles a snort.

I cannot believe she just called me that!

"I'm the new girl and I deserve to stand out," Alexis complains. "Haven't you heard about the ratings? It's my storyline that put us back on top."

"That girl is dead," Sky whispers angrily. "DEAD. Just wait till my contract renegotiations this year. If they think I'm putting up with this . . ."

I butt in. "She's a scene-stealing, no-name, two-faced liar, that's what she is! She flirted with my boyfriend, semi-knocked us in the press, and now she's telling off the nicest person in the *FA* family, all while she pretends to be America's new sweetheart? She's not getting away with it!" I immediately slap my hand over my mouth, shocked by what I just said, and Sky grins.

Yes, it felt good to have that outburst, but I shouldn't have done it in front of Sky. The only side Sky's ever on is her own. She could turn on me in a second.

"Renee, where are Sky, Alexis, and Kaitlin?" I hear Tom as he enters the room. He sounds beyond stressed. "I need them right now. Actually, five minutes ago."

"I sent Sky and Kaitlin out at least ten minutes ago." Renee sounds perplexed. Uh-oh. "But Tom, we have a problem. Alexis doesn't like any of the dresses. She, um, doesn't want to wear red."

Silence. Sky and I stare at each another. Neither of us can breathe. Tom is going to yell . . .

"Renee! I didn't say that," Alexis says with a nervous laugh. "Tom, I told Renee that her dresses are spectacular, but none of them are quite, well, me, you know?"

Liar!

"You've said it yourself — Colby is hot right now," Alexis adds. "She's the new, bad girl in town. I need to look unique. How would it look if I dressed like all the others? I'm sure you agree it wouldn't work."

Tom's walkie-talkie begins to make static. "TOM! TOM! Get the girls out here! We have to shoot the next scene in forty-five minutes if we don't want to pay the grips overtime! What's the holdup?"

"GIVE ME TEN, RICK." He yells back. "I see your point, Alexis, but I really want all the girls in red," Tom is firm.

HA! Take that, Alexis!

"Please?" Alexis begs. "Can't you make an exception this once? Pleeaasse . . . I'm sure the network wants me to stand out too. I'm just trying to do what's best for the show, Tom."

Sky grabs my hand and clenches it tightly. She feels like ice.

"TOM! TOM! We need them now!" I hear the walkie-talkie voice again and Tom grunts in frustration.

"COMING!" Tom barks. "Renee, find her something to wear. And make sure she accessorizes it with red. I want you outside in five, Alexis. Understood?"

"Tom, you rock!" Alexis purrs. "You won't regret it!"

Sky's grip tightens.

WHAT? Wait a minute — Tom gave in? "He never gives in when *you* throw a fit like that," I whisper.

Sky seems surprised too. "I know," she pouts.

Oh. My. God. The shoot! "We have to get out there before Alexis sees us," I realize.

"Renee, find me something tight, long, and slinky. And make it snappy," Alexis demands now that Tom is out of earshot.

When Alexis follows Renee into the closet, I dash out of the dressing room with Sky right on my Gucci heels. Sky and I race down the dressing room hallway to the sound-stage, slipping and sliding as we fight over who is getting through the doorway first.

"HA!" Sky announces triumphantly as she squeezes past me.

"Show-off," I grumble.

"Are you okay?" Matty asks me. "You look upset." I look around and realize other people are staring too. Sky and I usually don't stand within twenty feet of each other when the camera isn't rolling.

"Yeah, Matty, we're fine," I assure him even though I'm still shaking from what I overheard with Alexis. I can't believe it, but maybe my suspicions about Alexis were dead-on. Wait till I tell Nadine. "Are you ready for your first big *FA* photo shoot?" I ask, changing the subject. I ruffle his hair.

"Don't mess the 'do," he complains with a grin. "So where's Alexis?" he asks. I frown.

"Queen Alexis didn't want to wear the same color dress as us so she's taking her sweet time getting out here," Sky snaps.

Matt pales. "Oh. I, um, was just asking because I'm in the next scene and I only have three and a half hours left to work today and I don't want to miss out," Matty says.

"You have two lines. I'm sure they'll be able to squeeze it in," Sky snaps.

"HEY. I know you're upset about what just happened, but don't take this out on my brother," I admonish.

"I don't know what you're talking about," Sky hisses. "I'm completely fine."

She must have stood on her head too long this morning during her yoga class.

Before either of us says another word, Tom appears, looking in dire need of a double shot of espresso.

"People, we're ready," he says. Sweat is pouring down his bald head and fogging up his glasses as he walks across the stage. Alexis races in right behind him. Our executive producer looks like a munchkin next to Alexis the giant. She stands at his side, looking cool and relaxed in a green Diane von Furstenberg wrap dress with red earrings and a red bracelet. When the rest of the cast sees what she's wearing, they start to whisper to one another.

"We're going to do these photos and go right to the school hallway set," Tom explains wearily. "We're already running behind and some of you have time constraints." Matt clears his throat. "After this, you'll have fifteen minutes to change and touch up again and then we're shooting the next scene before lunch." Everyone starts whispering again. At this rate, we won't have lunch until three! All thanks to Alexis.

Alexis slips her arm through mine. "Hey, girlie, you look stunning in that dress," Alexis says admiringly. "Your boyfriend would melt if he saw you."

Huh?

"Um, thanks," I say. I have to remind myself that Alexis doesn't know I overheard her Oscar-worthy meltdown moment. Maybe she's bipolar.

"It's going to be ages before we eat today, but do you want to grab a salad later when we do?" Alexis asks. "I feel like we haven't caught up in ages."

She just bashed me to Renee and now she wants to be my lunch buddy?

"Shoot! I have a phone interview to do," I lie. "Maybe tomorrow?"

"I'm going to hold you to that," Alexis says with a wink.

I smell a rat, but until I know what Alexis is up to, I better play along.

MONDAY, 9/23
NOTE TO SELF:

Tues. call time: 7 AM
Wed., Thurs., Fri.: On location in Malibu. Call time: 5 AM
*Check driver's ed. Web sites!
*FIND A B-DAY GIFT!
Date w/ A – Fri. night, Slice of Heaven

INT. PAIGE'S HOSPITAL ROOM—DAY 7

PAIGE

(sounding weak) Girls, I want to talk to the two of you—I
mean the three of you—for a moment.

SAM

What is it, Mom?

PAIGE

I love you girls so much. I'm starting to feel so much
stronger thanks to Colby.

COLBY

Please don't thank me again. You've done enough
already.

SARA

Yeah, Mom. We've done enough. We gave her a nice hotel
room, some clean clothes, a warm meal, and it's not
even Christmas. You have enough to worry about. You
just woke up from a coma!

PAIGE

I can never repay you, Colby. You saved my life. You
gave me back my husband and my girls. For that, I

will be eternally grateful.

                    SAM
Mom, you said there was something you had to tell us.
Did the doctors say something about your condition?

Paige looks at Colby and reaches for her hand. The two
clasp hands and smile.

                    PAIGE
Girls, I'm going to be fine. I wanted to talk to you
about Colby, actually. I know you've been hearing
rumors and I wanted the truth to come from me.

                    SARA
(to Sam) Why is she holding her hand?

                    PAIGE
Sara, concentrate. This is important. You need to
listen to what I'm about to say. It wasn't just a
coincidence that Colby's blood saved my life that
day she walked into the hospital waiting room.

                    SAM
It was a miracle. We know that, Mom.

                    PAIGE
It was more than a miracle. It was fate. What you
don't know is what Colby told Dr. Braden. She is my

long lost daughter. We're having a DNA test done to confirm it, but I know in my heart it's true.

SAM

WHAT? NO! You would never cheat on Dad! You love him.

PAIGE

Girls, this was before your father and I even met. Granddaddy was so ashamed, so I.... (tearfully) gave my firstborn daughter up thinking I would never see her again. Colby and I have been talking and putting together facts and I'm sure she has her information correct. She's my daughter. (sobbing) Colby, I'm so sorry I abandoned you.

COLBY

I understand all that now. Don't get upset. You have to rest, Mom.

SARA

"MOM?" This is insane! A good story and a blood type don't prove anything!

PAIGE

Colby and the baby share the same birthdate and Colby says she was born at the hospital where I gave birth. She may not look like a Buchanan, but she is one.

SAM

(in shock) Mom, are you sure?

PAIGE

Certain.

COLBY

Can I say something? I know this comes as a shock.
But I'm hoping we can start slow. We're already
friends. Maybe we can work toward feeling like
sisters.

PAIGE

Well, you'll have plenty of time. I want you to move
into our home immediately.

SARA

WHAT? She hasn't even taken a blood test yet!

COLBY

The offer is so generous, but I couldn't ... I don't
want to cause problems.

SARA

Mom, are you sure you're thinking clearly?

PAIGE

That is enough. Colby saved my life and that makes

her family no matter what the blood test results
are. I expect all of you to make her feel welcome.
Alice is already home readying a room and I expect
you two to make her feel comfortable.

SARA

But ...

SAM

You heard her, Sara. We want Mom to get better. We
need to do whatever we can to help. Colby, we hope
you'll feel comfortable in our home.

COLBY

Oh, I'm sure I will.

Sam and Sara hug their mother as Colby watches with an
inscrutable smile.

FIVE: *I Heart Alexis*

"AND WE'RE ROLLING!" Tom yells into his megaphone.

FA's crew of almost one hundred people becomes quiet as the bright, scorching, overhead lights focus on Sky, Alexis, and me as we huddle around Melli, who is lying in a hospital bed. Tom oversees the scene from a monitor stationed in front of his director's chair while the guest director sits near us on the camera dolly. As usual, standing behind Tom are our writers, ready with pen and pad to fine-tune any clunky lines.

"Mom, are you sure you're thinking clearly?" Sky recites as Sara.

Melli, aka Paige, nods weakly. She's supposed to look like she just woke up from a coma, which is why she's wearing white pancake foundation and no eye makeup.

"That is enough," Melli says hoarsely, and on command I give her a drink of water from the plastic pitcher on her tray table. A huge basket of flowers from our "dad," Dennis (aka Spencer) and balloons of every color and shape fill the room. "Colby saved my life and that makes her family no matter what the blood test results are," she adds. "I expect all of you to make her feel welcome. Alice is already home readying a room and I expect you two to make her feel comfortable."

"But . . ." Sky protests.

I grab Melli's hand and with my other hand I grab Sky's. "You heard her, Sara," I say, shaking slightly. "We want Mom to get better. We need to do whatever we can to help." I turn to Alexis. "Colby, we hope you'll feel comfortable in our home."

"Oh, I'm sure I will," she says smoothly.

I wait for the camera to pan wide before breaking character, but Alexis doesn't. She scrunches up her face in disgust. "UGH! I sound so stupid!" she says to all of us. "I'm sorry to mess up the scene, but I don't get why Colby would sound so sinister."

"CUT!" The director yells. He and Tom walk onto the set. "I thought we went over this in rehearsal," says the director, sounding slightly annoyed.

Alexis trains her big eyes on him. "I know, and you explained it beautifully, but I'm still not sure the line is working. The viewers love Colby, you know? I don't want them to think she's pure evil just yet," Alexis pouts. "I mean, do you think the network would want that? I don't know. We might want the writers to tweak the line."

"Tweak," the guest director repeats. "Okay, let's take five and discuss it."

"Writers," Tom calls. "You're on."

Melli massages her neck. Sky rolls her eyes. I bite my lower lip. We're running behind again today and this is the second line Alexis has questioned this morning. It's been two weeks since the Priceless party and a week since our infamous cast photo shoot and Alexis has only gotten more brazen with her demands. Yes, the press and most of this cast still hold her high on a pedestal, but every diva-in-training needs to know when to keep quiet. Now is one of those times. NO ONE disrupts a scene with Melli. Melli has been on this show since day one, which gives her a certain unspoken respect that the rest of us don't command. Melli's like the Godfather. You don't upset the Godfather. I guess Alexis doesn't care about sleeping with the fishes.

"Tom, do I need to be here for this?" Melli asks. She pulls back the hospital sheet to reveal slim-fitting faded jeans under her puke green gown. Melli starts to get up. "I promised my kids I'd call them on their lunch break and I'm going to miss it if we take any longer."

"Mel, please," Tom begs. "Give us two minutes."

Melli sighs. "I'll use my cell. When you're ready, I'll be at crafty getting coffee."

I hesitate, wondering if I should follow her. I've been dying to talk to Melli about these confusing feelings I'm having about my future, Sky, and Alexis. Melli's like a second mom to me, and I can tell her anything. She doesn't look like she's in the mood to talk today though, so I stay put as a bunch of the writers run over carrying their scripts and PDAs.

We have about twenty writers, so you'd think they would crowd our already packed stage, but they don't. Our *FA* set is huge. There are several sets in the Buchanan household — the kitchen, which has real running water, the living room with its Restoration Hardware furniture, Paige and Dennis's bedroom (which doubled as Sam and Sara's up until a few years ago when we finally got our own set), and the long dining room, with an Ethan Allen table that seats twenty. It's perfect for large family arguments, which are *FA* staples. Our soundstage also has interiors of my aunt Krystal's bedroom and kitchen, Penelope's living room and bedroom, the Summerville Diner, the Summerville Hospital waiting area and patient room (where we're shooting now), and just this year, we added our own mock school hallway and a classroom so that we don't have to film all of Sam and Sara's Summerville High scenes on location. For exterior shots of the front of the Buchanan estate, we film on a fake idyllic street on our studio's backlot. That's an area behind the film studio headquarters with room to build, or use, exterior sets.

HOLLYWOOD SECRET NUMBER FIVE: Like many TV shows, when *FA* shows the exterior of a character's fabulous home, chances are the interior scenes are filmed somewhere else, like a soundstage. Real rooms with four walls are too cramped for a large camera crew, writers, and assorted higher-ups, so most sets only have three walls, or are larger than your average room so that a crew can fit inside. When you see a house on TV, chances are the studio has either paid to use someone's exterior for the shot or they've constructed a house shell on the back lot to serve as home sweet home. On our back lot, *FA* has a street full of homes that have been used on other TV shows or movies and now serve as the town of Summerville. When Paige and Penelope were in the Buchanan Manor house fire two seasons ago, they burned the falling exterior of an aged home on the block. The space made way for a park, which we use for outdoor school shots. Buchanan Manor is the grandest of all the fake homes. But don't bother putting on a bathing suit — our swimming pool is not on set. Those scenes are shot twenty-three miles away at a mansion in Arcadia.

"Hey, ladies." *FA*'s newest writer, Max Welsh, walks over and flashes us a gorgeous smile that makes me nearly faint. I can't lie: Max is beyond cute. He's "SoCal" tan, has short, spiky brown hair, brown eyes, and a tall, fit body he shows off with a metrosexual wardrobe. Practically everyone on set has a secret crush on the twenty-something. (I wouldn't call my feelings a *crush*. I just appreciate his cuteness. That's not betraying Austin, is it?) "How can we help you this afternoon?" he asks.

"I'm so sorry to be a pain," Alexis says in a whiny voice. She looks and sounds like a ten-year-old in a super tight Snoopy tee that grazes her belly button and low-slung dark jeans. Colby is supposed to be sort of trashy, which explains the wardrobe. "I'm tripping over this one line. Colby comes off as suspicious, which is great, but I really think she could be so much more than that. What if we gave her a great backstory that explains why it seems like she's trying to betray the Buchanans?" Alexis stops talking and waves frantically to some of the writers standing in the back. "Becky, that color looks amazing on you! Hey, Roger! Ready to shoot some hoops later?"

Peter, one of our veteran writers, frowns. "But Alexis, Colby *is* trying to betray the Buchanans," he says gingerly. "This line is giving the viewers a tease of what's to come."

"I get what you're saying, I really do, but maybe we're missing the chance to have a bigger storyline here," Alexis says hurriedly. "Does Colby have to be lying about being Paige's daughter? Look how the public has embraced this character. Do you really think they want to see her gone in a few months? What if we let her stick around and cause problems for everyone in town instead of just the Buchanans?" Alexis asks hopefully. "Every show needs a good bad girl."

"This show has already got one," Sky hisses. "Me."

Alexis ignores her. "I'd just hate to ruin a popular storyline when there is so much more we could do with it — and Colby. I think we're creating something really great here this season and I, for one, don't want to see it die out too soon." Alexis squeezes my hand. I resist the urge to pull away and smile sweetly.

"Alexis, we've talked about this," Tom warns.

"But . . ." Alexis's eyes begin to water.

It's not unusual for the writers to be called in to help tweak a joke that just doesn't fly or a line so snippy it makes everyone on set wince. But changing someone's whole character outlook? That's a decision that happens upstairs, not here on set. I can't believe Alexis would have the nerve to even make such a suggestion. I resist the urge to glare at Alexis. Even if I ignore the fact that I overheard her talking trash about me and caught her flirting with my boyfriend, I can't forget her recent interview in *Hollywood Nation*. I can't believe she had the nerve to talk about Sky and me not getting along.

After the story ran, Alexis sent me flowers with a note that said they took her quote out of context. I am so not buying it.

"You're right about the public, Alexis," says Tom thoughtfully. "But this storyline has a beginning and an end that was mapped out before you were even hired. Colby eventually reveals her true colors. She tries to blackmail the Buchanans for abandoning her as a baby, but Sam and Sara uncover proof that Colby isn't Paige's daughter. It turns out that Colby's dead mother was Paige's college roommate, so she knew all about the baby given away at birth. Colby knows so much about the Buchanans that she thinks she can pass herself off as kin. After her cover is blown, she leaves town in episode thirteen."

"I can't wait till episode thirteen," Sky quips.

Alexis shoots Sky a nasty look. "I know," says Alexis, composing herself. "But things are going so well that I thought maybe you'd consider changing your minds about that." The last words come out in a sob and one of the grips puts his hand on Alexis's shoulder. I look around. Everyone from the camera guys to Shelly, my makeup artist, looks sad.

Did Alexis taint the water supply? How is everyone falling for this act? Alexis knew her story arc when she signed her contract!

"I have an idea," says Max.

He always has good ones too, so everyone pays attention. Max has only been with us for a few weeks, but he's already famous for single-handedly writing Melli's heart-wrenching wakeup scene. Everyone says the dialogue will win Melli another Emmy.

"Tom, maybe we can drop this line and put something simple in its place so that things are left up to the viewer's imagination," says Max. "We don't start unfolding Colby's motive for a few more episodes anyway."

He's kidding right?

"That's true," says Sarah, an *FA* writer who has been around for years. "It's probably better to give the story a chance to breathe before we change gears. Besides, it's just one line."

No! Nooooo! It's not just one line! She's angling to get a permanent role. Why can't they see it? Tom, don't listen to them!

"It is just one line," Tom seems to agree. "I guess it's okay."

SOB!

"BUT," he warns, "Alexis, next time you want to make a suggestion about your character's fate, you take it up with me before filming, not during the middle of a scene." Alexis puts her head down and nods. "I have the final say when it comes to storyline, not the writers, not the cast. While I can't say your idea hasn't crossed my mind in recent weeks," Tom adds, causing me to feel a little dizzy, "it's not something I'm ready to change my mind about just yet. It's my decision and I don't want to be questioned again in front of my entire cast and crew. Understand?"

"Yes," Alexis says simply, a smile beginning to curl at the corners of her full lips. "Completely."

I'm a little rattled. Yes, Tom put Alexis in her place, but he also seemed open to possibly changing the course of Alexis's storyline. That means she could be sticking around longer! I think I need to go lie down.

"Good," Tom is saying. "Now I'll go get Melli. Let's try to get through the scene without another delay this time." He glances meaningfully at Alexis.

Max scribbles some notes on his script. "Let's try a few other sentence ideas."

Everyone flips to the page in question and starts throwing out suggestions. "Can't wait?" "You rock?" "Thanks, Sam?" They settle on "Thank you. Thank all of you," making Colby sound like a saint. I bite my lip to keep from screaming.

"Thank you!" Alexis coos, hugging Max. "You're the best writing staff in town."

Sky turns away in disgust. "How would she know?" Sky says so quietly that only I can hear her. "What did she do before this? A Kentucky Fried Chicken commercial?"

We both snicker. We look at each other, realize that we're sharing a moment, and quickly turn away.

Twenty minutes later, we wrap the scene and I walk off set. Nadine stops me before I reach the soundstage door leading to the dressing rooms.

"That scene took FOREVER. What was the delay?" Nadine asks. She's been holed up in my dressing room this morning finalizing next week's schedule and setting up some phone interviews. Today Nadine's wearing a fitted navy tee, worn jeans, and running shoes. I'm too tired to explain what happened. My stomach does it for me, growling in protest. "That upset, huh?" Nadine asks. "I'll get right to it then. Good or bad news first?"

I stop in my tracks, afraid to hear what's happened now. I fix the cuff on my capri-length Dr. Denim jeans. I'm wearing a fitted floral silk tank by Prada with a sash around my waist and ballet flats. "Did Mom find out about my permit test?" I ask, sounding worried.

Liz and Austin got me so pumped up about getting my license that I went right home that night and asked my parents if I could take my permit test. Mom looked at me like I had just asked to be a guest on *Jerry Springer* and said, "Why would you want to do that when you have a driver to take you everywhere?" I tried to protest, but I could quickly see I was getting nowhere fast. Mom didn't get the bigger picture. I thought Dad would, being a car junkie and all, but he was Mr. Serious about it. "Driving a car is like lifting the hood of your Cadillac and trying to fine-tune the engine," he said. "If you don't know what you're doing, you're going to make a mess. I don't think you're ready, Katie-Kins." I tried appealing to their career sense and asked them what would happen if a potentially Oscar-winning movie role came around and I couldn't take it because my character needed to know how to drive. How would I do that if I didn't have my permit? They both laughed and said stars don't usually drive cars in the movies anyway. It's easier to shoot a car scene if the car is pulled along by a flat-bed truck. I stormed out of the room after that.

Feeling slightly rebellious, and concerned about the

betterment of my career, I did something I've never done before — forged my mom's signature. Then I forced Nadine to sign me up for my permit test. Nadine thinks I should confess to my mom about the test and I will.

After I pass.

Nadine and I duck into an empty guest dressing room and Nadine pulls a magazine out from the Bible. That's what we've dubbed the binder she keeps my schedule — and basically my whole life — hidden in.

"Your mom hasn't found out about the permit test," Nadine assures me. I breathe a sigh of relief. "But I still think you should tell her." I give her a look. "Okay, fine. That's not the bad news anyway. The bad news is that the new *Hollywood Nation* is out and you're in it again," she says. "An unnamed source says that you held up filming last week due to exhaustion. Stupid, huh?" Neither of us laughs.

"I've never delayed filming!" I complain. "Not once. Mom even makes me come in when I have a cold!"

"I know." Nadine touches my shoulder comfortingly. "Everyone important knows you didn't actually do it."

"Sky just can't quit, can she?" I say angrily.

"If Sky planted it, she isn't laughing too hard. There's an article bashing her in here too." Nadine turns the page.

I look at the spread Nadine is holding and gasp. SKY MACKENZIE BATTLES BULIMIA.

I've always suspected Sky managed to get less negative press by giving reporters fake articles about me to run instead. I've never done it, but I know stars who do. Some will do anything to avoid bad publicity. But if that's what Sky did this week, it backfired. The article says that Sky is lollipop thin because she worships the porcelain throne. On the page, there's a huge picture of Sky wasting away next to one from last year where she's supposedly heavier. Personally I think it's just the dress she has on. One is a muumuu and the other is made of spandex.

"I can't believe I'm defending Sky, but I don't think she makes herself throw up," I admit. "Even she's not that insane." I frown, flipping back to the article about me with the head-line KAITLIN BURKE COLLAPSES ON SET! If Sky isn't out to get me, then someone else is for sure.

"We should do some damage control," says Nadine.

"Okay," I say, feeling suddenly depressed.

"Ready for the good news?" Nadine sounds more cheer-ful. "Guess who's waiting for you in your dressing room?" I shrug. "He's cute and couldn't care less what the tabs say about you."

"Austin's here?" I squeal. "Can I deal with this article later and go see him?"

Nadine nods. "I'll call Laney," she says and opens the door for me.

I sprint down the hall and trip over someone's foot as I reach my dressing room.

"Watch it!" Sky moans.

What is she doing here? "What do you want?" I ask, fold-ing my arms across my chest.

"I have a bone to pick with you about that vicious story

you planted in *Hollywood Nation*." Sky has a defiant look in her dark eyes.

I snort. "Please. Why would I tell them that? Even if *someone* did make up a story about my supposed exhaustion."

Sky actually looks surprised. "Well, it wasn't me."

Deep down, I kind of knew it wasn't Sky, but I don't have it in me to admit it out loud. Instead I shrug.

"So if I didn't give them that story about you and you didn't give them that story about me, who is planting this garbage?" Sky asks.

I'm so aggravated by the latest tabloid assault, and annoyed that Sky is ambushing me to discuss it, that for a moment, I don't even care. "I don't have time to discuss it," I say, knowing I sound unreasonable. I just want to get past Sky, kiss my boyfriend, and forget all about this morning's ugliness. "If you'll excuse me . . ." I trail off and reach for the door.

"Fine," Sky huffs and stomps away.

I take a deep breath and then peer inside my room. Austin sees me and grins. He's looking particularly cute in warm-up pants and a long-sleeved thermal with a blue lacrosse tee over it. He always looks hottest at his most casual.

"What are you doing here?" I ask, feeling flush with happiness. I lean down and give Austin a kiss and then see Matty sitting next to him. Oops.

"We had a half day for parent conferences." Austin grins. "I thought I'd surprise you. I ran into Matty down the hall. We're just hashing out a little problem he has."

"Are you okay, Matty?" I ask worriedly. "Is it the schedule? Is it too much on you with all your schoolwork and lines and everything?"

Matty shakes his head. "It's not that." Matty won't look at me. "Man, did you have to tell my sister?" he asks Austin.

"Just tell her," Austin insists. Matty shakes his head. He looks really embarrassed. I look at Austin. Now I'm nervous.

"It's girl trouble," Austin explains.

I breathe a sigh of relief. Awww . . . my younger brother has a crush! He's only thirteen and a half, but I guess it's about time. "Matty, that's adorable. Who is she?" I ask. "Are you going to ask her out?"

Austin nods encouragingly. "No offense, but I couldn't tell you first," Matty says slowly. "You're my sister. I can't talk about girls with my sister. Are you mad?"

"Of course not." I can't stop smiling. "I wish you had confided in me though."

"Yeah, but I wasn't sure you would approve." He frowns.

I hit him in the arm. "What are you talking about? Of course I approve of anyone you want to date." I look at Austin. "This is so cool. We can double-date!"

"Would you come with us on our first one?" Matty looks hopeful. "I'm so nervous. I was thinking of asking her to the Ivy."

I shake my head. "Way too public for your first date. We'll think of someplace romantic and very private. So who's the girl? Do I know her?"

"Yeah, you do." Matt shifts uncomfortably and looks away again.

Uh-oh. I clutch my chest. "Please don't tell me you're in love with Sky!"

"NO WAY!" Matt looks disgusted. "I would never disrespect you like that."

"Good." I'm relieved. "Then who is she?"

Matt looks at Austin. Austin looks at Matt. Then Austin looks at me. So does Matt.

"It's Alexis," Matt whispers. "I like Alexis."

"ALEXIS?" I screech. They both jump. "You CAN'T. You just CAN'T!" I blurt out. I sound like a maniac. I just know it. But I don't care.

"I knew you'd react this way!" Matt moans. "I told Austin you would."

"What do you mean?" I demand.

"You're jealous of her," Matt says.

"I AM NOT JEALOUS," I yell, feeling very flush.

"It's obvious." Matt sounds mad. "It's hard not to be the object of everyone's affections anymore, but take it like a lady, Kates. Alexis is hot right now. That doesn't mean everyone doesn't still like you."

"I know t-that," I stutter. I can't breathe. I seriously can't breathe. Someone must have just sucked all the air out of the room.

"Do you?" Matty asks. "Because all you do is complain about Alexis getting so much attention. I hear you talking to

Nadine and Rodney on the way to work. You should be ashamed. She has been nothing but nice to you."

I open my mouth to respond and quickly shut it again. What can I say? That Alexis is a two-faced manipulative diva? Matt is so blinded by his crush, he probably wouldn't believe me. Besides, what proof do I have? Overhearing her being catty in the wardrobe room or witchy on the red carpet? No. Until I know for sure that she's up to something, I've got to keep my mouth shut. "It's not that I'm jealous or I don't like her," I say instead. "I just think she's too old for you."

"Well, you're wrong," Matt huffs and he heads straight for the door. "And I'll prove it. Thanks, Austin." He slams the door behind him.

"Austin, I hope you tried to dissuade him!" I'm jumping up and down like a spoiled two-year-old and I don't care. "She's too old for him! She'll break his heart! But more importantly, she's not who she says she is. She's a FRAUD! I don't want her sinking her teeth into my baby brother!" My chest is pounding.

Austin chuckles and puts his arm around me, pulling me into a fierce bear hug. I bury my head in his chest, which smells like laundry detergent, and breathe deeply.

"Calm down, tiger," Austin says softly. "I'll talk to him again. I promise." He hugs me. "But you know how it is — when you fall for someone, you fall hard. You can't turn it off, even if you know the odds for success are as bad as a big star deciding to date an average Joe."

I blush. "I see your point."

He kisses me. "Hey, at least he has good taste, right? Alexis is gorgeous."

I pull away. "You think she's gorgeous?" I know I sound annoyed, but I don't care. I *am* annoyed!

From the wide-eyed look on his face, I can tell Austin immediately realizes what he's done. He's broken relationship rule number one: Never talk about another girl in front of your girlfriend. Austin begins hacking and I can't tell if it's real or fake, but it sounds so awful that I let him off the hook.

For the moment.

TUESDAY, 10/1
NOTE TO SELF:

Wed. BE AT "LOCATION" 4 PERMIT TEST AT 7:15 AM!
Wed. STUDY TONITE!
Wed. Call time: 8:15 AM
Thurs., Fri. Call time: 5:15 AM
Fitting w/ Kristen 4 next episodes: Tues. 3 PM (prepare 2 stay 3 hours)
Fri @ 7 – date w/ A :)
Spa day (hallelujah) w/ Laney, Liz, Mom – Oct. 5

SIX: *Bliss Interrupted*

Liz sighs. "Tell me again why we don't do this more often?" Her voice is muffled. Our heads are buried deep in plush face pillows as we lie on side-by-side massage tables at the Argyle Salon and Spa in West Hollywood getting four-hand massages. (Two massage therapists working on one person. It's pure heaven!)

"We should make a weekly appointment." I feel relaxed and woozy from the scent of the Jacqua Buttercream Frosting lotion that Liz and I requested for our massage. "I think I might have to reserve us a permanent room here."

"If you don't, I'll ask Dad to do it for us," Liz says, her voice jumping as the therapists pound her back. "I still can't believe this was your mom's idea."

"I know." The masseuses are busy working out the tiny knots that have taken up permanent residence in my neck and shoulders thanks to the recent bashings in *Hollywood Nation* and on *Celeb Insider* this week about my supposed bad behavior on set. I could blame them on Sky. She seemed agitated when we had that confrontation outside my dressing room after Alexis's line-tweaking delay last week. And she's done it countless times before. But Sky doesn't seem immune to the bad press either. No, Nadine and I have talked about it and we're convinced Alexis is behind this latest wave. Not that we have proof, but Nadine is working on it, and until she has it, I'm determined to keep quiet. I just don't understand Alexis's motive. She's getting enough great press to last for years. Why is she determined to take us down in the process?

"Mom even had Nadine cancel an interview I had today so that my schedule would be clear," I add. "She said I needed a day off."

"That's a first," Liz teases, her voice echoing in the cavernous room. Mom reserved Argyle's oversize spa suite, which can host up to eight people at a time, and invited me, Liz, and Laney (I thought Nadine would be upset about not being included, but she was thrilled to have a "Laney-free day," as she put it). The room is like a super-lush hotel suite, with fabulous silk drapes and a giant ninety-eight-gallon soaking tub for body treatments that is filled with rose petals and tiny candles. There was even a breakfast spread waiting for us when Rodney dropped us off. Since the spa is tucked inside the Sunset Tower Hotel, you can have meals catered to your room. Laney had a breakfast, and Mom said she had an appointment, so neither of them will be here till eleven, which is fine by me, because it gives Liz and me some much-needed bonding time.

"We're finished, Kaitlin," one of my masseuses whispers in my ear. "Take your time getting up. The herbal tea you requested is waiting for you on the table. Your manicure and pedicure appointments will start in half an hour."

"Thank you." I sigh happily. "That was incredible." We both lie on our tables till we hear the door close, and then Liz and I slowly get up, tuck ourselves into the plush white robes and slippers the staff have left behind, and meander over to the couch. On our packed schedules today are a group manicure and pedicure, facials, and then private body wraps. Liz and I chose the Argyle Signature body wrap, which is a mix of avocado, chocolate, almond, coconut, clove, cinnamon, orange, and vanilla. I rest my head on a pillow and breath in the deep scent of freesia that pervades the low-lit room. The only sound I hear is ocean waves, courtesy of the relaxation CD playing in the room. "I want to hear everything you've been up to this week."

"I think they should make this place a prerequisite for taking the SATs," says Liz, her wild curly brown hair tucked in a ponytail and a Louis Vuitton head scarf. "That's honestly all I've been doing — studying. That and working with Daniella on your movie. Wait till you see some of the scenes at the private screening in December, Kates. You look so fierce. You're definitely going to give Angelina Jolie a run for her money in the action business."

"I don't know about that." I laugh. My face feels so fresh for a change. Maybe that's because my ivory complexion isn't covered under a mask of foundation and bronzer. I didn't even wash my hair this morning. Instead, I fixed it into a low bun to keep the creams and oils away from my highlights. "Did I tell you I asked Monique to give me some SAT practice tests? They're really hard, but I think they're helping. I may not know what I'm doing about college, but at least if I get a good score, I'll have options."

"I think that's really smart, Kates," Liz agrees.

"Oh, I've got some other news too. I think I've figured out the perfect birthday gift for Austin." I can't help but smile at the thought. "You know how he loves watching NASCAR? Well, I talked to Rodney and he said that the Las Vegas Motor Raceway gives rides on the track. I thought we could fly to Vegas on his birthday — it's only an hour flight — and he could be a passenger in a race car. Then we can have dinner at SW Steakhouse at Wynn Las Vegas before flying back. What do you think?"

Liz frowns and her eyes shift downward.

"You hate the idea, don't you?" I worry. "Why? Do you think it's too over the top? I thought taking Austin somewhere rather than buying him an expensive present would make him less uncomfortable. Do you think I'm wrong? Or is it our moms? I didn't think about this, but maybe they won't want us flying out of state for a date."

"Kates, calm down," Liz says gently. "I think Austin would love the idea." I breathe a sigh of relief. "But there's still a problem."

"What?" I bite my lip.

"Austin's birthday falls on Homecoming this year, which

wouldn't be a big deal except that yesterday the nominations were announced for Homecoming court." Liz pauses. "Austin is up for the court. That means he's supposed to ride in the Homecoming game parade. Technically, he doesn't have to go to the dance, so I guess he could go to Vegas in the afternoon, but I've never heard of a nominee bailing on the dance. Maybe he could forfeit his nomination," Liz suggests.

I shake my head. "That's silly. I'll do the Vegas thing another day."

Liz smiles. "Definitely!"

"I wonder why Austin didn't say anything about the nomination," I question. "We went out for sushi last night and he didn't say a word."

"You know boys," Liz says dismissively. "He didn't tell me either. He told Josh. Josh said Austin knew you'd been planning a birthday surprise and he didn't want to disappoint you. Josh told him to ask you to the dance instead, but Austin didn't think you'd want to go after what happened at the Spring Fling."

"The paparazzi showing up and ruining the school dance again wouldn't make me that popular with the student body," I agree. "I'd be banned from Clark for life." I look up at the creamy white ceiling hoping for an answer. "The dance sounds fun," I say. "And if it's on Austin's birthday and he has to go, that's where I want to be too. I wish there was a way I could go with him."

We're both quiet for a minute. Then Liz says, "Why can't

you? What if the paparazzi had no idea you were going to be at the dance?"

"They'll find out." I frown. "They always do."

"Not if Austin thinks you're not going to the dance either." Liz sounds excited now. "This is what you do: Tell Austin you just found out you have reshoots for *Pretty Young Assassins* on his birthday. Apologize profusely and tell him you'll celebrate with him on Sunday instead. Austin's such a good sport, he'll feel obligated to go to the dance and won't feel bad about it anymore. When people ask if you're going to be his date, he'll obviously say no. The press will think you're not going. Then, that night, you can show up at the last minute, when it's too late to alert the paparazzi. That would be the ultimate birthday surprise!"

"Liz, you're a genius." I hug her. "I'll take Austin to Vegas on Sunday. He'll get two birthday presents."

"You see? I knew we'd work it out." She grins. "I'll buy you a ticket for Homecoming this week so you have it. Austin has to buy them ahead of time and he won't get you one if he thinks you're working."

"Perfect." I hear the door open.

"Morning, Katie-Kins!" my mother sings. "Are you and Liz having fun?" My mom is dressed casually in Genetic Denim jeans and a three-quarter-length sleeve ballet-neck navy T-shirt with flats.

"This place is amazing, Mom," I tell her. "You've got to ask them to use the Jacqua Buttercream Frosting lotion for your massage."

"Is that what smells so overpowering in here?"

Who said that?

I do a double take. Walking in behind my mom is Alexis. In addition to a super-sized smile, she's wearing hip-hugging J Brand jeans and a bedazzled burgundy tank top. Her long red hair is a little frizzy, but perfectly curled at the ends, like she'd gone to a party the night before and it hadn't been redone since. Laney is standing behind her and she looks really ticked off.

"Hey, Alexis." I manage to compose myself quickly. "I didn't know you were going to be here today."

"I invited Alexis to join us so we could tell her all about how Burke Management has enhanced your career," Mom explains happily.

What? NOOOOOOOOOOOOOOOOOO!

There goes my blissful Saturday.

I can feel my heart palpitations kick-start. With work being so busy this past week, and Mom's social calendar more packed than Nobu on a Saturday night, I haven't had a chance to tell her or Laney my suspicions about Alexis or about the stunts she's been pulling on set. Thankfully, from the look on Laney's face, I take it Nadine's told her a thing or two. But it's obvious Laney hasn't discussed them with Mom yet.

Laney slips out of the BCBG blazer that I gave her and plops down next to me. "I had no idea she was coming till I pulled up and saw her flaming red hair in your mom's Beamer," she whispers to me while Mom is busy introducing Alexis to Liz. "I was wrong about this girl. I want you to know

I'm not on board with this, Kaitlin. I don't represent frauds. Having *FA*'s biggest star on my roster is enough for me."

I'm so touched I want to reach out and hug her, but I know Laney doesn't like to have her neatly pressed clothes wrinkled. Instead, I smile brightly.

"Nadine has been filling me in about Alexis and her blatant attempt to woo the writing staff," Laney continues, her voice dripping with disdain. "Well, that's nothing compared with the disturbing set gossip I've been hearing." My heart lurches as Laney's dark eyes peer into mine ominously. "This girl is no good. I don't trust her and I don't like how she's infiltrated *FA*. You've got to be careful. I mean it."

"I know," I say, feeling light-headed. Laney has just confirmed what I've been thinking about Alexis for a while and I'm not sure how to process it.

"I'll straighten out your mother," Laney promises as my mom whips a large stack of papers out of her green Balenciaga tote and places them on the table in front of me. "Trust me."

"So is this why you wanted me to come here today?" I whisper to my mother as she takes a seat on the couch across from me. I smile sweetly at Alexis, who is making small talk with Liz. "So that you could woo Alexis?"

Mom purses her lips, which look thin again. I'm sure lip plumping is on her agenda today. "Shh," she says, looking over her shoulder at Alexis. "Don't look at me like that. We're here so you can have a relaxing, well-deserved day of pampering. I just thought it would be nice to write the whole expense off by doing some business as well, so I invited Alexis."

"Didn't the spa comp this whole thing because Kaitlin was a guest?" Laney asks. I try not to grin. She's probably right.

Mom raises her right eyebrow at Laney. Uh-oh. "It can't hurt to talk to her about my management firm, can it?" Mom asks us.

"I really don't think that's a good . . ." Laney stops talking when she realizes Alexis is listening. Alexis walks over and takes a seat next to me.

"I'm so glad we've got a chance to bond together today, Kaitlin," Alexis says to me. "I was just telling your mom that I rarely see you when we're not shooting." She looks like a sad puppy in a store window.

"She's good," Liz whispers in my ear.

"That's why you came today, Alexis? To hang out with Kaitlin?" Laney asks politely. "That's *so* nice."

TRAP HER Laney. At least someone other than me — and, well, Sky — sees through Alexis's sickingly sweet fake act.

"That's the main reason." Alexis smiles at me. "I'm dying to know more about Kaitlin Burke! What makes you tick? What do you like to do on your day off?" She stares at me, waiting for an answer.

"Nothing exciting," I say slowly. "I do the same things everyone else does."

"You're too modest!" Alexis laughs. "You can admit how fabulous your life is! I think it's great. But I have to admit, I do have another motive for coming here."

I hold my breath, wondering what Alexis is going to say.

"I wanted to meet the fabulous Laney Peters and talk to

your mom." Alexis grins. "I've heard you two are an unstoppable PR and management team."

Now it's my mom's turn to smile. All this smiling and someone's face is going to freeze that way during a facial.

"I didn't think I needed representation, but now I'm wondering if I do." Alexis frowns. "This town can be really tough."

Here we go.

"Hollywood's not meant for everyone," Laney says simply, as the door to our suite opens and five Argyle Spa employees file in with a manicure and pedicure cart.

"Oh good, our first appointment," Mom says excitedly. She glances at Alexis with a look of concern. "Alexis, dear, tell us what's going on. Are people giving you a hard time?"

"I'm having a problem with my contract." Alexis starts to tear up.

Wow, she's an even better manipulator than Sky.

"I didn't realize when I signed on that it was only for half a season," she moans. "The Colby character could be a huge asset to this show if they'd just keep her around."

When I hear Alexis say that, I almost want to laugh. So Alexis thinks my mom, Laney, and I can help her? I shake my head. Alexis's motives are clear to me now, but I still don't get what they have to do with me and Sky. Why is she talking trash about us? Is it jealousy because we've been on the show forever? There's still so much about Alexis I haven't figured out.

"That's TV," Laney echoes some of my sentiments out

loud. "You signed for a limited story arc and that's all they're going to give you."

Alexis looks annoyed with that answer and turns her attention back to my mom.

"But maybe we can help, Laney," Mom suggests. She looks at Alexis's sad face. "Is there anything we can do to change their minds?"

Alexis's face relaxes a bit. "Well, the more people say they like working with me, the better," Alexis confides. "*FA* is such a great TV family and I'd love to be part of it longer. I'm just so overwhelmed about how to do that. I'm not as savvy as Kaitlin, you know? I don't know all this fancy lingo and how to deal with the paparazzi." She pauses and turns to the woman preparing to do her man-icure. "After this, I'll be having a Hamman scrub, an Organic Boost facial, and if there's time a hot stone four-hand massage."

"She doesn't sound savvy at all," Liz whispers. I try not to giggle.

Across the room, I hear the familiar vibration of my Sidekick and take the opportunity to jump off the couch to retrieve it. Five minutes in the room with Alexis and already I feel my loosened shoulder knots begin to tense up again. I read the message.

WOOKIESRULE: How's my girl doing? It hasn't even
been 12 hrs. since I saw U and I miss U.

A smile spreads across my face, and for a moment I forget the beauty and the beast scenario I'm currently starring in. I carry my Sidekick back to my spot on the couch, noticing that Alexis has moved over to give me less room, and squeeze myself back into my rightful place. The manicurist sees the Sidekick and gets to work on removing the polish from my toes instead.

> PRINCESSLEIA25: U made my day. I'm in spa hell.
> WOOKIESRULE: Spa hell. Is that where supermodels go to die?

I can't help but laugh aloud. "Who are you talking to?" Alexis asks.

"Probably her boyfriend," Mom explains, sounding slightly annoyed. I glare at my mother. Did she have to bring him up?

Alexis smiles. "He's adorable. I was talking to him for a while at the Priceless party when you were off networking. You better watch someone doesn't try to steal him away."

I can't help myself. The words are coming out of my mouth before I can stop them. "Lucky for me, Austin — like most of Hollywood — finds me completely irresistible." I hit send on my Sidekick and smile smugly.

> PRINCESSLEIA25: I'll explain later, but miss U 2. Especially right now.
> WOOKIESRULE: Did U break the news about passing UR permit test yet?

PRINCESSLEIA25: Shhh! No. I wanted 2 wait till after my massage 2 break the news.
WOOKIESRULE: Uh-oh. Good luck. TTYL — if U R still alive.

Very funny! I slide my Sidekick safely back in my bag and resist the urge to hit Alexis over the head with my hardware. If she says even one more word about Austin, I just might.

"Oh, he's not famous." I hear Mom saying to Alexis. She's talking about Austin, I'm sure. "Kaitlin met him when she did that god-awful school stunt last year."

"School stunt?" Alexis asks, looking intrigued.

"I'm just going to run to the bathroom," Liz says, trying to slip out of the line of fire. I hear her slippers smack against the floor as she hurries out.

Laney clears her throat. "I feel for you, Alexis, but I really don't think Meg and I can help you," she interrupts, stopping my mother dead in her tracks. Mom's jaw drops, as does Alexis's. I try to suppress a smile. "Kaitlin is a huge client, and I don't think either of us have time to take on another client on the same hit show. It would be a conflict of interest." Alexis looks flustered. "I'd be happy to give you the name of other management firms and publicists at my company though. I hope we haven't wasted your Saturday. You're welcome to stay and hang out with Kaitlin, like you said you wanted to do." Laney's smile is thin.

Mom looks like she wants to say something, but I guess Laney's torturous stare stops her. If there is one thing

Mom isn't oblivious to after all these years, it's Laney's expressions.

"Thank you, Laney," Alexis says briskly. "I really appreciate your honesty, but I am disappointed. I've had plenty of offers, but having heard so much about both of you, and being so fond of Kates, I wanted to offer you both first crack."

"We appreciate that," Laney says sweetly.

"After all, even if the network hasn't extended my contract, they have awarded me 'and' status during the show's theme song." Alexis smiles at me.

"You're kidding!" I practically choke. "I mean, that's awesome."

I place my hand on the bag holding my Sidekick. I have the strong urge to hit her. I know that's mean of me, but I can't help it. I'm jealous, all right? I know she's not sticking around *FA* forever, but I wish she wasn't on our set at all. Laney's right — there is no way Alexis will be able to turn her contract around. She's on for a limited number of episodes and that's it. I just have to survive the next few months with her and then she'll be out of my hair for good.

"I thought *FA* reserved that status for full-season stars." Mom all of a sudden looks nervous.

"Apparently *FA* loves me," Alexis gloats.

HOLLYWOOD SECRET NUMBER SIX: Everyone knows that a TV show credit — which is a star's billing during the beginning of the program — is a coveted piece of real estate. When a cast's names are featured at the beginning of the program, usually the first and the last names to appear are reserved for the biggest stars. In *FA*'s case, Melli (Paige) has the first mention. Shows, and movie posters, usually reserve the "and" for a star who doesn't warrant top billing, but is a big enough name that they shouldn't be lumped in the middle of the credits, with everyone else (like me, who gets fifth billing, before Sky and after Spencer, who plays my TV dad). Billing is such a big deal that stars actually negotiate where their name will be placed when they're signing on to a project.

If they've given Alexis "and" status, they must think she's a star. Does that mean they're reconsidering her short-term contract? That would mean I'd have to put up with Sky *and* Alexis. Even if I had weekly Jacqua Buttercream Frosting massages, I don't think my neck muscles would survive.

"You must be thrilled," Mom says tightly. Maybe now she's getting the picture. Alexis getting so much love from *FA* is a threat to her daughter. "Well, I hope you'll still stay and enjoy the treatments."

"Of course!" Alexis says. "And Laney, I'd love that list." The manicurist is done with Alexis's toes, which are painted bloodred. Alexis slides into her slippers, gathers up her Gucci tote and strappy black heels, and walks toward the door. "I'm going to go get my facial before I do my manicure, but I'm sure I'll see you all a little later."

"Kaitlin, I feel like such a fool," Mom says after she's sure Alexis has closed the door behind her. "I had no idea she wanted to stay on your show! I can't represent her and my baby. Obviously I'd always want *FA* press for you over her." She hugs me tightly.

I'm in such shock I almost forget to hug her back. Mom gets it. For maybe the first time ever, Mom totally gets where I'm coming from!

"Laney, I'm so sorry," Mom adds.

"I could have you banned from Barneys for that." Laney's joking, but her voice is chilly and I know she means business. "Don't ever bring another potential client in like that without telling me first! I was going to tackle you to the floor before I let you sign her! That girl is trouble."

I fill Mom in on Alexis's Jekyll and Hyde behavior. How she's beyond nice to the stars and kisses up to the writers, but treats the underlings like dirt. How she's determined to be a regular on *FA* at any cost. How she throws fits and holds up filming.

"Classic overblown ego," Laney tsks. "I don't buy this innocent act either. That girl knows what's she doing with the press, the show, everything. Kaitlin, I wasn't kidding when I said you need to watch out. I don't care how nice she is to your face. She wants a permanent gig on *FA* and she'll stop at nothing to get it."

I shudder. "I know," I agree. "What am I going to do about her?" Before either of them can answer, Liz runs in and slams the door shut behind her.

"You're never going to believe what I just overheard!" Liz exclaims. "I was on my way back from the bathroom, when

I passed Alexis pacing in a room waiting for her next appointment. She was on the phone and she was yelling about how 'little miss perfect' gave her no dirt to use and how this morning was a waste of her time. Kaitlin, she was so talking about you!"

"I'm not surprised," I say angrily. "I've overheard her bash me before. This is what I was talking about. We have to take her down."

"We are definitely taking her down!" Laney echoes with a battle cry. "No dirt? That girl is totally trying to feed the press garbage about you! I'm sure that's where those new stories are coming from."

"I thought Sky was our problem with those," Mom says, looking very pale.

"I did at first too, but Sky is also getting creamed," I explain. "And I think Sky hates Alexis more than she does me at this point. It's got to be Alexis. I'm more sure of it now than ever." Wait till I tell Nadine what just went down.

"I've spoiled your whole spa day," Mom groans. "I can't believe I invited that awful girl here. How can I make it up to you, honey?"

Without skipping a beat, I reply: "You could let me take driving lessons."

Liz laughs.

My mom is flabbergasted. "You don't even have your permit."

"Actually I took the test and passed," I mumble. Mom hears me anyway.

"What? How?" Mom asks.

"The point is, I have the permit and I should learn how to drive," I tell her. "What if the next role I audition for requires me to drive a car? What am I going to say, I can't?"

"She does have a point," Laney says. Mom looks at me pensively.

"Mom, everyone my age is learning how to drive," I add. "I should be learning too."

"Okay, well, we can just teach you to drive on the back lot like everybody else," Mom says reasonably.

"The class has to be done with a licensed instructor," I explain. "I need six hours of driving time plus fifty hours in the car with a responsible adult over the age of twenty-five. So I Googled some schools online and there's a bunch near the studio . . ."

"UH-UH." Mom shakes her head. "We'll hire you some top-notch private teacher who can teach you on your lunch hour. I don't want you going to some public school."

"The paparazzi will have a field day if you enroll at some dinky driving school and crash a car," Laney agrees. I open my mouth to protest. "No buts, Kaitlin. You can learn to drive — if your mom okays it — but classes are out of the question."

"But this is Los Angeles!" I argue. "Stars go food shopping, to the park, to the dog run, hiking, and no one bothers them. Why should driving lessons be any different? Sure, there might be a few pictures, but I bet a school wouldn't even care that I'm enrolled."

"It's true," Liz adds. "It's totally 'in' to act as if you couldn't care less that a celebrity is in your midst."

"See?" I say. "I don't want a professional or special treatment like I get with everything else. I want a totally normal driving class where a cranky old instructor yells at me for making a left turn into traffic. Is that so much to ask?"

"Yes," Mom freaks. "And I'm sure your dad would back me up on this. You're not like everybody else, sweetie. We've been through this. You can learn how to drive, fine, but you have to do it our way. It's for the best. You don't need any extra excuses to get bad press right now. Not while we're still unsure what Alexis is really up to."

"But . . ."

"No arguing." Mom is firm. "Now let's talk about something more pleasant, like cars. The first car a celebrity drives makes a huge statement. Do you want a showpiece or do you want to be eco-friendly and drive a Prius?"

"Oooh! Maybe we can get her a Tango electric car!" Laney offers. "I know someone who knows someone who can get Kaitlin one for less than $100,000."

"Congratulations," Liz says as Laney and Mom continue yapping away.

Congratulations?

Oh wait, Liz is right! They may not have agreed to driving lessons, but they still okayed me learning how to drive.

If I can win them over about this, I'm SURE I can make them love the cute, small driving school in Burbank that I've been secretly talking to (shhh . . .). I feel so inspired, I think I'm going to call them this afternoon and sign up. When I come home after my first class (or maybe my second), I'll give Mom, Dad, and Laney a demonstration of my amazing driving technique, point out how I've kept the paparazzi at bay, and then they'll be so proud of me they won't care that I lied to them.

I think.

Nadine doesn't know I've been checking out schools behind her back (she agrees with Mom and Laney on this one), but I'm sure she won't be mad. Right?

SATURDAY, 10/5
NOTE TO SELF:

Tell A about driving classes — warn him not 2 tell
Nadine or Rodney.
First appointment: Fri. 10/11 7 AM
Call time: 10 AM (yippee!)
Finalize Vegas details. Ask A's Mom 4 permission 2 take
A 2 Vegas day after his b-day.
Find dress 4 Homecoming!

seven: *Learning Curve*

Three ... two ... one, and ...

"I know I said I wouldn't say anything else, but I can't help it!" Nadine is wigging out. "I can't believe you did this. I just can't!"

Okay, so maybe I underestimated. Nadine is *beyond* mad that I booked a driving class without telling her. She's downright furious.

Gulp.

"You're a smart girl, Kaitlin! How could you do this?" Nadine continues. At this point, she'll still be yelling when Ralph, my Wheel Helpers driver's education instructor, shows up. It's 7 AM and Nadine, Rodney, Austin, and I are standing at Ralph's and my agreed-upon top secret meeting place — the northwest corner of West Olive Street at an abandoned parking lot — and Ralph is ten minutes late. Or maybe he's lurking nearby and is just afraid of facing Nadine.

Nadine actually sounds a lot like Laney right now. Or

Mom. Or even Melli on the rare occasions that Sky and I have a spat in front of her.

"I thought you'd be proud of me finding a school on my own," I sniff. I think I'm getting a cold — my voice has been sounding nasally for days. I guess that explains why I feel so chilly. I stick my hands in the pockets of my olive green cargo pants to warm them. I wanted to look and feel like any normal teen taking her first driving class, so I'm dressed casually in Gap pants and a plain black V-neck.

Nadine glares at me as she zips up her blue hoodie and pulls it up over her nose. She doesn't say anything.

Now I feel bad. "Nadine, don't be like this," I beg. "I tell you everything. *Everything*. The truth is, I wanted to figure something out on my own for once." I pause. "And I didn't want to get you in trouble with Mom and Laney so I thought it was better if I kept you in the dark."

I had tried feeling Nadine out about the driver's class but she seemed to feel the same way my parents and Laney did — that I shouldn't take any lessons until we found a studio-approved private instructor who had taught the likes of Mischa, Hilary, or Lindsay (and probably been so easy on them they didn't even have to learn how to parallel park), *and* would agree to sign a confidentiality agreement. The whole idea of a private instructor seemed over the top to me. Why couldn't they see that a driving class at a school would be no big deal? Rather than continue to argue, I struck out on my own.

"But you always confide in me no matter what the consequences," Nadine replies softly. "And with good reason. When have I ever steered you wrong?"

That's true, but she's exaggerating because she's hurt. I know it. Even Yoda wasn't always right. Was he?

I thought the extra-early appointment time and top secret location would make Nadine proud, but no, she's still mad. Rodney picked up Austin on our way here and Nadine thought it was because he was coming for a set visit (on a school day?). Halfway to the studio, I told Rodney and Nadine the truth — my call time wasn't until 10 AM and Austin was here to offer his support for my first-ever driver's education lesson. Rodney took it well, but Nadine *flipped*.

Why couldn't Nadine understand that what it all comes down to is I just want the same experience everyone else my age gets when it comes to learning how to drive? This is one of the first major decisions I've made on my own — well, if you forget about the whole skipping Hollywood for high school thing — and I'm sure I'll look back on it proudly one day. If Jen Garner can hang out in the sandbox with her daughter every week and not be bothered, I can totally tackle driving school without a paparazzi entourage.

"Not only have I let you down by not stopping you from this suicide mission, I'm going to be fired!" Nadine is starting to get hysterical again. "When your mother and Laney find out what I let you do, they're going to put a hit out on me!"

I'm about ready to hand her the paper bag from Austin's sesame bagel and tell her to breathe in and out of it very slowly, but instead I say, "I'll tell them the truth — that you had no idea what I was doing." Nadine doesn't look relieved.

"Think of it this way. At least she didn't show up alone," Rodney says, taking a bite of an egg sandwich oozing with ketchup.

"I really have thought this thing — AH-CHOO — through, Nadine," I say. "The school is new, so no one knows it exists, and I've spoken to Ralph, my instructor, and he couldn't care less that I'm on a TV show."

"That's what he's telling you. I give this place fifteen minutes before helicopters are hovering overhead!" Nadine grimaces.

"Ralph assured me he would sign a confidentiality agreement when he got here," I say before sneezing.

"As your longtime assistant, I would have told you that you should always have them sign the agreement *before* they arrive," Nadine says. "Now they can show up with *Hollywood Nation* and you'd have no way to stop them."

I didn't think of that. "Ralph seemed very trustworthy," I argue. "I grilled him several times before I set up the appointment."

Nadine rolls her eyes. "Austin, talk some sense into her, will you? Remind her how many stars have been burned by people they thought were nice."

"I'm staying out of this," Austin says, holding up his hands in peace, and Nadine walks away in disgust.

"Between us, I have to say Nadine has some valid points," Austin says tactfully.

I would hit his arm, but I feel too weak. I'm sweating and freezing at the same time. Is that even possible? Thank God Austin is here to keep me warm. He's skipping his first two periods to cheer me on, which is not smart, but incredibly sweet.

"Seriously, everyone you know thinks this is a bad idea," Austin adds. "What if Nadine's right?"

I shake my head. "I'm going to lessons in the wee hours of the morning when Larry the Liar is still hungover from the night before. No one can leak this to the press, and besides, Ralph told me he couldn't care less about celebrity culture so I feel positive that he . . . that he . . ." I wrinkle my nose. "AH-AH-CHOO!"

"Bless you! Listen, Burke, I'm on your side no matter what," Austin says. "I just wanted to triple-check that you thought this thing through."

That's my problem, actually. I overthink everything I do! Like the other day on set. We were having a great time shooting a scene with Melli — which Alexis wasn't in — and I was actually getting along with Sky and having a great time with Matty, and Tom was giving me compliments left and right about how much my acting had grown and all I could think about was that I belonged here. I want to work on *FA* till I'm forty-something, just like Melli. Who cares about college?

Ten minutes later the voice in my head was saying, "What if *FA* goes off the air? What if your career dries up? Do you want to be hawking bad jewelry on the Home Shopping Network? Go to college like Austin and Liz and have a backup plan!" And then the other voice in my head said, "But if you leave *FA* for college, your career will flop," and so on. I wish I could just enjoy the ride and not worry about the long term. Today I was making a decision and sticking to it.

"Listen, Meyers, I'm in too deep to change gears now. Kind of like you and Homecoming," I tease, finding the perfect segue. I've been trying to keep up the whole "I'm mad I can't go to his Homecoming" thing so Austin doesn't get suspicious. It's good actor training.

"I don't care about Homecoming," he says, not very convincingly. "It's a stupid tradition. I didn't ask to be nominated." Austin's wearing his short-sleeved Clark High lacrosse shirt over a long-sleeved gray tee and distressed jeans. "I'd rather get the parade over with and spend as much of my birthday as possible with you."

I think it's cute that Austin is embarrassed about the nomination. And even cuter that he wants to protect me from the paparazzi — who Liz says have been hitting up students to find out if I'm going to the dance with Austin just like we hoped they would — but he doesn't have to worry. Just like the driver's lessons, I've got this figured out. The only thing left to do is get used to the idea that Austin could have to dance with his ex, Lori, who was unfortunately nominated for the court too. BLECH.

Nadine barrels over again, with Rodney behind her. "And another thing — you know what else your assistant would have handled if she was in charge?" she asks. "Making sure Rodney did a thorough security check of the location and a background check on the driving school."

Rodney takes another bite of his sandwich. "Nadine, the school is brand-new and the location is an abandoned parking lot. I think you're spending too much time around Laney." He chuckles, but he still looks intimidating with his bald head wrapped in the hood of his black sweatshirt.

I try to laugh, but I sneeze again instead.

"Burke, I think you're getting sick." Austin puts his hand on my forehead, like our housekeeper Anita sometimes does when she thinks I'm overexerting myself. "You feel warm."

"I'm fine," I lie. Actually I do feel hot, but I thought that was because I'm excited. Besides, I don't have time to get sick. Actors rarely take sick days.

HOLLYWOOD SECRET NUMBER SEVEN: Celebrities don't get sick. At least, they don't tell the world when they do — unless they're in serious need of some R&R and want to check themselves into Cedars Sinai for "exhaustion." (Sky's pulled that twice now.) Usually stars stick to the motto "The show must go on" and fight through the colds (with the aid of Emergen-C) and bouts with the stomach flu (delay filming for a few hours rather than a whole day). Of course, if you're a major cast member and you come down with the chicken pox, shooting usually is delayed, like it was when my friend Gina got sick and infected two other cast members on her TV show. I've never taken a sick day, but that could be because whenever I sneeze, my mom reminds me that Oprah has never called in sick in almost two decades on the air.

"You've been coughing and sneezing for two days, Kaitlin," Nadine says. "You should take some more Cold-EEZE. I bought orange and cream flavors."

"I told you, I'm not sick! Plus, I shouldn't drive while taking medication," I joke.

"FINE." Nadine rubs her temples. "Get sick. Get caught by *Hollywood Nation*."

I hug her stiff body. "That's not going to happen." Nadine grunts. "But thank you for always looking out for me," I tell her as an old white four-door sedan pulls into the lot with a glowing Wheel Helpers advertisement fastened on the roof. "He's here!" I say excitedly, sneezing and jumping up and down.

Rodney folds his arms across his chest and stares menacingly. "It looks like a legitimate Wheels Helper vehicle. And no one is trailing him."

When the car comes to a stop, I can see Ralph fiddling with his clipboard and a pile of paperwork that keeps falling into his lap along with his glasses. He pulls down the visor and smoothes his bushy eyebrows in the mirror. He looks over his shoulder a few times like he's forgetting something and then he finally opens the car door. The first thing I notice is the comb-over with his few strands of gray hair. He's wearing a wrinkled white button-down shirt, has a pocket protector filled with pens in his shirt pocket, and has on gray pants that are cuffed too wide at the bottom.

"Hi, I'm Ralph from Wheel Helpers," he says in a high-pitched squeak. His eyes are as wide as the cup saucers at high tea at the Ritz. He's staring at me so intently that I start to squirm. "And you must be Kaitlin," he says, shaking my hand with his own clammy one. He laughs goofily.

"Hi," I say, wiping my sweaty brow. "It's nice to meet you, Ralph. Thanks for meeting me at the crack of dawn."

"No problem. I'm good at keeping secrets, Kaitlin. Kaitlin Burke." He keeps fiddling with his pocket protector as he continues to stare at me and laughs nervously. This time it sounds like a hiccup. "This is so cool. I've never met a celebrity before."

Nadine clears her throat. "Do you have the confidentiality agreement Kaitlin discussed with you over the phone, Ralph?"

"Sure. Sure." He riffles through his papers and frowns. "I had it right here." He keeps looking. "I know I left the house with it. It must be in the car." Nadine glowers at him.

"So Ralph, I have to be at work by ten so I have to leave here by nine-thirty," I tell him. "How long do you think our first lesson will take?"

Ralph doesn't seem to hear me. "Kaitlin Burke. THE Kaitlin Burke! I can't believe she's talking to me." He nudges Austin, who looks at me with a withering glance.

"Kaitlin said you weren't into celebrities," Nadine quips.

Ralph looks hurt. "I'm not," he says quickly. "But it's still cool, isn't it? I have a secret with Kaitlin Burke. I can't believe you're taking my class, Kaitlin Burke."

Why does he keep saying my name like that? I avoid Nadine's gaze. "Just call me Kaitlin, Ralph," I say with a smile.

"Okay, Kaitlin," he says, still fidgeting with the pens. "Let's get started." Ralph leads the way to the sedan and we follow. Ralph turns around. "Uh, the others aren't coming, are they? Because I have a lot of papers in the back of the car."

"No, not at all," I say, looking at the three of them sternly. "They were just saying good luck." Austin kisses my cheek and Rodney slurps his milk shake.

"Before you go," Nadine says loudly, "we need that confidentiality agreement."

Ralph looks flustered. He throws open the car door, grabs the paper sitting on top of his passenger seat, takes a pen from his pocket, and scrawls his signature. "Here." He thrusts it at Nadine.

"Thank you." Nadine snatches the paper and puts it in her front pocket. "And remember, Kaitlin, we'll be RIGHT HERE if you need us." She glares at Ralph. I nod and head for the car.

With the grilling over, I start to relax. I open the front door and breath in the strong lavender air freshener and slide onto the blue vinyl seat. I quickly buckle my seat belt and then trace my fingers along the dash, the steering wheel, and the radio. Wow. The driver's seat. Cool! Just then the commander-in-chief ring tone blares from my cell phone. Laney. Ahhh! What do I do? If I don't answer she'll keep calling. I smile sheepishly at Ralph, grab the phone, and answer the call. "I can't talk now," I whisper.

"WHAT?" Laney yells. I didn't even know she got up this early. "I'M ON MY WAY TO MY TRAINER'S. WHERE ARE YOU? ON SET?" She must have the top down on her BMW convertible because the highway sounds much louder than usual.

Ralph stares at me with a goofy grin. "Yep," I lie. "I have to go."

"WHAT ARE YOU UP TO? YOU'RE ACTING STRANGE."

Oh God. Oh God. Ralph's playing with his pocket protector again. The pens make a clicking sound when they bang together. He begins tapping his arm on the back of his seat impatiently. "Nothing! I swear. Just busy. I'll call you later."

Laney cackles. "I'M JUST MESSING WITH YOU. I CALLED TO TELL YOU *HOLLYWOOD NATION* IS PRINTING A RETRACTION ON THE EXHAUSTION GARBAGE. I SAID, 'KAITLIN BURKE IS A HUGE STAR AND YOU CAN'T TREAT HER THIS WAY.' YOU DON'T HAVE TO THANK ME," she adds.

"Thanks anyway, Laney," I reply gratefully. "But I'm about to walk on set and it's really noisy here. I'll try you later," I yell, hanging up and quickly hitting the power button. I laugh nervously.

"On set?" Ralph repeats. "Does someone not know you're here?"

"My publicist," I admit. "And my parents. They were against the whole driving school thing. They wanted me to get a private instructor who teaches celebrities."

Ralph nods. "Overprotective," he says. "A lot of parents are that way." His pens click together again. The sound is kind of annoying. "But are yours more so than most? I've read your mom can be a bit of a barracuda, no offense." He leans in closer and I lean back against my door to move away.

"My mom's like any mom of a . . ." I wrinkle my nose. "Mom of a . . . AH-CHOO! Teenager. Always worrying," I say with a tight smile.

"Are you tired of the spotlight, Kaitlin?" Ralph's brow furrows as he stares deep into my eyes. "You can tell me if you want. I won't tell anyone. The stress is getting to you, isn't it?"

What? What is he talking about? I look through the rearview window and see Nadine, Rodney, and Austin deep in conversation. Nadine is pointing to a paper in her hand and looks like she's yelling. She picks up her cell phone and starts dialing. I don't need to call them over, do I? Ralph is just being a little forward, that's all. I've had fans do that before. "Should I start the car?" I ask, ignoring his questions.

He looks disappointed. "Sure," he mumbles.

I turn the key and the car roars to life. I wait for my first instruction.

"Now take your foot off the brake and ease on to the gas pedal. That's the pedal on the right," Ralph instructs me.

"Today we're going to stay in the parking lot. For the next class, I'll take you out on the streets."

I pause. "Don't you want to give me any safety precautions before I start?" I ask, feeling anxious.

Ralph looks flustered. "Oh yeah, uh, I forgot. Well, you seem like a smart girl. After all, you're a movie star. I'm sure you know everything already. I'll tell you if you're doing something wrong, okay? You can start driving." He smiles and I can see the yellow stains on his teeth.

What a weirdo. I guess he's just nervous. I do as I'm told. My big foot lies heavily on the pedal and we lurch forward. Ralph almost smacks his head on the dashboard.

"BRAKE! BRAKE!" Ralph says. "Okay, let's start with something simple. Put your foot *lightly* on the gas again and let's do some simple turns around the parking lot."

I steer slowly, putting my foot on the brake every time I see the speed dial go above twenty-five. I keep my eyes on the road, closing them only when I sneeze, which is a lot. After about ten minutes, I feel like I'm starting to get the hang of it. I'm driving! That's when I realize Ralph is staring again. Not at the wheel or the road, but at me.

"I have to ask you this," Ralph prods. "Is it true you and Sky Mackenzie don't get along?" He leans into me, but since the car is in motion, I really can't do anything about it. He's starting to make me nervous.

"Gee, Ralph, I thought you knew nothing about celebrities," I joke. "Why the sudden — AH-CHOO! — interest?" I desperately need a tissue.

He laughs nervously. "I started reading up on you last week after you called," Ralph says. "I wanted to know more about you so we'd have something to talk about."

Oh. I guess that makes sense. And he would have read about Sky. News about our feud is legendary. "AH-CHOO!" I feel myself sweating more profusely now that I'm out of the cold and I begin to feel dizzy.

"So do you like her or not?" Ralph tries again.

"Maybe we should try parallel parking," I reply, jerking the wheel too hard. I recover and try to straighten out. My hands grip the steering wheel so tightly that I'm afraid to lift one off to wipe my sweaty brow. It's definitely hot in here.

"In a minute," Ralph says insistently. "Come on, we're friends, right? I have to know the truth. Do you like Sky or not?" He leans over again. Why does he keep doing that? I take my eyes off the road and stare at Ralph's chest pocket. The pens are bulging out of the protector. For the first time I notice his pocket looks fat. Very fat. Fat enough to hold a tiny tape recorder. OH GOD.

Before I say anything, I feel a bump. It feels like it's coming from the backseat.

"What was that?" I ask, alarmed.

"Nothing," Ralph says quickly. "Just a box. IT WON'T MOVE AGAIN."

Why is he yelling? Wait. There isn't someone in the car with us, is there? I would have noticed, right? Right? But what if there is? ABORT! I have to get out of here, just in case. I steer the car toward Rodney and Nadine again and realize they're running toward me. Nadine is waving her arms wildly. Since Austin is in the best shape, he's way ahead of them, and he's yelling, "STOP!"

Something's wrong. They know it. I know it. I'm starting to feel faint. Okay, don't make it obvious, Kaitlin. Just get out of the car before Ralph sees your entourage freaking out. Walk away and you won't cause a scene. "Ralph, I'm not feeling so — AH-CHOO! — hot. I'm going to end the lesson here."

"What? No!" Ralph says sternly. "We've only been at this for ten minutes." He changes his tone, his voice much softer now. "Come on! I've got so much else to ask you — I mean, teach you."

"No, I've got to go," I interrupt. I can't just jump out of the car since I'm behind the wheel. Instead, I focus on driving toward the Lincoln and pulling in behind it.

"KAITLIN! STOP!" I hear Nadine yell.

"Just five more minutes, please," Ralph begs. He sees Nadine and Rodney barreling toward us and he looks like he's sweating. "I haven't even asked you about the Tom Pullman story in *Hollywood Nation*."

What? This is worse than I thought. WHY don't I listen to Nadine? WHY? Haven't I learned my lesson by now?

"Sorry." I halt the car and put it in park. I unbuckle my seat belt. "I don't want to talk about it. This session is over." My face is burning. I don't know if it's because I'm upset or if I'm not feeling well, but it's taking all my energy not to tell Ralph where to put his *Hollywood Nation*s.

"NO. Wait!" Ralph begs, grabbing my arm a little too tightly. He locks the door with his free hand and I feel my throat constrict. This isn't good. I push him off me and grasp for the door handle.

Austin's fists hit the closed window with a thud and Ralph and I jump.

"GET OUT OF THE CAR, KAITLIN," Austin yells in a scary voice I've never heard before. "NOW."

I don't argue. I grasp the door handle. Then I hear . . .

CLICK. CLICK. CLICK.

I whip around and see Macho Mark, from that Web site XLA.com, in the backseat taking pictures. "Hey, Kates," he purrs.

We call him Macho Mark because he's vain — with good reason. He has short brown hair and always wears tight tees that show off pecs worthy of a star turn on *General Hospital*. He's so cute that sometimes you forget to run from his camera.

Now isn't one of those times.

"I knew it!" I scream at Ralph and unlock the door. "You sold me out!"

"Do you know how much this lousy school pays?" Ralph says, his voice icy. "I had to call the tabs. Mark said he'd cut me a deal. A few pictures of you will cover my rent for a year!"

"You're awful, Ralph! I can't believe I trusted you. Give me that camera," I say, reaching blindly for Mark's equipment.

"No," Ralph says, and before I can stop him, he has thrown

the car in drive. In one quick move, his left leg is on the gas. I scream and thankfully Austin jumps out of the way before the car starts to move slowly.

"What are you doing?" Macho Mark bellows. "You're going to hurt someone!"

"I'm getting you a few more minutes of pictures," Ralph barks.

In a fit of rage, I wrestle the steering wheel away from Ralph and that's when it happens.

BRAKE. GAS. BRAKE. SWERVE.

BOOM!

Steam rises over the dash and Ralph, Mark, and I look up in horror. Ralph's sedan is pressed against our Lincoln, which has a huge dent in the rear bumper. OH NO! I look out the window and see Rodney's hand instinctively cover his face. Rodney's car! Our car! Oh God. I look around to make sure everyone — including Ralph and Mark — is okay. They look more shocked than anything. I burst into tears. I let out a loud sneeze and then have a huge coughing fit, which could be a panic attack. I'm not sure. My body is overheating. Is something burning?

"Kaitlin! Kaitlin!" I hear Austin and the sound of Rodney and Nadine running behind him. He throws open the door while Ralph and Macho Mark are still in shock. "Are you okay?"

"You idiot!" I hear Macho Mark say, smacking Ralph in the head. "That's not how we do things. She could sue!"

Austin guides me out. Mark shakes off the shock and he

jumps out of the backseat to keep taking pictures. Rodney barrels past him. He'd probably like to deck him, but he can't without risk of being sued. These photographers know all the loopholes and right now, we're in public.

UGH. Nadine was sooooooo right.

"Not only am I an awful driver, but I've made another huge mess," I sob.

"Get out of here!" Nadine screams at the top of her lungs, making a scene as she starts with Ralph and Mark, whose camera keeps snapping. "You've crossed the line! We could sue for this!"

"You're too late," Ralph gloats, pointing to his chest. "I have everything I need right here, on tape, just like the tabloids asked!"

OH GOD. "I didn't say anything! AH-CHOO!" I yell.

Rodney throws me in the back of the Lincoln and Nadine and Austin pile in as Macho Mark keeps shooting. I want to scream at him, but that would just make things worse. Rodney screeches away and I hear Ralph scream, "Who's going to fix my car?"

"Kates, are you okay?" Nadine asks, her voice full of worry. "I knew it. I just KNEW it. Right after you pulled away, I felt compelled to look at Ralph's confidentiality agreement. Look at what that jerk wrote." Her hand is shaking as she holds out the paper for me to read. In sloppy handwriting, I see the words "Mickey Mouse." "I tried calling you, but your phone was off," she adds.

A single tear falls onto the paper and I look up at Nadine and start to cry again. "I'm such a fool," I wail.

"Kates, don't say that," Nadine soothes. "You thought with your heart instead of your brain. It happens." She smiles and wipes away a tear from my right eye. "Tell us what happened when you got in the car."

I quickly explain — interrupted by a series of gulps, sobs, and sneezes — about Ralph's grilling, the fake pocket protector, and when I realized Macho Mark was in the car. I wait for Nadine to scream at me, but instead she says over and over, "Kates, I'm so sorry. I should have stopped you." She puts her arm around me as Austin wraps Rodney's sweatshirt around my shivering body. "I didn't want to be right."

"Kates, we're taking you home," Austin says. "You're really sick."

I shake my head, and I feel too weary to even answer. "Maybe just a nap and then I'm going to work. Can't miss work." I groan. "Mom and Dad are going to kill me," I sob, thinking of the twisted chrome on the Lincoln and Ralph's dented sedan.

"Ralph is probably already on the phone with *Celebrity Insider* and Mark's photos will be online before we even get home," Nadine says with disdain. "I've got to call Laney and try to fix things." I close my eyes, too dizzy to think about how she's going to want to kill me.

"I'll pay you for the car damage, Rodney," I sob.

"Don't you worry, Kaitlin, we'll take care of everything,"

Rodney promises. "Right now, let's just get you home and to bed."

I sit up and lay my head on Austin's chest.

Maybe when I wake up, this will have just been a really bad, AH . . . really bad . . . AH-AH-CHOO! Dream.

FRIDAY, 10/12
NOTE TO SELF:

Pay back Rodney 4 damage.
Think about asking Dad 4 an advance on allowance.

EIGHT: *Fever Hysteria*

101.7. That's what the ear thermometer read when Anita took my temperature minutes after Austin carried me fireman-style past my panic-stricken mother ("She's sick? Are you sure? She doesn't look ill.") and tucked me into bed. Anita was steps behind him with a thermometer, Tylenol, ginger ale, and a phone, so that she could call my doctor and ask him to make a house call. But between Mom pestering Austin about Nadine's whereabouts (she was calling Laney) and Dad asking whether I'd followed the proper protocol for calling in sick, Anita couldn't hear a thing the doctor said. She got that constipated look she gets when she's mad and ordered Austin ("Sweet dreams, Burke.") and my parents ("Are you sure that thermometer is working right, Anita?") out so that I could nap in peace.

That lasted for exactly forty-five minutes.

"WHAT DO YOU MEAN SHE SIGNED UP FOR A DRIVING CLASS BEHIND YOUR BACK?" My mother's voice startles me out of a deep sleep. "NADINE, ONCE YOU FOUND OUT, WHY DIDN'T YOU STOP HER?" Nadine's muffled voice seeps through the walls, but I can't make out what she's saying. I should be going downstairs, but my head hurts so much I can barely lift it off the pillow. Poor Nadine. She doesn't need to take the brunt of this. Wait till she tells Mom about Ralph recording me and Macho . . .

"MACHO MARK WAS IN THE CAR? HOW DID NO ONE REALIZE THAT MACHO MARK WAS IN THE CAR?" Mom screeches. "SHE DOESN'T NEED ANOTHER MEDIA FRENZY, NADINE! GET ME LANEY! GET ME LANEY RIGHT NOW!"

UH-OH. I sit up a little too fast and feel dizzy. I hold on to my distressed white nightstand table, pull myself up, and make my way to the door. I stop for a quick rest next to my Orlando Bloom poster. I grab my sage green robe hanging on the back of the door and peek my head out. Nadine's voice becomes clear enough that I can make out a few words. "Kaitlin . . . drive . . . Lincoln . . . dented . . ."

"KAITLIN HIT OUR CAR?"

"What kind of car was Kaitlin driving?" my dad asks, sounding not the least bit upset. If anything, he sounds excited to be discussing his favorite subject: automotives. "Did you catch the make or model?"

"Mom? Dad?" I try to yell, but it comes out as a whisper. My body feels clammy and I'm too weak to walk the long hallway. Instead, I slump down on the cream-colored carpet and lean against Matt's bedroom door. "Matty? Nadine? Anita?"

"Wow, Nadine wasn't kidding — — you look like a ghost," Matty observes as he bounds up the staircase in a rugby with a crisp white collar and carpenter-style jeans. His blond hair is hidden under a backward royal blue Dodgers cap.

"What are you doing home?" I close my tired eyes.

"Tom sent me." Matty sighs. "When word got out that you were sick, somebody in the cast freaked out about germs and worried I would infect the whole set. Monique has to tutor me here today." He pauses. "By the way, why are you lying in the hallway?"

"I was trying to get downstairs to protect Nadine." Did someone turn up the heat in here? "By somebody, do you mean Sky?" I ask.

Matty is silent. "Not exactly."

Hmph. I guess Sky doesn't make sense. She would have been thrilled I was taking a sick day and would have catered a smoothie cart to celebrate. She also would have kept Matty around to report back and make me crazy. "Well, then who wigged out?" I speak slowly, trying to catch my breath.

Matty mumbles something I can't understand. "Who?" I ask. He mumbles again. "I don't understand what you're saying."

"Alexis," he tries again very quietly.

"ALEXIS?" I dissolve into a huge sneezing fit. "Alexis sent you home? She's unbelievable! How could you like

135

her, Matty? Please don't like her. She's no good for AH-CHOO!"

"Cover your mouth," Matt says. "I don't want to need a sick day tomorrow."

"Sorry," I say and strain to hear Nadine again. "What did Alexis say about me?"

"She was really nice," Matty says a tad defensively. "She took up a collection to send you flowers and couldn't stop telling anyone she saw how awful it was that you weren't feeling well."

"Show-off," I say under my breath.

"HOW DID SHE MANAGE TO BOOK A DRIVING SCHOOL WITHOUT ANYONE KNOWING?" I hear Mom scream.

"What's going on down there?" Matty asks. "Is it true you cracked up the Lincoln?"

"You've got to help me downstairs, Matty," I beg. "I've got to rescue Nadine."

Matty offers me his arm. "I'll help you back to your room, but that's it. You're in no condition to go toe-to-toe with Mom. Nadine can handle the fire."

I'm so tired, I don't argue. Matty helps me back to bed and I sink into my pillows and six hundred thread count sheets. I push aside my used tissues and the large box of Kleenex and take a sip of the ginger ale Matty is holding out for me. I look around my bedroom. I wish I got to spend more than just sleeping hours in here. I absolutely love my whitewashed furniture, canopy bed, serene blue walls, and striped bedding and I feel like I never see it during the daytime. Hello, room!

"Do you need anything else?" Matty asks.

"No." I feel very groggy. "Thanks, Matty. Oh wait. There is one thing. Wake me in ten minutes so I can see Nadine. Need . . . to . . . see . . . Nad . . . ZZZZZZZZZZZZZZZ."

"Kaitlin? Wake up." Matty nudges me gently.

I jump up. "What?" I ask. "Has it been ten minutes already?"

"More like eight hours," Matty says.

"Eight hours!" I sneeze violently.

"Anita wouldn't let me wake you, but everyone has been calling. Austin checked in three times, Liz twice," Matty rattles off. "Tom called and even, um, Sky."

"Sky?" Wait. I must still be dreaming. "Sky called?"

My door swings wide open and Laney saunters in wearing a three-quarter-length-sleeved black-and-white-striped top and wide-leg black trousers. "I'm assuming Sky was calling you about this."

I brace myself for a major lecture from Laney. But instead, she silently turns on the TiVo box and Mom, Dad, and Nadine file in behind her. Nadine looks like she's been tortured. She gives me a weak smile and I feel my stomach do a series of somersaults. Nadine got in trouble with my mom and it's all my fault. I have to tell Mom and Dad that. I open my mouth to speak and *Celebrity Insider*'s Maggie Swanson beats me to it. I glance at the TV and see the sleek, rail-thin blond model-turned-celeb-anchor standing in front of a video screen showing pictures of Sky and Alexis.

"Family Affair's Sky Mackenzie lying about her age? It's true, and we've got the video to prove it. You'll only see it here, next on **Celebrity Insider!***"*

I'm flabbergasted. This is what Laney wants to talk to me about? Not my driving disaster?

"When was *Celebrity Insider* on set?" Matty frowns. "I didn't know they were coming to talk to us."

"I guess it was after you were quarantined," Nadine says. Matty glares at her.

I forgot *Celebrity Insider* was going to be on set today! The whole cast was being interviewed about being the longest running primetime series on television. I was looking forward to it. Maggie Swanson is one of my favorite interviewers.

"Tonight's piece was supposed to be about life on the set of *Family Affair,*" Maggie says. "But we're saving that for next week because while I was on set today, I witnessed longtime star Sky Mackenzie having an altercation with darling newcomer Alexis Holden. Take a look."

OH NO. I watch as Maggie's interview begins. Maggie and Alexis are standing on the *FA* set and Alexis is wearing a way-too-revealing beige low-cut monochromatic sundress. "And now the girl everyone is talking about, Alexis Holden,"

Maggie beams, her smile laser-white. "Tell us about life on *Family Affair*, Alexis."

"I love it," Alexis gushes. "By the way, Maggie, awesome top. Where did you get it?"

Maggie looks down at her cute brown knit halter. "Thank you! I just got it at Intuition. I bet you get to wear a lot of cute clothes like these on *Family Affair*."

"Definitely," Alexis says. "And I have some breaking news about Colby that I want you to hear first. I just found out myself and I'm busting. Originally she was only supposed to be on for a few episodes, but after fans reacted so strongly to the character, the network decided to let my story arc continue indefinitely."

"WHAT?" I attempt to yell (it sounds more like a cough). Indefinitely? I can't handle working with Alexis indefinitely! What does that mean? I can't deal. How is she managing to change things so quickly? Matty tries to turn away so that I won't see his face break into a grin so wide it could crack his face in two. Traitor.

"What great news! Alexis is sticking around, and you heard it first on *Celebrity Insider*," Maggie says. In the background, I see Sky in a bright yellow floral halter-style silk minidress. "Did you hear that, Sky?" Maggie yells across the stage.

Sky hurries over, all smiles for the camera. "What's that, Maggie?" Sky asks sweetly, avoiding eye contact with Alexis.

"Your new costar is staying on indefinitely!" Maggie marvels.

Sky blinks nervously.

"This is such a great day, Maggie," Alexis gushes. "And do you know what makes this news even more special? Today is Sky's birthday."

"No, it's not," I tell the TV. Everyone in the room looks at me and I forget for a moment the hot water I'm in. "Sky's birthday is in January. She turns seventeen a month after I do. She never lets me forget it."

Back on TV, Sky is laughing. "Alexis, my birthday is in January. I'm sixteen," Sky tells the camera. "I'm a month younger than Kaitlin Burke." She winks.

The camera pans wide and we see Alexis pull a license out of her handbag. "Oh, I'm sorry," Alexis says. "I got confused when I saw this." The camera closes in on the California State license. There's no doubt about it — it's Sky's. "I've never been great with math, but doesn't this mean you're seventeen going on eighteen today?" Alexis asks.

"Oh. My. God," Nadine says. "Sky lied about her age! Why?"

"Every year counts in Hollywood," Laney explains. "Maybe her family worried she wouldn't have gotten the part if the studio knew she was older. A year makes a big difference when you're four."

Matt falls back on my bed and dissolves into uncontrollable laughter. I'm too shocked and weak to say anything.

"This is good," Laney says as they break for a commercial to heighten the anticipation of Sky's meltdown. Why do TV shows always do that? "Maybe the press will be all over this

Sky age fiasco and forget all about your driving mishap." Laney gives me the evil eye.

Oh. I guess I'm not off the hook.

"I know you're sick so I won't grill you, but that was a pretty silly thing to do." Laney's voice is cool. "I'm going to have a tough time coming up with a convincing statement for this one."

Mom looks at me and raises her right eyebrow in solidarity.

Gulp. "I know that now," I whisper. "Can we talk about this later?"

"Kaitlin, I'm just so disappointed in you," Mom starts, but Matty interrupts.

"Can you guys chill and let her rest? We can deal with this later." I smile weakly at Matty. He can be really sweet when he wants to be.

"Besides, look at the TV," Nadine points out, her face pale. She grabs the TiVo remote and rewinds to the image that startled her.

"Where did you get that?" We see Sky squeak. She lunges for the license. Alexis falls backward, landing on her backside, and Maggie helps her up. "You broke into my dressing room, didn't you?"

"No, no," Alexis says innocently. "I swear. I found it on the floor."

"Yeah right," I mutter.

"I didn't know you would be upset about me mentioning

141

your birthday," Alexis says to Sky and then to Maggie. Her eyes are wide and she's totally playing the ingenue card. "I thought I was just being nice."

The camera turns to Sky. "You two-faced, conniving shrew!" Sky grits her teeth. "I'll get you for this!" She storms offscreen. I half expect Sky's face to turn green, a witch's hat to appear, and for her to say, "And your little dog too!" But it doesn't happen.

Alexis is teary. "I didn't know she was lying about her age," she sniffles. "I just wanted everyone to know today was Sky's birthday so we could celebrate." Maggie looks mournful and hugs Alexis. I'm still speechless as the camera cuts to co-anchor Brian Bennett and Maggie standing on the *Celebrity Insider* set.

"Wow, Sky Mackenzie has some explaining to do, huh, Maggie?" Brian asks, looking picture-perfect in a pin-striped suit (Brian always dresses as if he's a news anchor rather than a tabloid reporter).

What Alexis did to Sky is awful. I can't believe I'm saying this, but I actually feel bad for her. Mom and Laney are so busy yapping about how Sky will lose out on younger roles that we almost miss Maggie's segue to the next segment.

"But what our viewers are probably wondering is where Kaitlin Burke was during this fiasco," says Maggie. "Producer Tom Pullman said she was sick, but our cameras caught her out of bed and behind the wheel of a car taking driving lessons."

OH NO! Maggie, I thought you liked me.

"But I'm really sick!" I say hoarsely, clutching my tattered teddy bear. "The lessons were just a coincidence." I think I'm going to throw up.

"They've got footage of your accident already?" Laney's face is flush. "I thought there were no video cameras there, Nadine."

"Don't blame her," I beg. "None of this was her fault. It was mine."

"There weren't any cameras," Nadine cuts in. "I don't know what they're talking about. The only people there other than us were Ralph and Macho Mark."

Celebrity Insider flashes to a picture of the West Olive parking lot I was at only this morning. Standing in front of his dented sedan is Ralph, his few strands of hair combed neatly.

"Oh God, please tell me you already contacted this guy about paying for his car," Laney groans.

"Not exactly," Nadine says quietly. "Things have been kind of hectic today."

"It was only this morning that Kaitlin took her first-ever driving lesson with Ralph Abersam of Wheel Helpers auto school," Maggie's voice-over explains. The Dave Matthews Band's song "Crash" plays in the background. "Tell us about Kaitlin."

"You mean other than the fact that she can't drive?" Ralph snorts.

D'OH! I cover my burning face in shame. On-screen, Ralph is explaining how I told him I was going behind my family's back to take driving lessons and how inexperienced I was behind the wheel. While he talks, they show a few pictures Macho Mark must have taken of me once I realized he was in the car. In one, I look like a madwoman as I lunge for his camera. In another, my mouth is contorted in a crazy scream.

HOLLYWOOD SECRET NUMBER EIGHT: Tabloid shows and reputable magazines that rely on celebrity cooperation and access don't like to print photos of a celebrity looking ticked off. (The exceptions being a mug shot or a "celebs yelling at the paparazzi" E! special.) They know that an unflattering picture only pisses off the celebrity more, makes the shutterbug who took the picture look incompetent (What? He couldn't get a good shot?), and bores readers, who hate the idea of their favorite stars acting, well, like normal human beings who get a little mad like everyone else.

But according to Nadine, who is pretty chummy with a few less reputable tabloids and gossip Web sites (she feeds them positive stories and quotes when necessary. Shhh . . .), some rags eat up the meter-busting furious rants because they know, deep down, the public loves to see them.

In my case, the absurdity of the situation — combined with the fact that I wasn't actually trying to hurt anyone — is probably too good for the media to pass up. Those pictures will make Ralph and Macho Mark a bundle and be in all the magazines by week's end. I pull up my comforter and try to disappear. Then the phone rings.

"Don't answer it!" Mom says in alarm, but Matt has already picked up.

"Hello? Oh hi, Tom." Matt's voice deepens. "Yeah, she's doing fine. She can talk to you." He pushes the phone under the covers.

"Hello?" I answer weakly.

"How you doing, champ?" Tom asks, trying to sound upbeat. But I know Tom. I can tell something's up. "For you to take a sick day, you must be pretty bad. I won't keep you, but I had something important to tell you."

"I'm glad you called. I was going to call you," I tell him. I take a deep breath. "Tom, I'm not lying about being sick. My mother can vouch for me." Mom coughs. "I admit I had a driving lesson before work, but I swear, I fell ill there. It wasn't because of what happened that I . . ." Tom cuts me off.

"Kates, don't worry about it. I believe you. That's not why I'm calling. I wanted to tell you that Alexis was on *Celebrity Insider* today."

"We just saw it." I grimace at the memory.

"I want to apologize for you hearing about Alexis staying on from a TV show and not from me," Tom says.

"Thanks, Tom." There is so much I want to say about this, but now is not the time.

"You should know that no permanent decisions have been made about her character," Tom adds. "We just felt that the character was testing so well that we couldn't let her go.

And, between us, since so many people have contract nego-tiations this year, and not all will be picked up, the studio felt it could spare the extra expense to keep her around."

The words *contract negotiations* make me feel dizzy again. Doesn't Tom realize that I'm one of those people? What is he saying?

"I'm not thrilled she announced her stay before I could tell you all," Tom continues, oblivious to the torture he's causing me. "I will talk to her about that. But because she will be around for at least a while longer, I want her to feel comfortable, especially with all those rumors about her not fitting in, and today's blunder with Sky."

Not fitting in? I wonder who started those rumors. I won-der who planted those stories of Alexis feeling alienated. Probably Alexis herself, to get me in trouble! "I have no problem with Alexis," I say through gritted teeth.

"Good!" Tom replies happily. "Then you won't mind tak-ing a trip with her."

"Excuse me?" My heart is starting to thump a thousand beats a minute.

"The network is so excited about how great the ratings have been that it's rewarding its main players with a trip to Vegas," Tom explains. "Melli and Spencer can't get away be-cause they have kids, so they'll get something else, but all the younger cast members are heading to Vegas. Doesn't that sound fun? I'm coming with you guys as a chaperone and everyone will have a chance to bond with Alexis."

"Bond," I repeat. What can I say? If I tell Tom how I don't

trust Alexis, I'll look like the bad guy. "Um, okay," I reply. "But Tom, you know we can't gamble, right?"

"With the spas, the food, and the shows, you won't even care," Tom says. "Tell Matty he's going too, will you? I'll call you over the weekend and give you more details when I have them. We're chartering a private flight on Tuesday and you'll each have your own room. The network wanted you to bunk up, like sleepaway camp, but I figured it would be for the best if you, uh, had some space."

"Space is good," I agree.

"Now go rest," Tom says, "and forget all about the stupid car. It took me three times to pass my driver's test." He chuckles to himself.

"Thanks, Tom." I poke my head out from under the comforter and I hang up. "Tom wants the cast to go to Vegas," I tell everyone.

"That's interesting. I was just about to ground you from taking Austin there." Mom looks stern.

"But Mom, it's his birthday," I protest.

"You lied to us, Kaitlin," she says. "You can't expect us to reward your behavior."

My face fills with tears. "Don't take it out on Austin. It's his birthday gift."

Mom shakes her head and looks at my dad. "An *FA* trip I have to agree to, but I'm not about to say yes to another trip to Vegas till I see how your behavior improves."

I could continue to argue, but I'm on such unsure footing as it is, I know it will just make everything worse. At least she didn't give me a definite no. I can't believe how badly I've screwed things up.

"Do I get to go?" Matty asks. I nod. He hollers with joy.

"Vegas news later," Laney yells over the commotion. "First let's see the end of this." Laney pushes play again on my TiVo and we hear Ralph's reply to Maggie's question about the type of person I appear to be. ("Scared and lonely.") Mom keeps trying to talk over Ralph to ask questions. ("Kaitlin, what were you thinking?") The clip ends with Ralph's hopes for me to continue lessons.

"Kaitlin, if you're watching this, I know we had a rocky start," he says solemnly to the camera, "but you'll find no better driving school than Wheel Helpers. I'll even give you the next lesson for free to make it up to you. What do you say?"

Not in a million years, Ralph!

"This is bad, but not as bad as it could be," Laney reflects as she turns off the TV. "We have two things working in our favor — Sky's age will take off some of the heat and we can play up Kaitlin's illness and say she wasn't thinking clearly."

"Oooh!" Mom squeals. "Maybe Kate-Kate should be sick on Monday too." They begin to file out of my room and I grab Nadine's hand.

"I'm so sorry," I say. "I didn't mean to get you in trouble."

"It's okay. It's my fault," Nadine says. "I know better. I should have dragged you out of there."

I squeeze Nadine's hand. "You couldn't have stopped me."

We both start to chuckle. We're still laughing when Anita walks in a few minutes later with soup, some fresh ginger ale, more Tylenol, and cold medicine.

"The doctor will be here in the morning," Anita says. "I've told your mom and Laney not to disturb you again tonight. You need sleep."

I swallow the Tylenol and smile gratefully at Anita and Nadine. "Slwp sunds goo," I admit, feeling very groggy. And I drift off in a haze of meds.

FrDy, Still 10/1111111111111111111
NOT 2 SLF:
SLWP. SLEEP. SLWP. SLEEP.

October 14

Family Affair Hot Gossip—Are Sky Mackenzie and Kaitlin Burke in or out?

by **Christi Lemmon**

The *Family Affair* cast has spats and quarrels on set like any regular family would, but have tensions escalated to the point that certain family members are actually on the verge of being disowned? That's right, kiddies—our on-set sources say that the top brass is getting sick of the off-screen shenanigans of some members and a few may be on their way out the door. The word is they'll look toward new blood to fill that void.

Whose jobs are in question, you ask? We've already reported that Peter Hennings (who plays Dr. Braden) is in jeopardy of not having his contract renewed after his screaming match with a grip turned downright nasty. (Peter, it isn't nice to name-call. Especially when your profanities are politically incorrect.) Peter is currently in therapy to work through what he calls "the hatred inside of me that I never knew existed." Word of his contract renewal has been nonexistent.

While Peter's possible departure might be obvious, the latest names to appear in the questionable column are ones that really hurt—Sky Mackenzie and Kaitlin Burke. Yes, they've been feuding for years, and yes, it's always enjoyable to read about, but apparently the studio is growing tired of the drama their actions cause.

"Usually the fighting is just between the two girls and it doesn't really affect anyone," says a source too close to the stars to name. "But over the past few months, the girls have taken their dramatics to new levels—interrupting filming, causing delays, and being difficult with cast members. It's like they think they've become too big for the show. This last outburst from both of them—Sky lying about her age, Kaitlin lying about being home sick when she was supposed to be filming—really upset the higher-ups. They feel Sky and Kaitlin are making a mockery of the show and they don't want to let it continue."

Hmm... both girls' contracts are up for renewal this year, making it the perfect time for the studio to give them the old heave-ho, no? "The girls' salaries and demands have only increased over the years," added the source. "While the girls are popular, so are less expensive stars, like newcomer Alexis Holden, who is an absolute gem to work with. There is not a diva bone in her body. A lot of people think it would be easier to add her to the roster and drop the troublemakers. Plus they would save a bundle."

Sky Mackenzie's rep wouldn't return calls, but Kaitlin Burke's publicist, the always-fiery Laney Peters, said: "As usual, you guys stick to reporting outrageous lies. The truth is, the studio adores Kaitlin Burke and her job at *Family Affair* is not in jeopardy."

Stay tuned...

nine: *Alexis Exposed*

An all-expense paid trip to Las Vegas is the perfect vacation from reality. With the five-star hotel accommodations, fine dining, tickets to sold-out Cirque du Soleil, VIP club passes, and private poolside cabanas, I've got everything I need to forget all about being semi-grounded, possibly ruining Austin's birthday, and facing the aftermath of my driver's ed class fiasco. This trip couldn't have come at a better time and to a better place. Vegas is Hollywood's favorite playground and I, for one, have been itching to hit the sandbox.

I just hope I don't get in trouble for throwing sand at Alexis.

It's only been a few days since my ill-fated driving class, so maybe I'm still keyed up about being betrayed by Ralph. But the fact remains that I can't stop thinking about traitors and Alexis's true motives. Everyone from the media, to our network, to the staff, to my own baby brother, seems to adore Alexis, except Sky and me. So I can't help wondering, has my jealous streak warped my true perception of her? I mean, maybe she was just having a bad day when Sky and I over-heard her bashing us in the wardrobe closet. Maybe she was honestly being friendly to Austin and not flirting with him at the Priceless event. And the nasty tabloid stories, like the recent round about Sky's and my contract renewals being in jeopardy, could have come from anyone.

Two days into our *FA* trip, I decide I can't hash it out on my own anymore and I need to bounce my thoughts off Lizzie. She'll tell me whether I'm being paranoid or not. When I call, I start off telling her all about my first night in town, which included a private dinner at Emeril's restau-rant, which he cooked for us himself, and tickets to the Beatles tribute show, Love. I got Austin a tee as a souvenir. It was the least I could do after I found two dozen roses wait-ing in my suite when I checked in with a note that said, *You can drive my car (when I actually get one) anytime. Keep your chin up. Can't wait to see you in a few days.* I can't believe I'm so lucky. I haven't told him yet that our Vegas trip might be on hiatus. I'm hoping Mom will reconsider.

"You have the best boyfriend ever," Liz admits. "Except for mine, of course."

"Of course." I laugh. "So listen, I wanted to ask you some-thing —"

"So I haven't told you my big news yet." Liz doesn't hear and is yapping away. "Guess where I'm going next weekend?" She doesn't wait for me to answer. "New York! My dad sur-prised me with a weekend getaway so we can check out New York University."

"Liz, that's fantastic," I gush.

"I've been telling him all about the drama program and he agrees it could be a perfect fit for me," Liz exclaims. "Can't you see me living in New York City, Kates? I would totally fit in. I'll have this awesome roommate, be a short walk from the coolest clubs and restaurants. All we need is for you to shoot a few films in town so that I can see you all the time and we'll be set."

"Definitely," I reply. "I'll get right on it." But in my head I'm thinking how much easier life would be if Liz didn't get into NYU at all. Then she wouldn't move so far away.

I slap myself on the head. WHAT AM I DOING? This is my best friend! Of course I want her to get into any college she wants. I want her to be happy! I'm beginning to think my brain has been taken over by an alien life-form. I have to stop it before I become a totally conceited, ultracompetitive star who only cares about her own happiness — and career trajectory.

I'm so ashamed of my thoughts that I make up some lame excuse about having a headache. I hang up quickly, never asking Liz about Alexis. I put my sleep mask on and think about how I can fix things. If I'm conjuring such awful thoughts about Liz, who is my best friend, then maybe I'm so blinded by jealousy that I have Alexis all wrong too.

In the morning, I hit the spa doors running in a fitted brown velour Gap track suit. Our whole group is scheduled for a day of fitness and beauty, starting with a ten AM spin class, so I know Alexis will be here. Canyon Ranch's 21,000-square-foot fitness center has Pilates, yoga, and a three-story-high rock wall. Austin always raves about rock climbing with his teammates, so I'm itching to squeeze in a session.

But first I'm going to find Alexis, tell her all about Canyon Ranch's Rasul treatment and convince her to get one with me, and then totally win her over with my friendly personality. She won't be able to pass up the Rasul. It's this Middle Eastern–inspired body wrap where you're covered in therapeutic mud, placed in a beehive-shaped room with heated seats and a fake starlit sky, and given an herbal steam. At the end of the treatment rain falls from the "sky." Even Alexis will have to be impressed by that.

I don't have to look very far to find her. Alexis is standing with Tom, Matty, Trevor, and the gang outside the aerobics room. I'm sure Matty is drooling over what Alexis is wearing: a ripped pink tee that flaunts her taut belly and skintight black bike shorts that accent her giraffelike long legs.

"Hey, Kates," says Trevor, bounding over in lacrosse shorts and a muscle tank, looking like the cover of *Men's Health*. His blond hair is matted to his sweaty face, like he's already gotten in an early morning workout, and his blue eyes are playful. If anyone is having a great time on this trip, it's him. The girls have been throwing themselves at Trev everywhere we've gone, making his infatuation with Sky a thing of the past. "Ready to spin?"

"Yep. Can you save me a seat next to you?" I ask. "I have to talk to Alexis for a minute."

"No problem." Trev eyes the cute instructor with curly brown hair and miniature waist walking past us to the aerobics room door and follows her.

Everyone will be going inside in a minute so I have to move fast if I want to get Alexis alone. I quickly walk over and flash Alexis a big smile. "Hey!" I sidle up to her. "Having fun? I feel like I haven't seen you the whole trip."

Alexis stops talking to Hallie and looks at me strangely for a moment, but she quickly recovers. "Hey, you!" Alexis enthuses. "I haven't seen you either and I've really wanted to hang out." She pouts. "I've been bonding with Hallie here and trying to get over the whole thing with Sky." Her eyes well with tears. "I still feel SO bad."

"I keep telling Alexis it's not her fault," Hallie says. "She had no idea Sky was lying about her age."

I nod. "By the way, maybe I missed this part, but did you ever say how you found Sky's license in the first place? Sky doesn't usually carry a wallet on set." The Alexis hater in me is taking over again and I can't seem to help myself.

"Like I've said, it was on the floor. I don't know how it got there." Alexis is smiling, but her voice is slightly strained.

"Gotcha. Well, do you care if I join you guys? I'd love to bond now that I've found you," I say. I could swear someplace nearby Matty just snorted. He's got a distinctive snort. I ignore it.

Alexis looks taken aback. "Of course! Hal, will you give us a sec? I just have to talk to Kates alone about something and we'll be there in a jif."

Good! A minute alone. I'll say my piece, we'll make up, and we'll be off to the Rasul treatment in an hour.

"Sure," Hallie says. "I'll save you both bikes."

The doors to the studio open and Tom pats me on the shoulder as he walks by with Hallie and the rest of the group. I don't see Sky. "We'll see you inside," Tom says with a grin. "I want to remind you about tonight's all-important dinner at Tao. I've got *Celebrity Insider* and *Hollywood Nation* coming by to do some positive interviews with the cast."

"We'll wow them, Tom," Alexis says. "Now get inside and find a bike. I'm going to whip your butt in there." She laughs. Once Tom's out of earshot she stops laughing and looks at me.

"So what's up, Kates? I feel like you've been avoiding me," she scolds.

The words get caught in my throat, instantly giving me away. "A little," I admit.

"Why would you do that?" Alexis looks aghast. "I've been nothing but nice to you."

"Well..." I'm not sure how to word this. "I just... I've heard you talk about me behind my back." There. I've said it.

For a moment, I think I see Alexis's cool, confident demeanor crack. "No way. Who said I have?" She waves her hands madly. "It doesn't matter. Whoever told you that is lying to your face." She reaches out and clasps my hand. "I admire you, Kaitlin. If anything, I want to be just like you."

I look into her face, so bright and hopeful. Maybe this nagging feeling I'm having is wrong. Alexis might not have meant to say those things we overheard. She could have uttered them in a moment of anger. I've certainly done that. "You want to be like me?" I can't help asking. It's kind of flattering.

"Absolutely." Alexis squeezes my hand tight. "You have the career that I want, I mean, I aspire to have. That's why I want to stay on *FA* for as long as possible. To learn from you."

Really?

"And I would never, never, ever say a bad word about you *ever*," Alexis adds with a big smile.

Not meaning what she said is one thing. Saying she never said it is a bold-faced lie. Why can't she just admit she talked about me? I open my mouth before I can stop myself. "But you did say things, Alexis," I try gently. "Maybe you didn't mean them, but I heard you with my own ears." Her right eye flinches slightly. "Talking to Renee. Sky did too. And then Liz heard you that day at the Argyle Spa."

Alexis's face turns to stone. "You heard wrong. Your friend too. And that leech Sky, she'll say anything to get ahead." She rolls her eyes. "I thought you said you wanted us to get along. Why are you pushing this? Why won't you believe me?" She sounds agitated now and it's sending up red flags.

"Alexis," I try again, needing to be certain. "It's okay. Everyone gets bent out of shape sometimes, but I need to know the truth. With all those phony tabloid articles about my set behavior and Sky's, I don't know who to trust anymore."

"Are you saying I planted those articles?" Alexis's voice is shrill and, for the first time, I notice she looks angry. She lets out a little grunt and runs her hands slowly across her face. When she's finished, she looks at me and I can see her expression has totally changed to one of eerie calm. "You know what? Forget it. I'm done pretending," she says. "You've caught me."

"What?" I can't breathe. What does she mean?

"I don't like you, Kaitlin," Alexis says flatly. She glances around, making sure no one is within earshot other than me. "Sky was too smart to fall for my act. But I tried to be nice to you because everyone loves you and I thought being friends with you would get me what I want, but I can see now you're not biting." She shakes her head. "To tell you the truth, it's a relief that you know. Now I don't have to pretend with you. I'm not the type of girl who likes having girlfriends anyway." She smiles weakly. "There's too much competition and jealousy."

I'm too shocked to speak. My mouth is hanging to the shiny, tiled floor.

"You're jealous of me, Kaitlin," Alexis says quietly. "I've seen it from day one. You can admit it."

"I am not," I lie.

"You don't like that I'm moving in on your precious turf." Alexis points her ruby red manicured finger at my face. "Well, tough. It's time for some new names to get some action on *FA* and I'm going to be one of them."

"What does that have to do with me?" I ask stonily.

She laughs bitterly. "Everything. Don't you think I've seen how much Tom and everyone adore you? And even that troublemaker, Sky? At first I thought it was a good idea to get in tight with you and your posse, since you have so much influence on Melli and Tom, but I could tell you were suspicious of anyone who wanted to get close to you." She shakes her head. "So I moved on to being sweet to everyone else on *FA* so that I'd be so adored on and off set that they couldn't let me go. But when all my baking and other good deeds still went unnoticed, and there was no talk of extending my storyline, I finally pleaded my case to Tom." She rolls her eyes. "You know what he told me? He didn't have room for another major teen player because they already had you two. Well, that answer didn't fly with me."

Her tone is icy and I feel chills run down my spine.

"So the answer became obvious — if there isn't room for three of us, then maybe I had to get rid of you two so that I could have a fighting chance. I knew Sky was onto me, which is why I had to find out one of her skeletons. Revealing her true age did the trick." She smiles smugly. "But you, I figured I'd keep you close until I could find a better way to take you down. Now I can see you already know what I'm up to, so why hide it anymore? You can't stop me. You've got enough problems handling all that new bad press about your set behavior." Her eyes squint menacingly. "Want to know the best part? If I continue buttering up the writing staff and being nice to everyone else, they'll never suspect me of trying to ruin your reputation." She laughs to herself.

I KNEW IT. It wasn't an alien invasion after all. I was right about Alexis! She's totally out to destroy Sky and me. She's *nuts*. "You're not going to get away with this," I seethe, my voice eerily calm. It's taking all my strength not to reach out and smack her across the face. "Tom will never get rid of Sky and me because of some bogus tabloid articles." I'm so angry I'm shaking, but the truth is, I'm not sure how much more the studio or Tom is willing to swallow. Suddenly I feel very afraid. Alexis could get away with this and here's the reason why.

HOLLYWOOD SECRET NUMBER NINE: How do the tabloids get away with printing such outlandish lies? They're brilliant at manipulating words. According to Liz's dad, my lawyer, in order to sue a tabloid magazine for slander or printing false information and win, a celebrity has to prove that the magazine was being malicious. So if someone says "Kaitlin Burke is pregnant" and I'm obviously not, but burning mad they said it, I have to prove that the magazine was deliberately trying to hurt me by printing that remark. That is tough to do. Usually when a magazine comes under fire for a particularly dirty item, all they have to say is that they *believed* the item was true at the time they printed it and they have their get out of jail free card. Pretty sneaky, huh?

"The public may like you, but you're not the sole reason our show is doing so well this year," I tell Alexis. "If you weren't such a complete amateur, you'd know ratings have to do with a number of things." Like the fact that we're not opposite *CSI* anymore, Melli's got a hot storyline, and we've got a crackerjack team of mostly new writers.

"You idiot. Don't you see, I don't even have to crow about the ratings anymore." Alexis is smug. "Those tabloid articles are going to keep coming, and believe me, they're going to get worse. And you can't prove I have anything to do with them." She laughs. "Your increased hostility toward me will be enough to send you and Sky packing."

I'm going to hit her. I'm going to hit her and it's going to be all over. And that's exactly what she wants. "You wish," I hiss.

Her eyes turn to slits again. "It will happen. And if you even think of telling someone what I just told you, I'll bury you. Who do you really think they'd believe? The beloved, sweet new girl who's upping the ratings or the has-been who's giving them nothing but trouble?" She smiles smugly, turns on her heels, and heads into the studio while I stand there breathing fire.

I lunge for her hair, wanting to yank it out of her head, but someone grabs my arm.

"Let her go." I turn around. Sky is standing right behind me and she looks as ticked off as I am. She unzips her sweatshirt and reveals a pink sports bra and tight black pants. In her navel is a Cartier diamond double-C piercing.

"Did you hear what she just said to me?" I still can't believe what just happened.

"No, but I can imagine. I've been watching you two for a few minutes and I've never seen you angrier — even at me," Sky points out. "I told you I had that praying mantis pegged."

"Well, I believe you now." I'm still shaking and it's hard for me to speak. "She's out to get us both, you know."

"I've known for a while." Sky sounds sad. "She already made a dent in me with the age thing. Not that I'm worried," she adds quickly. "My agent says my real age getting out won't affect me too much." She doesn't look like she believes him.

"Hang in there," I tell her awkwardly. "I'm sure the whole thing will blow over. My scandals always do."

Sky gives me a small smile and I see her brown eyes are puffy. "Yeah, but that's because yours are always made up by the same unnamed source," Sky says, not acknowledging that the source was usually her — until recently, that is. "Mine are real. At least this one is."

"It's no one's business how old you are, Sky," I argue. "Although I can't figure out how you passed for a four-year-old when you were five and we started the show." Sky just shakes her head. "But for the record," I add, "I think what Alexis did to you was cruel."

"Thanks," Sky says, casting her eyes downward. I think that's the first time I've ever heard her utter that word to me.

"So what are we going to do about the — what did you call her? Praying mantis?" I try not to smirk.

"It fits, doesn't it?" Sky looks pleased with herself. "We'll think of something. But first, let's blow off steam. What do you say we skip that spin class and hit the rock wall instead?"

163

"You're on," I say.

The enemy you know is always better than the one you don't, right?

FRIDAY, 10/18
NOTE TO SELF:

Call Nadine & Laney ASAP!

TEN: *What Happens in Vegas, Doesn't Always Stay in Vegas*

A few hours later, after Sky and I have sweated, climbed, and tortured our bodies enough to curb our anger toward Alexis, I've gone back to take a long soak in my room's over-size tub. That's where I replay the conversation I just had with Sky. It was probably the most we've said to each other in years. Alexis wants us to look like we're too difficult to keep around, which is why we both agreed that starting with her while we're on a cast trip would be suicide. We need to keep cool until we figure out a surefire way to get rid of Alexis, once and for all. Not that we've come up with one yet.

With my head clear, I head downstairs to meet Matty. We're having a cast dinner at Tao, which is in our hotel. The Venetian is like its own mini city!

"You're going to love this place," I tell Matty, linking arms with his and trying to sound upbeat. We're both dressed up for the occasion. Matty is in a black pin-striped suit and a white shirt with no tie, and I'm in a killer blue Marc Jacobs dress the designer sent me from his upcoming collection. "They have the most amazing sushi."

"You're not going to brag about going to the one in New York, are you?" Matt groans.

I hit his arm. "No, cranky, I'm not."

"Sorry," he says. "It's just that Alexis wouldn't speak to me after her fight with you."

I stop walking and turn to look at him. "How do you know we had a fight?"

"She ran into spin crying about how you said you were going to get her fired because you can't stand her," Matty explains. "I overheard her telling Ava."

Wow. Alexis is a more cunning opponent than I realized. "Matty, do you think I would say that?" He shakes his head. "So why do you think she'd say something like that? The truth is, she wants me gone. She wants to take my place." He looks away. I feel awful upsetting him, but he has to know the real deal. There is no way I'm letting Alexis anywhere near my brother.

As we enter through the circular hallway filled with tubs of floating flower petals, I see that Sky, Brayden, Hallie, Trevor, Ava, and Luke are already waiting. Alexis is noticeably missing and Ava is glaring at me. Hmm . . . I've got to win her over again without stepping on Alexis's toes.

"Tom is running a few minutes late," Trevor tells us. "He took two more treatments at the spa and they ran long."

"And Alexis?" Matty asks.

"She's, uh, running late too," the Zac Efron–clone of a host tells us. "She called and she said she'd be late."

"But we have reason to celebrate in the meantime," Trevor says and throws an arm around Hallie, who blushes.

"Tell me," I beg, looking forward to hearing something positive for a change on this trip.

"My agent just called," Hallie says shyly. "I signed on to that new JJ project for ABC."

"YES!" I yell giddily. Hallie has been nervous about her meeting with JJ for weeks and I've kept telling her it would be fine. Within seconds, I'm hugging her and the two of us are screaming in delight.

HOLLYWOOD SECRET NUMBER TEN: Want a sure sign that the grim reaper is coming to visit one of your favorite TV characters? Keep your eye on the front pages of *Variety*. If you read that your favorite star has signed on to do a pilot or do a recurring guest spot on another show, they probably know what we don't — their character is going to be snuffed out. In Hallie's case, her character is about to be taken hostage during a robbery. *Tome* keeps giving quotes about how "This pivotal episode will change the lives of everyone on *FA* forever," hinting that someone won't make it out alive (a big ratings draw these days). It's safe to say the probable demise — or long stint in rehabilitation — is Hallie, considering her new role on another network.

"Great. Now that the celebrating is over with, can we at

least sit down while we wait?" Sky gripes. She's wearing a sheer white dress with a pink ruffled slip underneath. Her long brown hair is pulled back in a loose twist. She looks pretty if you ignore the pout on her face. She's obviously having a tough time concealing how mad she still is about Alexis. I give her a stern glance and she looks away.

The host clears his throat. "I believe your table isn't ready yet. We thought you'd all prefer the mezzanine level so they're, uh, still setting up."

"Why are you so nervous?" Sky demands.

"Geez, Sky," Ava huffs. "Wouldn't you be if you were surrounded by celebrities?"

"I hope you're not referring to yourself," Sky sniffs.

Trevor holds Ava back. "Play nice, you two, this is a goodwill trip, remember?"

I take a look around. Well, from where I'm standing. The host won't let me move out of the waiting area. "It upsets our guests already seated," he explains to me. I don't argue. Even if there are only about twenty people or so eating at such an early hour. Even from where I'm waiting, I can see the restaurant/nightclub/lounge is huge. According to the description of the Chinese, Japanese, and Thai cuisine eatery I read in my room, it's actually 42,000 square feet. Large enough to have a 20-foot-tall carved Buddha floating over an infinity pool filled with Japanese carp. There are waterfalls, plenty of greenery, wood carvings, stones, and velvet-draped walls. I'm so busy taking in the scenery that I barely notice it at first. Up on the mezzanine level, where we're supposedly going to be eating, are a ton of photographers and they're taking pictures of . . .

"ALEXIS IS UP THERE ALREADY!" Sky screeches, apparently seeing exactly what I hoped I hadn't seen. "AND SHE'S GOT THE PRESS ALL TO HERSELF!" She grabs the trembling hottie host by his collar. "YOU KNEW, DIDN'T YOU?" she bellows.

He lowers his blue eyes and nods. "She gave me a hundred bucks and her room number," he boasts. "She moved the interview up an hour."

"She wouldn't!" Ava says, getting visibly upset. "She said she was looking forward to doing the interview together. Tom said it was important for us to do it together. Why would she do that?"

"Because she's a manipulator," Sky tells her and the rest of us. "Well, it ends now." She stomps off to the elevators with the rest of our angry mob in tow.

I run after them and try to make my way to Sky. "Remember what we talked about," I warn her. "Don't do anything stupid. She's probably charming the pants off them right now."

"She'll *wet* her pants when she sees me," Sky growls.

"You'll look like the bad guy," I tell her.

Sky hits the elevator button. "It's too late. I already am one."

When the elevator doors open upstairs, the scene is worse than I could have imagined. It's not just *Insider* and *Nation*. There must be at least a dozen reporters, cameramen, photographers, and lighting guys. In the middle is Alexis.

She sees us and grins. "There they are!" she says, clapping her hands. "My wonderful costars. I told the press you wouldn't stand them up. They were worried since you were an hour late." She frowns. "Didn't anyone tell you the press time changed to six?"

"That's funny. You told me it was still at seven." Ava folds her arms dramatically and her face is bright red. "You called me an hour ago to remind me!"

"Me too," seconds Hallie.

HA! We've got her.

"Hal, Ava, I got confused with all the changes." Alexis pouts. "I'm SO sorry. Well, it's all good now. You're here. Let's get started."

Thankfully Ava and Hallie don't look convinced. I know I'm not. But I'm not sure I want to get in a screaming match when there are so many tape recorders present.

"Did Alexis tell you guys that she paid off the host downstairs to keep us away while you interviewed her?" Sky asks the press while trying to remain calm.

"Sky!" I hiss. She's only going to make things worse.

Alexis laughs nervously. "Don't be silly! Sky is such a liar! I love my *FA* costars, but you guys all know Sky and Kaitlin will say anything to get some of the good press you have been giving me."

That's it! Something inside me snaps and I can't keep quiet. "You've manipulated the press pretty well, haven't you, Alexis?" I ask, getting mad as a flashbulb pops in my face. "It's amazing how many unnamed sources there are to talk about how wonderful you are and how rotten we are." I look at the press crew. "Well, we can play at that game too. Maybe you want to take a few minutes to get the real story and hear how Alexis threatened me earlier." A few reporters move toward me.

"Don't fall for it, guys!" Alexis blocks their path. "Think about it: Why would Kaitlin ever take Sky's side? The only reason those two are getting along at the moment is that they're hoping you'll forget all about Kaitlin's car crash and the fact that Sky is old as dirt."

"That's it," Sky says and she grabs a fistful of Alexis's red hair and pulls.

CLICK. CLICK. CLICK. There is a flurry of camera flashes.

Alexis screeches, turns around, and shoves Sky, knocking her backward into Trevor. Sky races at her again. Matty tries to pull Sky off Alexis, but he gets knocked down. Trevor runs over to break the whole thing up and winds up with a bloody nose. CLICK. CLICK. CLICK.

Suddenly it's pandemonium. Everyone is throwing themselves on top of each other. Matty, Luke, and Brayden (who also apparently has a thing for Alexis) are trying to pull Alexis out of harm's way — meaning Sky's — and Ava and Hallie are still yelling about Alexis tricking them. Trevor is trying to mediate as blood drips down his face, but it's no use.

Me, my feet are glued to the floor. My heart is pounding and I can't move a muscle. All I want to do is get in there and fight, but I know how these things end and I've already done enough damage by yelling in public.

CLICK. CLICK. CLICK.

"Oh my God," I hear someone behind me say.

It's Tom. He's arrived just in time to see Sky dragging Alexis by the hair. Tom falls into the nearest chair and covers his face in his hands. This is not good.

CLICK.

FRIDAY, 10/18
NOTE TO SELF:

Call Laney & Nadine. AGAIN.
Tell them 2 ready another statement asap.

IN THE KNOW

Family Dysfunction

by Hayley Lamar

Family Affair stars Sky Mackenzie, Alexis Holden, and Kaitlin Burke have their sisterly banter down pat—it's their off-set flare-ups they have to work on.

Ever since their very public brawl at Las Vegas's Tao restaurant, each *FA* costar has retreated to her own corner to let their publicists do the talking—or should we say do the classic not talking.

"It was a minor incident that I won't dignify with a statement," said Burke's mouthpiece, Laney Peters, about the fracas.

"Sky Mackenzie has nothing but the utmost respect for her costars, onscreen and off," said Mac's new-est mouthpiece (her sixth in four years), Amanda Reynolds. "Vegas is old news."

And since Holden has no rep to speak of, the show issued a statement on behalf of all the cast members involved—which is everyone too young to order a drink. "The mood on set is great," said show runner Tom Pullman. "*Family Affair* is a family in the truest sense of the word. Some days we have a great deal of fun, and on others, we have our differences, but in the end, our family is one that sticks together."

Oh really Tom? In the Know sources hear differently. According to our peeps in play, *Family Affair* has never been an uglier place to work. Corroborated accounts have bickering costars Burke and Mackenzie siding together for the first time in years against newcomer Holden. And plenty of set sources are starting to see why. "Alexis plays nice for people in charge, but her true colors came out in Vegas. She moved up the goodwill interview everyone was supposed to do with *Nation* and *Celebrity Insider* and didn't tell anyone," complained one weary crew member. "It's no wonder they came to blows."

> **"… in the end, our family is one that sticks together."**

Others, though, are coming to Holden's defense. "She left word for all her castmates that the interview time changed and they didn't bother to check their hotel voicemail boxes," sniffed a source. "Sky and Kaitlin are just jealous that Alexis is the one getting the spotlight this year. They've been giving her a tough time because they can't handle being reminded that Alexis is more talented than they are. Alexis is the reason ratings are up and they hate that."

We're told the cast trip to Sin City was Tom's effort to bring the young ins together, but it only drove the wedge further. Rumor has it that *FA* had to shut down the set for a few days to deal with the fracas, which has cost the studio close to a million in shooting delays and future missed on-air dates. The show's number one star, Melli Ralton, (who plays the girls' mother Paige) is so upset, she's thinking of leaving the show if Tom doesn't figure out a solution to this catfight fast.

Just who would be thrown out is another story. While Alexis's fans seem to think it's time for some new blood, Burke and Mackenzie fans are sticking by their favorite twin sibs. Either way, In the Know hears if things don't shape up soon, someone will be getting the ax.

> **"Sky and Kaitlin are just jealous that Alexis is the one getting the spotlight this year. . . . Alexis is the reason ratings are up and they hate that."**

"Tom is really upset about all the squabbling," said a source. "He told me one more incident and he'll tell the network someone's head has to go on the chopping block." ●

eleven: *Dance as if No One's Watching*

Now this is the kind of mission I don't mind being disguised for! Thanks to a curly red wig, my Dodgers cap, Gucci shades, J Brand jeans, and a plain tee; an on-purpose late arrival; and Rodney's promise to maintain his distance and blend in (he's in parent mode, wearing a button-down Ralph Lauren Polo shirt and brown chinos), I was able to foil the camped-out paparazzi and go to the Homecoming parade. I got to see Austin wear a corny plastic crown, smile, and wave to the cheering crowd from the back of a pickup truck. Watching him do that was a better high than logging on and seeing I'm not being crucified on perezhilton.com today. Ducking Larry the Liar didn't feel too shabby either. It's the first time in over a week they haven't accused Sky and me of being the most unruly teen stars of our generation.

I'm not worrying about the Alexis problem now. Today is about Austin and how I can make his birthday spectacular. Even the sight of Austin's ex, Lori, hanging her bony arm on

Austin can't crush my mood. I get to play dedicated girl-friend for once without a box of hot-off-the-presses *Holly-wood Nation* issues falling on my head.

After the Homecoming football game (which Clark loses 17-5), Rodney and I hop into our undercover car — we use Nadine's beat-up Nissan — and drive to Austin's house without being followed. YES! For once, things couldn't go smoother.

"Boo," I whisper, walking up behind Austin, who is alone and sneaking a lick of frosting from his birthday cake. The Meyerses' kitchen smells like vanilla and raw cookie dough and looks like a country catalog. Their farmhouse table and restored icebox freezer are a faded green and the wall-paper is a dizzying pattern of apples and roosters. I start singing the "Happy Birthday" song and my oxygen supply is cut off with a long kiss.

"Guys," Rodney whines. "You know I hate when you do that in front of me."

"Sorry, Rod." Grinning, Austin gently pulls the curly mop off my head and removes my sunglasses. "Aren't you sup-posed to be at work, Burke?" He frowns slightly. "I don't want you getting in any trouble on account of me."

"I'm not in trouble." I was a little panicked that my lie to Austin was going to be reality. I thought we were going to have to work because of the delay in filming all last week, but Tom was so backed up in postproduction that he gave us the time off anyway. Not that he was happy about it.

I wipe a smudge of chocolate frosting off the side of Austin's mouth. "I lied about working today," I admit with a grin, "so that you couldn't give Rod and me a hard time about checking out the game."

"You were there?" Austin asks, his blue eyes wide. "But . . . how? The paparazzi were crawling all over the place. Larry the Liar even tried to get on the field! Principal P. made an announcement about how you weren't there, hoping they'd all leave."

I tell Austin about Rodney's security plan and how everything went smoothly. "Which means that since no one saw me at the game, and Principal P. announced I wasn't coming, and you and Lizzie told everyone at Clark I was working, the coast is clear for me to go to Homecoming with you and see you crowned as part of the court," I ramble. Austin opens his mouth to protest and I take a spoonful of the leftover icing from the bowl on the counter and stick it in his mouth. "Laney and my parents know where I am and they're okay with it too," I promise, reading his thoughts. "And I agreed Rodney could shadow me so I won't be caught off-guard if Larry or any of the other persistent stalkers show up. I promise we'll leave at the first sign of trouble, not that I think there will be any," I cut him off and babble quickly. "One last thing — the dress I got for tonight is not to be missed. I wouldn't be surprised if it caused you heart palpitations. So what do you say, birthday boy? Aren't you going to ask me to the dance?" I bat my eyes.

"Kates," Rodney whines again.

"Sorry, Rod." I take a spoon and scoop up some frosting myself. Wow, is that fudge?

"You really want to go with me to some lame dance?" Austin asks, grinning.

"Yes," I say. "Homecoming doesn't sound lame to me. It sounds like more fun than I've had in months."

"You won't be saying that after you see what we have planned for your birthday." Austin winks. Then his bright smile fades. "Wait. We can't. I only have one ticket for me and you can't get any at the door."

I pull a shiny orange ticket from my J Brand jeans pocket. "Not a problem. Liz bought me one weeks ago."

Austin kisses me again and Rodney coughs. "You're amazing," he says.

"I'm glad someone thinks so." I look deep into Austin's blue eyes. "But don't thank me too much. I still don't have a replacement birthday gift for you." After what went down in Sin City, Laney and Mom vetoed a return flight anytime soon, nixing all plans I had for Austin's NASCAR experience. How could I argue? I'm not proud of what happened in Vegas. Especially since it didn't stay there.

Austin squeezes my waist tighter, and my body feels warm. "Vegas is overrated anyway, and I told you that gift was too elaborate. It makes me uncomfortable when you spend so much." He nuzzles my chin. "Besides, figuring out a way to go to Homecoming with me, even after I claimed I didn't care about going, is the best birthday present you could give me." He kisses me softly on the lips again. I hear footsteps, but I'm enjoying the moment too much to pull away.

"I didn't know you two were back," Austin's mother says. She grabs the bowl of leftover frosting from the kitchen counter. "How was the game?"

"You knew Kaitlin was going?" Austin asks.

She laughs. "Why do you think I set two extra places at the table? For Kaitlin and Rodney! We've got to eat dinner and have cake early so you two can get to the dance," she adds. Her blond hair is pulled back in a ponytail and she's wearing a navy blue velour warm-up suit. If Mom were here, she'd probably convince Mrs. Meyers to change, claiming velour is "too mainstream now."

"Rodney, you'll be staying for dinner, won't you? I made lasagna and there's plenty of cake," Mrs. Meyers adds.

"Thank you. It all smells amazing," Rodney says happily. "Tell me, is that homemade fudge frosting? I couldn't help tasting a spoonful."

Dinner moves quickly and the phone doesn't ring for me even once! Mom and Laney haven't called to ask me about another damage control interview, fittings for my next Fever cosmetics commercial, or whether I'm free for dinner next Thursday to meet a producer about a potential project. I think even Team Burke knows I need a day off after how stressful work has been.

The post-Vegas fiasco vibe on set has been colder than a Vanilla Ice Blended. No one under the age of seventeen is talking AT ALL, except when they go to the principal's office — aka Tom's, with whom everyone is setting up private meetings to discuss the tense situation and all the rumors about one of us being canned. The only bright spot is that Alexis is busy trying to do damage control with Ava and Hallie and it's not working. The pair of them have been so turned off by Alexis's betrayal that they've told anyone who will listen the true version of Vegas events.

I'm clinging to the hope that my meeting with Tom goes well so I can tell him what happened too. But Tom's assistant hasn't given me a date or time for mine yet. I know Sky doesn't have one either. That can't be a good sign.

Things at *FA* are messier than they've ever been, and that includes the season Melli fought with our director every week over lighting. Speaking of Melli, she and the older players, like Spencer, are so disappointed by the Vegas thing that they aren't talking to us either. It's killing me not to have Melli to talk to. Throw in the crew, who is bitter about having to work weekends, and you've got tension thicker than a smoggy Los Angeles morning. I'm fixated on what Tom is going to do. How does the network not realize Alexis is the root of all evil? The Darth Maul of actors? The Voldemort of TV?

Whenever I've thought of leaving *FA* (being wooed away to star in a blockbuster trilogy . . . taking a break and attending school full-time . . .) the one scenario I didn't think of was being fired. Tom's always praised me for being a professional and now here I am, along with everyone else, in the middle of a major feud. I want my *FA* run to end when I say so, not because of some stupid costar.

"Are you okay, Burke?" Austin asks. He gives my hand a squeeze and shakes me loose from my dark thoughts as Rodney drives us to Clark High School a little while later in Nadine's Nissan. "Do you want to back out? We can turn this car around, you know. I wouldn't blame you after what happened at the Spring Fling." He looks worried.

My other worst nightmare come to life reenters my mind. I can see Sky outing me when I went undercover as "Rachel Rogers," in front of a gym packed with my classmates and camera crews. I think of the media scrutiny of my life that followed and I stare at Austin intently to calm my nerves. His hair smells of coconut shampoo and is gelled. He's wearing his Armani suit, the one he was gifted when he was supposed to be my date to the Teen Titan awards. Well, before I canceled on him and we broke up for a few weeks. I ran after him hours before the show started to apologize, and we got back together again. I'm exhausted just thinking about our crazy courtship. I quickly push the stalkerazzi images away. "I'm going." I'm firm. "Tonight is your night and I'm not missing it."

"This is not going to be a repeat of the Spring Fling," Rodney tells us. "I've done a thorough study of the gym this time. I know all the exits, how many paces it will take to get to Nadine's car, how to handle any undercover paparazzi who might show. Nothing is going to go wrong."

I smile at Rod, who has changed out of his football duds and into a tailor-made gray suit.

"Rodney, your bodyguard skills rock," Austin says. I freeze, moving only my eyes to look at Rodney's. OOPS!

HOLLYWOOD SECRET NUMBER ELEVEN: If you're a celebrity, you never refer to the person you've hired to protect you as your bodyguard. Rod, and all the guys he knows in the biz, seem to think the word *bodyguard* sounds like a mindless thug, while the term *personal security* has a more intelligent ring. They've certainly earned the right to be called whatever they want. Rod is responsible for protecting me 24/7, drops everything in his life to fit my schedule, has to worry about getting sued over altercations, and is stuck following me everywhere, even when I do something as unguyish as get a pedicure. No wonder we pay him almost $200,000 a year.

"Thanks," Rodney mumbles as we pull into the familiar parking lot. I'm sure he'll forgive Austin for the slipup.

There are no camera vans in sight and I breathe a sigh of relief. Still, Rodney gets out of the car first and moves us swiftly to the back entrance of the boys' locker room. He raps on the metal door three times and I give myself a once-over while I wait. I chose a Dolce & Gabbana pale pink satin dress for tonight. The lingerie-style gown clings to my every curve, ends at my knees, and is held up by spaghetti straps. My hair is pulled back in a smooth low bun.

The door slowly opens and Principal Pearson peeks out.

"Right on time," she squeals with a clap of her hands. "I'm so happy to see you!" We hug.

"Principal P. was in on this too?" Austin sounds incredulous. We both nod.

"Everything okay on the inside?" Rodney asks her.

Principal P. nods. "Not a camera in sight, well, if you ignore the disposable ones the students are using. I can't do anything about those, but I did ban camera phones. I'm sure that was slightly suspicious of me, but I had them confiscated at the door."

"You're incredible," I tell Principal P. as she guides us out of the dark locker room, which smells faintly like old gym socks. We head down the long corridor to the gym. "Thanks for helping me so I could be here."

Principal P. pauses. Her round face crinkles slightly and she pushes her short salt-and-pepper hair out of her eyes. Tonight she's put away her eclectic dresses and chosen a floral purple pantsuit. "While I have you, Kaitlin, I was hoping you could tell me a bit about . . ."

Oh no. I forgot Principal P. is a *Family* fanatic. Please don't say Alexis or Vegas. Laney made me swear on any future Oscar nominations that I wouldn't let the words *Alexis* or *Vegas* cross my lips tonight.

". . . Alexis Holden."

UGH. "What about her?" I ask, trying not to sound nervous.

"I hate her," Principal P. says without hesitating. "She's a dreadful actress. What does the show see in her?"

"Principal P., I love you!" I gush, letting go of Austin's hand and throwing myself around her large frame. She laughs. "Ask me anything about the show. Anything! If I have the answer, I'll tell you."

See? I didn't say Alexis's name.

Rodney chuckles. "You have no idea how happy you've made her."

Moments later, we're standing at the open gym doors. The Clark High School gymnasium had been transformed into a fall festival. There are bales of hay stacked up along the walls that are topped with pumpkins and mums in plum, orange, and yellow. Scarecrows stand guard at the punch stand where orange-iced cupcakes are arranged in a cake tower. So far I've spotted candy and caramel apples and even a cotton candy machine. Yum. The only bad move, it seems, is that someone decided to partially cover the floor in hay, which is proving to be a dance hazard. Organza-clad girls are sliding around in their open-toe sandals.

"You made it!" Liz shrieks. She pulls Austin and me into a group hug. When she lets go, I see she's wearing the sparkly blue Jenni Kanye dress we bought at The Grove. Her curly hair is down. It bounces as she bops to the beat of the music.

"I can't believe you were all in on this and no one told me!" Austin laughs.

Someone covers my eyes and whispers, "Guess who?"

"Beth!" I turn around to hug her petite frame. There's no hiding Allison's tall ballerina body standing right behind her. "Ali! I've missed you guys!" The pair of them, plus Lizzie and Austin, were the only people nice enough to befriend me when I masqueraded as Rachel at Clark. I haven't seen either girl since they visited me this summer on the set of *PYA* a few months ago.

"The best part about you being here is watching our favorite Homecoming court princess's reaction." Allison tosses her brown hair over her shoulder and I see Austin's ex-girlfriend, Lori, standing ten feet away with her right-hand minion, Jessie. Both girls are staring at us with their mouths wide open.

"She so doesn't deserve to rule," Beth laments and pushes her tortoiseshell glasses back onto her nose. Beth is wearing an ankle-length strapless olive green dress that contrasts nicely with her brown skin. "She's evil! What any guy sees in her, I have no idea. No offense, Austin." Beth blushes.

"None taken." Austin smiles easily and turns his attention to his pal Rob Murray, who is Beth's boyfriend. Austin seems oblivious to the crowd of people whispering about us. Larry the Liar, however, is still nowhere in sight. All is good.

With Austin not paying attention, Allison whispers, "I hate the idea of Austin and Lori having to dance together when the court is introduced." Her black cocktail tank dress shimmers in the low-lit disco lights.

"Maybe we should cause a scene and spill cider on her dress," Liz suggests.

"Lizzie," I warn. "The last thing I need is more drama.

Don't worry about it. The dance is tradition. I can deal. Tonight is all about Austin." I don't say it out loud, but I also want to enjoy a night off from any cattiness or girl fights.

"Just look at her smiling and staring at your boyfriend," Beth complains anyway. "It's not fair. Girls like Lori always get what they want. And you want to know why? Because they don't care what anyone thinks of them. They do whatever they have to do to stay on top and squash anyone who tries to stop them." I can't help but think of Alexis and then just as quickly I push her out of my mind. Across the room, I see Lori and her friends staring at us. I look away.

"Liz is right," Allison says, squinting her eyes at Lori. "Let's dump cider on her!"

"Everything okay?" Austin asks as he rejoins the conversation. We all jump.

"Uh-huh," we say at the same time, making us sound quite suspicious.

"Good." Austin grins. "Mind if I steal my girl away for a dance?" He takes me by the hand and swings me onto the dance floor. It's a fast song so I try not to be self-conscious about all the people staring as I sway to the beat. I don't worry long because soon Allison and her date, Tim Corder, Beth and Rob, and Liz and Josh have formed a small circle with us. The eight of us stay on the dance floor, in that very spot near the DJ booth, without anyone bothering us the entire night. It helps that Rodney is continually circling our group with his "I'm a big, bad personal security dude" face on. Not that he needs it — aside from people using their disposable cameras to take poorly lit pictures, there's not a photographer in sight.

"It's time to introduce our Homecoming court and pick our Homecoming king and queen," Principal P. finally announces into the microphone. The room roars with approval. "Would all of the court and the nominees please join me at the DJ booth?"

Austin winks at me before walking over to Principal P. I see Lori push aside her fellow court members so she can stand on the other side of Austin. Ugh.

Lori's blond hair is long and curly. She's wearing a dress I own in my closet — a slinky nude Marc Bouwer number that if it didn't glitter would make her look like she's naked. It would look fabulous if she could wipe that smug look off her face. Lori sees me staring and smirks confidently as she gives her lips a quick pucker. I do my best *True You* face and repeat to myself quietly, "I don't care about Lori. It's only one dance. Three minutes of my life." But I'm having trouble believing myself when Lori tucks a stray blond hair behind her ear and grips Austin's arm. Liz grabs my hands in support and Beth and Allison put their hands on my shoulders. I hold my breath.

Principal P. begins announcing the court. We clap politely for the freshman and sophomore members and pretend to be talking to one another when Lori's name is called. Out of the corner of my eye I can see her waving and bowing to her fans like a complete cheeseball. The group of us can't help but giggle. Finally it's Austin's turn. He blushes violently as we all hoot and holler.

After the king and queen are announced and share a ceremonial dance, I hear the words I've been dreading. "And now our court will take the floor for a spotlight dance," Principal P. announces.

We move back to make room for them and I watch somewhat anxiously as Austin leads Lori onto the dance floor. Lori smirks at me as she holds Austin's hand and I dig my own into Liz's. I smile politely even though it's killing me. I am not going to let her get to me. Instead, I focus on Austin. When he sees me, he smiles brightly. Then he turns to Lori and whispers something in her ear. While Austin talks, Lori's smile begins to fade. She turns and glares at me before stomping off.

"What was that about?" Liz asks, but before I can guess, Lori walks to the edge of the circle and pulls a guy I recognize from Clark's basketball team onto the dance floor. The next thing I know, Austin is standing in front of me.

"May I have this dance?" he asks.

"But you're supposed to dance with Lori," I point out. "It's okay with me. I know it's tradition." I don't want Austin to think I'm the jealous type, even though every girl is a little.

Austin smiles. "Well, I'm starting a new court tradition. It's my birthday and on my birthday the only queen I want to dance with is my own."

I blush furiously. I don't know what to say to that. It's

terribly romantic. I take his warm hand and let him lead me back into the spotlight. Liz and the gang are cheering, but I can barely hear them. I don't even care that Lori is still glaring at me. I close my eyes and rest my head on Austin's shoulder as we move ever so slightly to a slow song.

I haven't felt this free, this relaxed in . . . I don't know how long. I feel like Cinderella. The only difference is that at midnight, I'll turn back into a tabloid-plagued TV actress instead of an enslaved housekeeper.

"Tonight has been amazing," I murmur. "The only thing that would make the evening even more perfect would be if I had a birthday present to give you."

"Would you stop?" Austin says. "I told you earlier. I don't want you to buy me anything. All I wanted for my birthday was you and you're here."

Aww . . . my boyfriend is amazing. "Okay," I say because I don't know what else to say after that. "So what about you? Are you enjoying being royal?"

"It's not too shabby," Austin says. "But I think my queen is enjoying it even more than I am. I've never seen you this calm before. Burke, do you realize we're having a tabloid- and Hollywood-free night?"

I laugh. "Shh! Don't jinx us," I joke. "Can't I just enjoy a completely normal, totally un-star-related high school experience like the rest of my peers?"

"You're not like the rest of us, Burke. And it's more than just your star status," Austin says seriously. "That's what I love about you."

190

WAIT A MINUTE. Did Austin just say love as in LOVE LOVE? Or does he mean he *loves* different things about me?

I can't breathe.

Seriously, I think I'm going to need oxygen or something.

Any minute, Austin is going to realize I've stopped breathing. I can hear a whooshing sound in my ears like I'm going to pass out.

OH GOD. Am I supposed to say it back? I don't know.

I really, really, REALLY like Austin, but do I *love* him? The seconds are ticking away. If I'm going to say it back, I have to say it right NOW.

NOW.

Say it NOW, Kaitlin.

I don't say it.

But Austin said it! Right? He said he loved me!

I think.

I don't know. This is very confusing.

In my head, the music stops. The room is quiet. My heart is beating out of my chest, but my mouth feels dry and I can't speak.

SAT. 10/26
NOTE TO SELF:

Ask Liz 2 download dance pics.
Look up SAT definition of love.
Order pics A's mom took pre-dance from Snapfish!
Mon., Tues., Wed. call times on set: 6 AM

12 INT. BUCHANAN MANOR — FOYER — AFTERNOON

                    DR. BRADEN
    (out of breath) Thank you for agreeing to see me. I
    didn't think we should discuss this over the phone.

                    PAIGE
    Of course. Is something wrong? Did you find
    something on one of my tests?

Dr. Braden hesitates. He fumbles with his leather portfolio,
looking for the right papers.

                    DENNIS
    Please, Dr. Braden. My wife and my family have
    been through so much. Don't leave us in suspense.
    Whatever it is, we can handle it.

In the doorway, the viewer can see the outlines of Sam, Sara,
and Colby.

13 INT. BUCHANAN MANOR — DINING ROOM — AFTERNOON

                    SAM
    What's going on in there?

                    SARA
    (spying) It's Dr. Braden. Mom was on the phone with

him an hour ago and he rushed over. Something must
be wrong.

                    COLBY
Do you think we should be spying on them? Maybe it's
something they don't want us to know.

                    SARA
How do you think we find out stuff around here,
Colby? Watch and learn. Whatever it is concerns all
of us.

                    SAM
Mom and Dad have been so stressed over those tests
Dr. Braden gave us. I don't know what they'll do
if he finds out any of us have the same gene that
caused Mom's blood mutation.

14 INT. BUCHANAN MANOR – FOYER – AFTERNOON

                    DR. BRADEN
According to the results of the blood work
conducted on your daughters, not all three girls are
a match for Paige's DNA.

                    DENNIS
Are you saying Colby is not Paige's daughter?

                    DR. BRADEN
(pauses) The opposite, actually. I think Colby is her
daughter.

                              PAIGE
(hugs her husband tightly) I knew it! I could feel it.
She's come back to me, Dennis.

                           DR. BRADEN
There's more—according to these results, Sam and
Sara might not be.

                              PAIGE
What? That's impossible!

                           DR. BRADEN
According to our tests, the fraternal twins share
the same genetic makeup, but neither of them matches
your blood type, which leads us to believe that
your girls may have been switched at birth with the
Moxley twins, who as you may remember went missing
in a boating accident.

                             DENNIS
You must have mixed up the bloodwork! Why would
someone switch our girls? We had tight security on
the hospital at the time because Paige was receiving
death threats.

                           DR. BRADEN
Yes, I remember. But that doesn't mean someone from
the inside couldn't have made the switch. Natalie
Bennett, one of the night nurses, feuded with Paige

for years before her car went over the Summerville
Bridge. Maybe she ...

                    PAIGE
No. This can't be! No. NO!

                  DR. BRADEN
I'm so sorry, Paige. But according to this, it looks
like the girls you've raised as your daughters are
not your daughters at all.

Sara lets out an ear-piercing scream. She's inconsolable.
Dennis runs to her and holds her.

                    DENNIS
Don't listen to him! We'll have them retested. We'll
figure this out.

Sam faints and Colby rushes to help her up.

                    SAM
What's going on? Was I dreaming?

Colby brushes her hair and shushes her. There's a contented
smile on her face.

                    COLBY
Actually, princess, I think you're finally waking up
to a whole new world.

TWELVE: *Read It and Weep*

"So do you think he meant he *loves* me or he loves *being* with me?" I've just finished telling Nadine what happened at Homecoming and am waiting to hear what she thinks about Austin's use of the L-word. I bite my lip anxiously. It's been almost a week since he said it and I still don't know what to think. Not that I'm counting.

Nadine looks reflective. She's been out sick the past few days herself (I think I gave her whatever bug I had), so her milky white skin is still beyond pale. "So he said, 'That's what I love about you?'" I nod hurriedly. She looks perplexed. "Well, it's not a clear-cut 'I love you,' but it certainly sounds like that's what he meant. You know boys. It's like pulling teeth to get them to say what you want to hear."

I'm not sure if I should jump for joy or cry. "But I didn't say 'I love you' back," I say regretfully. "Now Austin probably thinks he made a huge mistake saying that he maybe loves me!" I bury my face in the script I'm memorizing.

"Do you love him?" Nadine asks.

"I think so, but how do I know for sure?" I ask my script. I'm so freaked out by this entire topic that I can't even look Nadine in the eye. Love. Do I possibly *love* Austin? Does he love me? How do you know for sure? Suddenly our six-month relationship seems a lot more complicated.

I hear a *swoosh* sound and look up in time to see a set of crisp white pages fly under my dressing room door.

"I thought you had this week's script already," Nadine mumbles as she munches on an Oreo. They're our favorite go-to cookies in times of stress and deep reflection and this is definitely one of those times. If Alexis stays put or this love thing gets more complicated, Nadine and I are going to have to order Oreos by the caseload.

"We already started shooting, but maybe there've been some changes," I tell her, scanning the first sheet.

HOLLYWOOD SECRET NUMBER TWELVE: As detail-obsessed film director Hutch Adams taught me, a script isn't final until it airs. (And even then, they can tweak things for years to come on director's cut DVDs.) I'm used to tweaking dialogue on set in the middle of shooting. Melli is famous for correcting the writing staff when they give her lines she doesn't think Paige would say. But major script changes, like the eight pages I just received, are pretty rare.

I back myself into my cozy leather club chair and start reading. The scene being rewritten is the one where Dr. Braden gives the Buchanans the results of Colby's blood test. Oh. That's nothing. Since next week's episode was supposed to be Alexis's last, the original script had a scene where Dr.

Braden determined Colby was not Paige's daughter. Now that Alexis is sticking around a little longer, the writers probably rewrote Dr. Braden's results. They can milk the Colby character for a few more episodes by ordering new-blood work, having the results get lost or stolen, and keep Alexis around indefinitely. I shudder at the thought.

But . . . hmm . . . this new scene is really different.

"Your mom and Laney want you to do a chat with E! Online," Nadine reads from her BlackBerry. "It's the Vegas story again, but you haven't talked to them about your side and Alexis was just interviewed by them and hinted that you and Sky caused the fight. You definitely have to speak up. Sky should too."

Sky and I are united in our determination to get rid of Alexis, but so far, the positive press and the interviews we've done on the subject have still been separate. We haven't said this to each other, but I think we both still think we're better off tackling the Alexis issue — and how it affects our careers — on our own.

"Fine." I read faster and faster, glossing over small phrases and lines to reach the outcome. When I get to Dr. Braden saying "the girls you've raised as your daughters are not your daughters at all," the pages slip out of my hands and fall to the floor. "WHAT?" I can't breathe. "THIS HAS TO BE A JOKE!"

"What does it say?" Nadine asks in a panic. "Kates? What does it say?" Nadine dives to the floor and scrambles to put the pages back in the right order.

I grab the empty Coffee Bean and Tea Leaf bag from this morning's latte off the table and breathe slowly into it, but it makes me cough. The bag smells too much like Colombian roast.

"Oh my God," Nadine whispers as she finishes reading. It's official. I wasn't hallucinating. The writers are cutting Sam and Sara out of the family and adding Colby into the fold. After all I've given this show, this is how Tom treats me? He can't even tell me to my face? They're keeping Alexis and not renewing Sky and me? How can this be?

I grab the script back from Nadine and bolt from the room before she can block me. "Kaitlin, wait!" she yells. "We've got to get Laney and your mom on the phone. Don't do anything rash till I call Tom!" she says.

"Do you hear me? KATES!"

"TOM!" I yell.

"TOOMM!"

"TOOOOMMMMMMMM!" I screech again as I run down the hallway. "I need to find Tom!" I grab a scrawny P.A. by his Dane Cook comedy tour T-shirt. "WHERE IS TOM?" I bellow. His blue eyes grow wide in alarm, but I don't care. "I need to see him immediately."

"I don't think he's here," the young guy squeaks. "He's barricaded himself in the postproduction office to finish next week's show since we've had so many delays. He isn't taking calls." I grab his shirt tighter. "But I could be wrong."

I let go of his shirt and run in a new direction. I know how I can find out if Tom is here. I can have the receptionist page him over the intercom. I run toward the *FA* studio's main entrance. I can barely see where I'm going because my eyes are glazed over with hot tears. I'm in the middle of screaming "TOM!" again when . . .

Smack!

Boom!

Groan . . .

I'm lying flat out on the floor looking up at the fluorescent overhead lights. I cradle my aching head and try to sit up and look around. The receptionist desk is empty. WHOA. I feel dizzy. I look over to see what I crashed into.

But it's not a what, it's a who. Sky.

Sky sits up and I see mascara is running down her cheeks. She looks like a ghoul on the way to a Halloween party.

A lump starts to form in my throat. This is real.

"You read the new script, didn't you?" I ask Sky tearfully, unable to hold back my emotions.

Sky nods and gets choked up too. "They can't be real," she sniffs, not caring for once that the person she's crying to is, well, me. "They can't be choosing not to renew our contracts. They just can't! They can't be writing us off the show. Why would they pick Alexis over us?"

"I don't know," I admit. "Melli would never let them get rid of us, would she? She has our back."

"Does she?" Sky asks as she stands up. She dusts off her stockings and clingy black mini using her lace fingerless gloves. I decide to face the music too. My black trousers have Swiffered the floor, but my satin Belle Gray cami made it out of our crash unharmed. I collect my missing Bally black pump and put it back on my foot.

"Of course she does." I hope I don't sound as unsure as I feel.

"K, she's not speaking to us," Sky points out, not that she has to. Her dark, puffy eyes say it all: We're doomed. "Tom is barely talking to anyone. The writers' room is agitated. Almost everyone here, including your brother, is still under Alexis's spell. The press is having a field day with the drama and all they can write about is someone getting axed over what happened in Vegas. Even *Vanity Fair* is doing an exposé."

I knew the tabloid drama had hit rock bottom when Laney showed me *Hollywood Nation*'s latest issue. I thought last week's In the Know piece was the worst, but this week they ran a four-page article on the Vegas melee and included a one-page article called "She Said, She Said — The Scene of the Crime." It was an artistic reenactment of how the Tao fight went down, using eyewitness accounts. *Nation* drew a picture of the Tao balcony and placed Sky's, Alexis's, and my heads on stick figures to show where we stepped, what we supposedly said, and who hit who first. They also polled readers on whether or not they were turned off by *FA* after what happened. Seventy-six percent said they were. Gulp. Then they asked whether someone on *FA* should be fired for causing all this drama. Eighty-six percent said yes. Double gulp. I was thankful they didn't ask them who should be axed. I guess now it doesn't even matter.

"So that's it then," I say, absentmindedly pulling my long, curly hair off my neck. "After all these years, they're getting rid of us both."

"Don't wallow, K," Sky snaps. "I don't know about you, but I'm not going down without a fight. Especially when kicking us off doesn't make sense. Even if Alexis keeps blaming us for feeling alienated, the ratings are up despite all the hoopla, which would make them want to keep all of us bickering babies around."

"Do you think the script might be fake?" I ask hopefully.

"Wake up, blondie." Sky rolls her eyes. "Even Alexis couldn't pull off a move this big. This thing comes from above her."

Before I can even imagine which coworker besides Alexis would be scheming against us, the intercom crackles to life. "*FA* cast members in the Buchanan Manor foyer scene report to set immediately for taping," the voice tells us.

"Oh God, the new scene." I freak and start to hyperventilate again. Where is a paper bag? I need a bag!

Sky's icy hand grabs mine. "Relax. It's probably just a rehearsal," she says. "They wouldn't tape the scene without a rehearsal first."

"We've got to find Tom and bring him to his senses before the cameras roll," I say.

We've only taken ten steps before encountering a setback. Sky shrieks. When I look up, I notice that what was once a blank, slightly dirty white wall next to the *FA* cast portraits is now home to a new picture of Alexis. Her red hair is windblown and her face has barely a stitch of makeup, allowing you to connect the dots with her faint freckles. Her eyes and smug smile seem to gloat, "Good luck getting rid of me now."

"I think I feel faint," Sky says.

I glare at Alexis's face and feel a newfound determination. "Come on," I grunt, pulling Sky's arm. We teeter down the long hallway, our heels clicking and clacking on the slippery floor, slowing down before we reach the large soundstage. Please, please let that P.A. be wrong about Tom. He's got to be here.

But he's not. Alexis is standing in the foyer set and Matty is reading her lines. Since he isn't in today's scene, Matty's dressed casually in ripped jeans and a navy thermal T-shirt. Alexis, on the other hand, is in super-tight black leggings with a long bright purple V-neck sweater gathered at the waist with a fat black belt. As if she can sense the rays of hate, she looks up, sees Sky and me, and snickers.

After what happened in Vegas, Matty told me he was forcing himself to stop liking her. So what's he doing with her now?

"I'm going to kill her," Sky declares, moving swiftly to the stage. I try to pull her back, but it's no use. She may be bony, but she's got strong upper body muscles.

"Our bigger problem is finding Tom, remember?" I hiss as Sky pushes aside a P.A., a grip, and two cameramen to reach her target. Alexis folds her arms across her chest and waits defiantly as Matty stares at my approaching frame in horror.

"Kaitlin, I . . ." Matty starts to say nervously. I look away and he stops talking.

"What do you two want?" Alexis snaps. "Are you here to pull another five-hundred-dollar extension out of my hair?"

"You mean ninety. Fake strands like yours could only come from the Jessica Simpson hair collection," Sky retorts, smoothing her black hair, which is back to its natural fullness thanks to a very good weave.

Alexis stares at us. "Shouldn't you two be off cleaning out your dressing rooms?"

"What is she talking about?" Matty asks.

"Your sister and Sky have been fired," Alexis says giddily. "The network has decided to get rid of the problem."

"Nice try," I reply bitterly, "but guess what? No one has canned us. Sorry, but your dreams of *FA* being a one-woman show will have to stay in fantasyland."

Alexis smiles. "It may not be a one-woman show yet, but it's a one-daughter show, that's for sure."

"What?" Matt whispers. Sky thrusts her new script pages at him.

"You love causing drama, don't you?" I ask Alexis, not expecting an answer. Something about her coy expression makes me more furious. "It just goes to show how inexperienced you are. Let me give you some advice: I don't care how great the ratings are, no one puts up with a manipulative amateur like you for too long." Take that! "And you can forget about Sky and me cleaning out our dressing rooms.

We're not filming these new pages till we talk to Tom." I fold my arms across my chest to keep from shaking.

"Then you really will be fired," Alexis purrs. "I'm sure the press would love to get an anonymous tip about how you two held up production yet again."

"Oh, you're good," Sky comments. "But I'm better. Don't mess with the master of deception. I've been ruining K's set life for years."

"Yeah," I back her up. Oh wait . . .

"And if you go so far as take your cell out of your bag, I'll text Brian Bennett and tell him all about your little trip to Palm Springs for lipo."

"How do you know about that?" Alexis stutters.

"I have my ways," Sky says smugly.

Wow, Sky's good. It's kind of fun to watch her in action when I'm not on the receiving end.

"This says Sam and Sara aren't Paige's daughters!" Matty exclaims to no one in particular, having finished reading. "These pages can't be real."

"Oh, they're real all right, Marty," Alexis says, not taking her eyes off Sky and me.

"It's Matty," he corrects her.

"Your sister is a goner," Alexis continues unphased. "The studio has finally decided that they're tired of her and Sky's behavior on set. These pages prove they've finally decided to get rid of them. And they're keeping me full-time instead."

Alexis steps closer to Sky so that the two of them are

face-to-face. I move closer too. I try to slide in between them. "Try something," I dare. Matty grabs my arm. I smack it away. "Two against one are great odds."

"You wouldn't make a move, cupcake," Alexis taunts. "Not in front of all these people. You wouldn't want to ruin your pathetic good-girl image."

"Watch it," warns Sky.

"Ladies, is there a problem here?" Phil Marker, this week's guest director, asks. He's shot several shows for *FA* over the years.

I turn around. "Yes, we have a *big* problem with the new pages and we're not filming a word of them till we see Tom."

Phil nods. "I know. I was just talking to Becky about them, and the whole daughter switcheroo seems to come out of left field."

Phil understands! Thank God. I always knew he was a reasonable guy. "So then you agree we have to talk to Tom before even proceeding with rehearsals," I say.

Phil frowns. "Well, Becky said she wasn't in any writing meetings where they talked about switching gears on the Colby storyline, but that's why we think maybe it came from the top. The bottom line is, Tom wouldn't have distributed the changes if it wasn't what he wanted, and he told me not to call him unless the set is on fire, we've been canceled, or there is a sudden flu epidemic."

"I think this qualifies as an emergency, Phil," I point out.

My mind is racing. Think, Kaitlin! "What if these pages weren't approved by Tom? You admit they're totally out of character. Can't we shoot another scene until Tom emerges?"

Phil shakes his head. "I wish we could, Kaitlin, but this is the scene we're set up for and we're already so behind and over budget because of the delays that we don't have time to change things. I have no choice."

"It's okay, Philly," Alexis coos. "We know you're just doing your job."

"Maybe we can start shooting another scene in the foyer and shoot this one tomorrow after we talk to Tom," Sky says desperately. "Something just seems fishy here, Phil. I'd hate to waste the network's money on a scene that isn't written that well."

"Are you saying our writers are shoddy?" Alexis tsks. "I'd hate for them to hear you say that. They work so hard."

Sky glares at her.

"You sound just like Melli, Sky," Phil says. "I just spent an hour in her dressing room trying to coax her out here and fifteen minutes in Spencer's. She was unbelievably upset when she got the pages and she and Spencer begged me to track down Tom. They're on their way down here now to talk to you two."

I look at Sky. Maybe we can all band together and stage a mutiny!

"I told them the same thing I'm telling you: Tom is the head honcho," Phil is saying. "I'm surprised he didn't warn me about this new direction with the show, but I don't think I can argue. We have to assume he wouldn't have printed these pages unless he wanted to end the episode this way."

"Oh my God." I am hyperventilating. "This is really happening." I can't breathe.

"Kaitlin, you've got to calm down," Phil says, grabbing my arm with concern.

"Sky? Kaitlin? Are you okay?" Melli and Spencer have just busted through the double doors and are running toward us with looks of deep concern. Melli's still wearing her between-scenes bathrobe and Spencer is in gym shorts and a basketball tee. Neither of them looks ready to film. Melli pulls us into a hug, much like our real moms would.

"Don't get upset," Spencer says in his deep voice. "We're going to get to the bottom of what's going on. You two aren't going anywhere."

Phil looks at his watch. "Now that everyone's here, we should really start filming. If you wouldn't mind getting into wardrobe —"

"Phil!" Melli reprimands, cutting him off. "How can you ask us to shoot right now when the girls are so upset?"

"I'm sorry! We're really behind and I have to get this to postproduction today!" Phil is starting to sound agitated. "Tom will kill me if we don't shoot this. Please, just do this and I promise you can talk to Tom later."

Sky shakes her head no. I do too and stand next to Sky in solidarity. I can hear my heart. The beat is faster than a freight train.

Phil shakes his head. "Ladies, *please*. If you don't shoot, I'm going to have to dock your pay and call the network, who will probably say you're in breach of your contracts."

"I don't want that to happen." Melli glances back and forth between the two of us, her voice soft yet stern. "You don't need more problems right now. Let's do what Phil says and then afterward Spencer and I will both go with you to find Tom."

I look at Spencer and he nods. "We promise."

Sky's eyes are welling with tears again just like my own. I know I can't go through with this. I can't film this scene. Not like this. Not now.

"Make the call, Phil." I'm shaking. I've never defied Melli or Spencer before. "Sky and I are not filming anything until Tom calls us and tells us to do it. He's the only person we trust."

"I agree," Sky says solemnly. "We're not filming a word of this crap. You know Kaitlin and me. You've shot scenes with us since we were little kids! Tom wouldn't do something so drastic without telling us first." Sky sounds strong and her voice echoes in the cavernous room. I notice some of the cameramen stop what they're doing and stare.

"Please," Melli tries again. "Think of your future."

"Kates, be reasonable," Matt begs. "We'll get ahold of Tom. Just film the scene, okay? Can you imagine what Mom will say when she hears you refused to film?"

"I'm sorry, everyone," I say hoarsely. "Sky's right. You don't make important, life-changing decisions like this without telling your actors first. This isn't *Lost*. You can't just practically kill us off without warning. We're a big part of *FA* and we both deserve some respect. We've been on this show our whole lives!"

Phil has his head in his hands. "ENOUGH," he says. "You have ten minutes to hit your marks. After that, I'm calling the network." He walks off to get ready and Melli and Spencer trail after him, badgering him not to do this.

"Wow, girls, thanks," Alexis says gleefully. "I thought I had to kick you guys off to get more airtime. Who knew you would go so willingly?"

"Alexis," Matty says, looking beyond hurt. "My sister's right about you. You have it out for her. What did she ever do to you?"

"Truthfully, nothing. But she's standing in the way of me getting what I want, and I can't let that happen," Alexis admits with a sick smile. "She's hogged the spotlight for years. Now it's my turn. Don't look so wounded, Marty," Alexis adds. "It makes you look pathetic."

"I'll tell you what's pathetic," Sky declares. "Filming this crap. You want a solo show, Alexis? Shoot this one alone. Kaitlin and I are out of here."

Sky grabs my arm. I hesitate for a moment, looking from Phil yelling into his cell phone, to Matty, to the group of grips and workers who have slowly gathered to watch the latest altercation. I can't believe it, but for the first time ever, I'm about to walk off set in the middle of a workday.

"K, let's go," Sky says through clenched teeth. I see her mascara has started to run again.

"Kaitlin, don't do this," Matty begs.

"I'm sorry, Matty, but what's right is right," I say over my shoulder, and with that, Sky and I exit stage left.

FRIDAY 11/1
NOTE TO SELF:

Call Nadine. Warn Laney. Have her calm down Mom.
Reach Austin and Lizzie.
Make Nadine unplug all TiVos in the house 2 avoid them seeing *Access* or *Celeb Insider.* We're going 2 be on it.

THIRTEEN: *Crossroads*

"Where are we going?" I ask as Sky drags me from the building and into the street in front of our soundstage. "I thought we were barricading ourselves in our dressing rooms and waiting for Tom." The back lot is buzzing with activity as usual and golf carts and Range Rovers whiz by. A loud honk tells us to move our debate onto the sidewalk.

Sky shakes her head. "Melli and Spencer will find us and push us to shoot the scene. We're better off getting as far away from *FA* as we can."

I think for a moment and realize I actually agree with her. "We'll leave Tom a message and tell him we urgently need to talk to him," I suggest. "That way no one can accuse us of completely bailing." I quickly dial his number and it goes right to voice mail. I leave a message from the two of us and hang up, my stomach doing cartwheels. "Maybe we should call our managers and publicists and tell them what's going on too," I add.

"Are you crazy?" Sky snaps. "My mom-ager will force me

to go back without even listening to why I left in the first place. Maybe your mom is different, but I'm certainly not calling mine."

On second thought, maybe I shouldn't call Mom or Laney yet.

Sky's eyes begin to brim with tears and I awkwardly put my arm around her. As I pat her back, Sky stops crying and starts to laugh.

"This is weird," she says as she uses her right index finger to fix her smudged mascara. "You're the last person I thought I would ever cry in front of."

"I always thought if I walked off set, it would be *because* of you, not with you." I feel myself getting teary too. "But here we are."

"Here we are," Sky repeats. She takes a deep breath. "Okay, enough moping. Let's get out of here before someone spots us. Do you have a car? My driver dropped me off this morning and my security is off today so he can take his Prius to the shop."

I frown. "We'll have to call Rodney. I don't have my license yet."

Sky wags a long red manicured finger at me. "That's right, I forgot about your little driving snafu. Dumb move going with a Joe Shmo school. What were you thinking, K?"

GRR . . . Sky's sudden mood swing reminds me why we're nowhere close to being friends. If I'm going to do something as crazy as side with her on this *FA* thing, then there've got to be some rules.

"Let's forget about my driving record and focus on the nightmare at hand, shall we?" I say coolly. "Until we figure out what to do about *FA*, can we at least *pretend* we're costars who get along? There's no bad blood between us, no tabloid feuds, no past mistakes, and no rude comments . Deal or no deal?"

"You're so cheesy." Sky rolls her eyes.

I start to walk away.

"FINE!" Sky blurts out. I turn and see she's got her hands folded in prayer like she's a sweet little girl making her first communion. "I'll play nice, but first we have to figure out how we're getting off this lot."

"KATES! KATES!" Rodney barrels toward us, moving like a freight train. His round face is contorted in panic and sweat is dripping down his bald head. He throws me over his shoulder and begins to sprint away like he's carrying a football. "What are you doing with her? Did she hurt you?" Rodney growls as he runs.

"Rod, put me down! Sky didn't do anything." He places me back on the pavement and looks at me with confusion. "Sky and I, um, walked off set together in a show of solidarity," I explain, knowing the idea of me working with Sky is as crazy as Darth Vader helping Luke Skywalker. Oh wait. He sort of did that in *Return of the Jedi*.

"I heard you left, but I didn't know it was with *her*." Rodney stares at Sky.

Sky doesn't seem fazed. She's whipped out a nail file and is buffing away. "Take it easy, big guy. Your precious paycheck is safe for now. I'm just here for a ride."

Rodney looks at me. "Let me handle her. Please?" I beg. "I need you to drive us off the lot."

"Us?" Rodney asks. "I have to take both of you? Kates, what's going on?"

"Just trust me, Rod," I tell him. "Can you get the car and meet us back here asap? We've got to move before someone realizes we left the building."

"Then you two better walk with me to the car," Rodney suggests. "The set is in an uproar. Melli and Spencer told Phil he can call the network about them too. They're not filming anything till they talk to Tom. Phil is having a meltdown over having nothing to shoot and is frantically trying to reach Tom himself. And Alexis is telling anyone who will listen that she thinks both of you should be immediately dismissed from the show."

"Wench," Sky mutters under her breath.

"They're sending out a search party to look for you guys," Rodney adds.

"You're right, we can't wait here for you," I agree as my cell phone starts to ring. Shoot, Nadine must already know. "We better run." The last thing I want is for Phil to see me and try to fire me on the spot.

"Come on, princess," Rodney says to Sky, who looks horrified at the idea of not having a curbside pickup. "You're going to have to hoof it in heels."

It takes us fifteen minutes to get to the Lincoln. It should have taken eight, but Sky whined the whole way there about her uncomfortable Miu Miu stilettos. Our cells drowned out most of her complaining though. If it wasn't Rodney's *Rocky* ring tone or Sky's phone blaring a new Justin Timberlake song, then it was my Motorola playing the commander-in-chief theme (Laney) or Nadine's personalized voice recording of the word "URGENT!"

"The only call I'm taking is from Tom," I say stubbornly as we climb into the backseat of the Lincoln and I hurl my cell phone across the seat. It's too late to call Nadine back now. She's already heard what happened and if I call her she will lawyer me into returning to the set.

Sky slides in next to me and looks around. I forgot she's never been inside my car before. "Is this a 2005 model? My driver has an '08."

"Did we decide where we're going?" I ask as Sky peeks in the backseat pockets. My phone beeps again and against my better judgment I fish for it. It's another voice mail. That brings the total to six.

"Don't check it," warns Sky, reading my thoughts. "The only thing you're going to hear is bad news."

But I can't help myself. I dial in my secret code, 1026 (Austin's birthday), and I hear Nadine's voice. "KAITLIN, YOU'VE GOT TO CALL ME BACK. PHIL IS FLIPPING OUT AND I DON'T KNOW WHAT TO DO ABOUT..."

I skip to the next message. It's Laney. "KAITLIN BURKE, YOU PICK UP THE PHONE THIS INSTANT OR I'LL... YOU SIGNAL BUDDY! I'M ON A CALL! KAITLIN? DO YOU HEAR ME? I'M WARNING..."

Skip. "KAITLIN, THIS IS NOT A JOKE." It's Nadine again. "THEY'RE GOING TO FIRE YOU TWO FOR REAL. IS THAT CLEAR ENOUGH FOR YOU? I'VE LEFT AN URGENT MESSAGE FOR TOM ABOUT THE SCRIPT. IT DOESN'T MAKE SENSE, KAITLIN. SOMETHING STRANGE IS GOING ON, I KNOW IT, BUT YOU CAN'T JUST LEAVE THE SET IN THE MIDDLE OF A WORK-DAY! AFTER ALL THAT'S HAPPENED, DO YOU THINK THEY'RE GOING TO TOLERATE THAT? DON'T LET ALEXIS GET THE BETTER OF YOU. COME OUT OF HID-ING AND WAIT TO HEAR WHAT TOM HAS TO SAY ABOUT . . ."

I hang up, feeling numb. Fired for real? I thought Alexis was bluffing and it would come out that the pages weren't approved and all would be forgiven. But I was wrong.

"What did they say?" Sky asks as Rodney pulls off the lot. "Are we to report to the principal's office at once? Being held a day's pay? What?"

"Guys, where are we going?" Rodney asks.

I stare at Sky. "Nadine said they're going to fire us."

Sky rolls her eyes and begins to laugh. "I've done far worse plenty of times and never been fired. Don't sweat it."

I shake my head. "No, Nadine sounded serious. She said the network wouldn't tolerate more bad press. Sky, forget whether the script is real. They're going to can us for this whether we were being written out of the show or not."

Sky stops laughing and the car grows quiet. Fired for bad behavior? Me?

"Guys?" Rodney asks softly. "Should I keep driving around in circles or am I going someplace?"

"Sky?" I ask, trying not to cry. "Do you think they're serious? Should we go back?"

"I need time to think," Sky says to herself. "Really think."

I look at her expectantly. "Sky?"

"Rodney, take us to Guy Anthony's bar on Beverly Drive in West Hollywood," Sky says abruptly.

"Sky, a bar?" Is she crazy? The press will really love that one. "I don't think a margarita will fix things," I reprimand.

"That's not why we're going to Guy Anthony's."

I don't like the sound of this. Suddenly I feel the urge to grab the wheel from Rodney and steer us back to the studio. Maybe there's still time to save our jobs.

"K, trust me," Sky says after seeing my skeptical expression. "We need an hour to clear our heads, and Guy Anthony's is just the place. Give me an hour."

"I don't know." I feel like I might hyperventilate. Is Sky playing me? What if she found a way to cover her own butt and is leaving mine out to hang? It wouldn't be the first time. "How do I know I can trust you?" I ask. "How do I know this is not just you trying to ruin my life again?"

"You don't," Sky admits. She pulls a black Bobbi Brown compact out of her candy apple red Marc Jacobs Totally Turnlock Bowler bag (I have the exact same one in green) and looks at her face in the mirror. "But what other choice do you have right now?" I bite my lower lip. "We've been on *FA* a long time," Sky reminds me. "If they're going to fire us for leaving over a script that basically said RIP, then what are we running back to? Give me an hour."

"Kates, Nadine and Laney keep calling me and I'm sure your mom will hear what's happened any minute. What do you want me to do?" Rodney yells.

Sky's right, even though I hate the idea of her having all the answers today. "Ignore their calls. Take us to Guy Anthony's," I tell him, looking straight at Sky. After that, we drive along in silence, listening to a symphony of cell phone rings until we reach our destination.

I've never been at an event inside the popular celeb hangout, so I take my time looking around the small, intimate space. It reminds me of a New York City–style lounge Nadine and I once went to. The walls are swathed in black drapes from floor to ceiling and leather banquettes surround the silver dance floor. At the center of the back wall is a long glass bar you can see through.

HOLLYWOOD SECRET NUMBER THIRTEEN: Ever wonder how celebrities know about the hottest hangouts or have invites to the coolest restaurant openings? They could have an amazing publicist (like mine, who tells me about all the best bashes), or they could have well-connected celeb friends. But chances are, some of those stars turned up because they've been paid. Sometimes when a club wants their opening splashed across all the papers they pay a big star to "host" the event or make an appearance. And when I say pay, I mean dough to appear plus an all-expenses paid trip to get there if the club is out of town. Stars can be paid for other outings too — like singing at a girl's bat mitzvah. Stars don't do those things out of the kindness of their hearts. They do it to fatten their already bulging wallets.

"Okay, we're here," I say to Sky. "How's this place supposed to help us?"

"You'll see," Sky says as she sashays up to the bar to talk to the lone person in the place. He's a cute bartender with ringlets of brown curls. "Hey, Cody," she coos.

"Sky, my love," he says in a thick British accent. He's busy drying martini glasses, but he smiles at her and you can see the dimples in his cheeks. "You know we don't open till much later."

"I know," Sky whines in a baby voice I've never heard, "but my, uh, friend and I are having one of those days. Can you help me out again? Please?"

Again? What is she talking about? Rodney and I look on at the odd exchange in silence. I watch Cody. His curls are bouncing all around as he shakes his head. He's definitely going to say no.

"You look hot in that shirt," Sky adds.

Cody laughs and puts down the glass in his hand. "Okay. But this is the last time." Sky crosses her heart. "Don't tell anyone I did this."

Sky pulls herself up on the bar and leans over to give him a kiss on the check. "Love you, Codykins," she coos.

"You're lucky I love you too," Cody says as he walks inside a door behind the bar and disappears.

"Are you two . . . ?" I start to ask, but Sky shakes her head.

"He thinks I'm too young for him." Sky shrugs. "And that's the end of the story."

I can take a hint. "Where's he going?" I ask instead. Within seconds I have my answer. Cody appears out of a door behind the DJ booth. He turns on the speakers and the sound system comes to life. I watch as he plugs in two microphones and places them on top of the turntable. Then he reaches underneath the booth and pulls out a tattered black binder overflowing with white pages and vinyl CD covers. Wait a minute. That's not a . . .

Sky runs over and grabs the karaoke book. "Come look," Sky encourages me. I walk slowly over. "Pick a song," she suggests.

I look at her like she's nuts. "This is your idea of fixing things?" I ask, getting angry "This is why we had to leave the studio? To do karaoke? I was stupid enough to believe you had a master plan to keep us from getting fired!" I'm frantic and it's not just because I can't sing. I've never sung in public and I'm not about to start now in front of Sky, Rodney, and Cody. I need oxygen fast. Why did I leave that paper bag in my dressing room? "Cody, do you have any paper bags behind the bar?" I ask. He shakes his head.

"K, what are you getting so wound up about?" Sky asks in a baby voice, which only makes me madder.

"Is this some sort of game to you, Skylar?" I say. "I walked off set with you because I thought you had a valid point back there. I thought we really needed each other to get through this. But here we are, in a bar, in the middle of the afternoon, and you want me to sing! How is that supposed to help us?"

Sky rolls her eyes. "You really don't know anything about me, do you?"

I don't answer. I listen to the nonstop ringing of our cell phones.

"Well, since we've called a temporary truce, I'm going to let you in on a little Skylar Mackenzie secret." Her dark eyes light up. "When I'm upset, I sing. I thought if we could get our mind off what happened till we hear from Tom, maybe you'd chill enough for us to come up with a game plan. From what I can tell, K, you're more tightly wound than the thread from my old pashminas."

"I know how to relax," I reply defensively.

"Oh yeah?" Sky replies. "That's one of your biggest problems, K. In all the years I've known you, you're always worried about something, and I sure as hell haven't caused all of your problems."

"You've caused plenty," Rodney pipes up from the bar area.

"What are you getting at?" I ask, waiting for Sky to strike again. She's like a python, and they never leave a prey when they're vulnerable.

"You've got to chill and just let life happen sometimes." Sky shrugs. "You can't control everything. Do you think I love being paparazzi bait all the time? Or seeing my latest boy failure trampled through the mags? My mom can be just as demanding as yours, maybe more, but you don't see me sobbing about it at crafty."

"You don't know anything about me," I spit, angry because she's partially right. "Nor do you care. Don't pretend to start now."

"Calm down," Sky says with another eye roll. "I'm just suggesting you take up some sort of hobby that's yours alone. It's made it easier for me to handle some of Hollywood's less flattering moments." Sky picks up the nearest microphone and tosses it gently from hand to hand. "I sing. I sing in the shower, in my car, and I come here on Tuesday nights for karaoke. A lot of stars show up. Just last week Ashley, Vanessa, and I did 'Lady Marmalade' and brought down the house. Kiki Dunst couldn't stop clapping. Neither could Cody."

"She's really good," Cody yells. He's behind the bar, cleaning the highballs.

"I've never read about star karaoke night before," I admit, feeling my shoulders begin to ease up as Sky stops analyzing me.

"That's because it's pretty low-key." Sky flips through the binder and finds the CD she's looking for. "No one talks about it and we've only been written up in *TV Tome* once. Cody told them it was a one-night charity thing so the press hasn't come back."

Sky puts the disc in the system and offers me a microphone. "Want to give it a whirl?" she asks.

"No way," I reply nervously.

Sky rolls her eyes again. "K, don't be a baby."

"You didn't even let me pick a song," I point out. "How do I know you picked one that I know?"

Sky sighs. "We'll do the first one together, okay? The lyrics are up on the screen so you can't mess up." She adds with a sly smile, "That is, if you can actually belt out a tune."

I know a challenge when I hear one. I take the microphone and step up on the platform next to the DJ booth. I can feel my body shaking, but I try to breathe deeply and focus on the flat screen TV where the lyrics will scroll. God, I really can't sing. Rodney sips a soda as he watches me. I think I may hurl.

"What are we singing?" I ask with a squeak.

Sky smiles. "'I Will Survive,'" she says.

The hokey instrumental version kicks in and I recognize the classic Gloria Gaynor song immediately. Sky nudges me in the ribs to join her, but I'm frozen.

I. Can't. Sing. In. Front. Of. People.

Sky doesn't seem to care that I've given her a solo. She gets more into the song by the line and I find myself riveted. Her Lip Venom–injected lips are turned up into a complete smile, her eyes are closed, and her whole body is swaying as she sings. Not only is she good, she's having fun and I'm a little envious.

Hearing Sky sing reminds me how much I like this song. Sky stares back at me as she belts it out and nudges my ribs again. At the bar, Cody and Rodney are clapping to the beat. My heart is beating rapidly and I'm sweating under these glaring strobe lights, but I'm feeling an itch as I watch Sky get into the lyrics as she reaches the chorus. All of a sudden I find myself singing with her in a small voice.

Okay, I don't sound *too* bad. At least I know this song by heart. Lizzie and I used to sing it during our sleepovers. Sky grins and signals me to speak up. Within seconds, I'm practically yelling. We face each other, mic to mic, and sing so loud that I can barely recognize my own voice. I don't know if I sound good or if I stink like expired milk, but I don't care. Sky is right. This *is* fun.

"*I will surviiiiiiiiive!*" we holler on the last chorus, and I hear my voice crack as I hold the long note at the end. Oops.

Cody and Rodney applaud loudly and Sky takes a bow. I join her, feeling giddy.

"Wow, that was actually okay," I manage to get out. I'm out of breath.

"You were great," Sky enthuses.

I look at her. "You're just saying that."

"No, K, I swear. You have a decent voice," she says, and from Sky, I take it as a compliment. "So how do you feel?"

"Like a survivor," I joke. "Seriously, you were right. This feels great. It feels like my birthday." Sky purses her lips. "What do you want me to say?"

"I want you to say you feel relaxed enough to find a solution to our problem," Sky admonishes. She pauses. "And that I was ten times better than you." We both laugh.

"I do feel great. And I'm not just saying this because you asked me to, but you sounded awesome." Sky's face turns pink. Who knew Sky got embarrassed?

"Thanks," she says, moving the microphone away from her lips. "I love it up here."

"Have you ever thought of doing an album?" I ask. "I bet labels would jump at the chance to produce you."

"We've had talks with lots of labels, actually, but I don't know if I want to be just another actor who sings," Sky says. "We all know how well that worked out for Lindsay."

"True," I admit, "but having her first single be about hating the paparazzi probably wasn't the best move either."

"I just . . ." Sky hesitates. Her voice is serious. "I couldn't handle having an album out and being number two, you know? Knowing the public liked someone else more than me would kill me. I play to win and I haven't been winning many battles lately."

I look down. That was definitely about me even if it wasn't intentional. Now I feel guilty, because I'm obviously the reason Sky is afraid to try something new and fail. It's probably the same reason I'm worried about Liz going off to college. I'm not sure I want to go myself, but I don't want to feel left behind or rejected either.

"Now I feel depressed," Sky says, almost as if she's read my thoughts. "Cheer me up with a solo so I can make fun of you." She flashes me a wicked smile.

"No way," I say in alarm. "I couldn't." Behind us, our cellphone rings seem to have gone up a notch. "Rodney, has Tom called us yet?" I try to stall.

Rodney looks at our cell phone screens and shakes his

head. "A lot of Amandas for Sky, and Kates, your mom, and Laney won't let up. Kates, don't be mad, but I told . . ."

"Maybe we should go," I cut him off, but Sky shakes her head. "I have told you more about myself in this one afternoon than I have in over twelve years. You owe me, K. Sing."

"I don't owe you anything." Still, I reluctantly take the microphone and walk over to the binder to pick a song. I know what I'm looking for, even if I'm not sure I can pull it off. I flip the page. There it is. My theme song if there ever was one. Not that I've ever told anyone that before. Even Austin.

"Kelly Clarkson's 'Breakaway'?" Sky complains after I pop the disc in the system and the title screen comes up. "I thought you were cooler than that, K."

I take a final swig of the soda Cody brought me and clear my throat. I take a deep breath, wait for my cue, and close my eyes. I sing with all of my might, feeling the words rock me as I repeat the lyrics my massaging showerhead knows I sing so well. Breaking away from the world is one thing I can emote with no problem.

Sky's right. Singing is really freeing! My hands have stopped shaking and I'm feeling the music. I'm enjoying myself up here, more than I could have imagined. I know the words by heart so I close my eyes and belt them out, trying to shut out the image of Cody, Rodney, and Sky watching me.

When I let go of the final note, all I hear is silence.

No applause. I have to admit, I'm a little disappointed. I actually thought I sounded pretty good. "Was I that bad?" I ask as I open my eyes. I look out at the dance floor and see Lancy, Nadine, and Mom. They don't look happy.

OH GOD. Behind them, Sky's publicist, Amanda, is whispering angrily in her ear. Sky looks up at me, smiles, and mouths what I think is "You rocked." Either that or "Your socks," but that wouldn't make sense. I smile back. Then I look at Rodney, who seems nervous. "I tried to tell you," he says. "I had to call Nadine and tell her you were okay and where we were."

"Kates, you sounded amazing," Nadine gushes.

"Nadine, that's not important right now," Laney snaps. "Although you were quite good."

"LANEY," Mom yells. I've rarely seen her so flustered. "Kaitlin, get off that stage this instant. Nadine told us everything. We're going over to see Tom Pullman."

"But, Mom," I hesitate, "he's not taking calls . . ."

"Melli reached him and he's furious," Mom says.

I hang my head. So it's true. We're toast.

"The script pages were fake. Someone purposely tried to get you guys to film a bogus scene and waste even more of the network's money."

Really? Our hunch was right? But why would someone do that? I look from Nadine to Laney. Oh my God. Sky and I were right! "You mean, you mean, we're not being written off the show?"

"Not yet anyway," Laney says with pursed lips. "But Tom isn't happy. With anyone, it seems. He's tired of all the fighting and the stories in the press and the tension between you two and Alexis. And now this bogus script . . . a few people could lose their jobs. It's not a good time to stage a walkout," Laney says flatly.

"But we . . ." I begin.

"You two made things worse for yourselves by disappearing," Amanda interrupts. Amanda has a short black bob, tanned skin, and the body of a dancer. She's dressed in proper publicist wear just like Laney — Rock and Republic jeans and a simple baby blue cashmere sweater with small heels. "Tom is so upset that he's ready to cut his losses and fire the problem people."

"Are we the problem people?" Sky asks. She looks worried. "This couldn't be helped. Phil said we had to tape."

"You should have demanded to wait," Amanda says. "Alexis looks like a team player while you two look bad for causing more delays."

"Both of you will call Tom immediately and apologize," Laney says. "It will probably go right to voice mail because he's crazed with edits and now this script mess, but do it anyway. Then we'll work on setting up one-on-ones with Tom for the two of you to tell him your side in person. His assistant said that might not be till next week though."

"But what about that script?" Sky asks. "If it's bogus, one of the writers had to be behind this, right?"

Amanda shakes her head. "All of the writers were questioned, and of course they swore they had nothing to do with it. Obviously someone did it so there's going to be an inquiry and a huge cast meeting, not to mention a couple of corporate ones with the studio. This means more delays and more money lost for the network. Tom is not going to stand for this."

"The thing you two have on your side is that the new script had to do with offing your characters," Laney explains. "Neither of you would write that."

"Wait, they think we did it?" I ask incredulously.

"They didn't say that, but they will be questioning everyone, including you two," Amanda says. "And neither of you have been happy at work lately with all these problems with Alexis, so ostensibly you could have done it to place blame or get out of your contracts."

"We would never *choose* to end our contracts." Sky is defiant. "At least I wouldn't."

Who ever thought we'd be on the same side for once, however temporarily? I resist the urge to laugh.

"They even questioned Alexis," says Nadine. "A few grips and a cast member saw Alexis getting nasty with the two of you and they realized something was going on. It's become clear, *finally*, that she has a real problem with you two."

"It took them long enough," I grumble.

"That doesn't mean they don't still adore her," warns Laney. "We'll have to see how this plays out. After Alexis composed herself, she expressed deep regret at her spat with the two of you and begged the producers to give you your jobs back." Laney snorts. "She's good. I'll give her that. The best thing we can do now is come up with a strategy to keep you guys in the show's good graces and Amanda and I agree on how to do it," Laney adds, glancing at the other publicist. "We're not here to yell at either of you. We're here to talk about saving your butts. We've all agreed that doing it together is stronger than trying to do it separately anymore."

Sky and I nod. "So have we," I reply for both of us.

"Good," says Laney, looking at everyone. "Because, girls, this is going to be heavy. Heads are going to roll and you don't want them to be your own."

FRIDAY 11/1
NOTE TO SELF:

Send Tom huge flowers from Sky + me.
Order Coffee Bean & Tea Leaf cart 2 set 4 day 2 serve crew/grips/wardrobe from Sky + me.
Do preemptive strike w/ Sky + call *Hollywood Nation* + *Celeb Insider* 2 give joint statement.
Have Nadine send Austin + Liz breakfast baskets to arrive before next week's SATs.

November 13

Messy Affair

by **Miana Demultz**

Firing family? That's the inside word from the sources on the set of
Family Affair after a walkout disrupted filming again. Network and
FA honchos are tired of the in-fighting, rumors and delays that
have disrupted the once peaceful set and have vowed to find out
who is responsible for the worst debacle yet.

Tabloid-plagued stars (Kaitlin Burke, Sky Mackenzie, and Alexis
Holden, we mean you), delays, and a Vegas catfight witnessed by
major media are nothing compared to what happened on set just
recently. According to *Tome* sources, new script pages for an episode that questioned the maternity of twins Sam (Burke) and Sara
(Mackenzie), instead of newcomer Colby (Holden), were given to
cast to film that day. The news sent already stressed-out staffers
into a tailspin. "It appeared Kaitlin and Sky were taking the fall and
being fired for all the bitter backstabbing and rumors," says one
staffer, "and Melli and Spencer (who play parents Paige and Dennis) were beyond upset. Everyone adores Kaitlin and Sky is a
great actress, so the decision appeared to come out of left field."

"Kaitlin and Sky were in tears all morning," confided another
staffer. "They couldn't believe they were getting the ax and no one
had the decency to tell them before sending them the script." They
refused to film the scene till they could talk to show producer and
creator Tom Pullman. But Tom was on location finishing edits for a

delayed episode. When the guest director insisted the girls film anyway, they walked off set together, sparking a new round of delays that will force *FA* to air even more repeats.

Here's where the story gets downright bizarre though, *Tome* readers—while Kaitlin and Sky were off sobbing about their potential lost paychecks, Pullman arrived on set and flipped out about the new script pages. It turns out the pages, handed out to everyone from the grips to the guest director, Phil Marker, were FAKE. "Tom was knocking over camera stands, throwing scripts, and basically screaming so loud that we thought he would have a heart attack," says another source. "He's not going to rest till he finds out who released the bogus pages. He's had it with the problems at *FA* lately. He has to make a big gesture to show he means business. Whoever did this is out of here."

So who's getting the ax? The official word is no one. "The rumors are unequivocally false," said Pullman when called for comment. "We have no intention of letting go of anyone in our cast."

Hmm . . . sounds like another *Affair* attempt at cleaning up their PR.

"Everyone is going to be on their best behavior till Tom makes his decision," claims *Tome*'s source. "But it's too late. Someone's taking the fall for all this and we're just waiting to see who it is."

Subscribe to this feed   Permalink   Comments (52)   E-mail to a Friend   Next

fourteen: *Do or Die*

When Nadine and I arrive at Liz's, the only thing I feel confident about is what I'm wearing. I have on a Thakoon Panichgul knee-length black-and-white-striped dress with a corset-style waist; my legs are in black tights and my feet in Cesare Paciotti heels. My hair is pulled in a simple low ponytail. According to my stylist, Tina Cho, the look says I'm "a young Audrey Hepburn–type who is sleek, smart, and totally ready to take on any reporter who comes knocking."

HOLLYWOOD SECRET NUMBER FOURTEEN: Everyone knows that the person usually responsible for a star's great taste in fashion isn't the celebrity — it's her stylist. We're quick to accept their wisdom (and the designers who lend us the free threads) when we're on the red carpet. But when we're stepping out on the town or braving a live interview, that's when we need our fashion gurus the most. A stylist can single-handedly transform a B-lister from a blip to a bona fide star overnight. Top stylists like Tina know the skinny on fashion trends present and future, attend all the runway shows, and know how to make a star feel comfortable in her own skin. Tina is a whiz at playing off my personality and chooses a lot of whimsical, romantic, or tailored pieces for me. She knows how to flaunt my assets (a tiny waist) and hide my flaws (my thick ankles and large hooves look tiny in a high heel). But our biggest weapon in deciding what I wear is Polaroids. Tina snaps pictures of every ensemble I try on so we can see how the threads look on film. If it's a great shot, then I know that nautical dress is ready for its closeup.

I'm glad I love today's outfit because pictures of me wearing it are going to be around for a while. Tina picked it for the day-long round of interviews they scheduled to boost my public image a week after Sky and I walked off set. ("I'm only sixteen," I said several times today, just like Laney and I practiced, "and sometimes I make mistakes, but I'm also smart enough to know how to correct them. Sky and me walking off set was not the answer to this problem.")

"Are you okay?" Nadine asks as she rings the Mendeses' doorbell. "Are you mad I'm babysitting you?"

"I'm glad you came," I assure her. Laney and my parents are afraid I'm going to be ambushed by reporters so they've insisted I have a Team Burke member with me at all times till this *FA* thing blows over. Or blows up. Whichever comes first.

Liz opens the front door. I can hear Gwen Stefani blaring from the stereo. "You made it!" Liz cries.

Liz and Austin took the SATs today and to celebrate, Liz decided to throw a "Thank God the SATs are over" bash. I'm glad for the excuse to party, even if I won't be taking my SATs till at least the spring. With everything that's happened, I've had to put any thoughts of taking the test on the back burner and that's probably for the best. If I tried to take the exam now, I'd probably choke like Meredith did on her intern exams on *Grey's Anatomy.* I'm not sure the proctor would have as much sympathy for me as the Chief did for Mer either.

Liz's olive face is flush and I can tell she's been dancing because her brown tweed dress is damp when she hugs me. "I thought for sure Laney would keep you tied up in interviews straight till Monday. Are you okay?"

I shrug. What I am is tired. Normally I really love interviews and talking about *FA,* but today's scripted session — Laney had me rehearsing quotes all last night (like: "The *FA* cast is the most dedicated one you'll find. Family fights sometimes, but we always stick together.") — was exhausting.

"She's a real trouper." Nadine smiles. Since Nadine has been at my side for all my interviews today — Mom had a date with Botox that she couldn't miss — she's traded her normal Saturday getup (sweats) for a fitted beige button-down shirt and wide-leg black trousers. "I've never been more proud of the way she's handled herself."

Liz steers us through the Mendeses' pink marble entranceway, down the long hall past the state-of-the-art kitchen, and into the eight-hundred-square-foot den with sweeping views of the Los Angeles skyline. "I know just the thing to cheer you up," Liz promises me. About fifty of my former Clark High classmates are here — dancing in the middle of the room, hanging out on the leather couches, watching *Bring It On* on the fifty-inch plasma screen that hangs above the fireplace, or making out on the pool deck — but the person Liz has in mind is right in front of me.

"You're a sight for sore eyes," Austin says. He wraps his arms around me tightly and I feel like a burrito. He looks adorable in an untucked white linen shirt and deeply distressed jeans that are frayed slightly at the thigh. "How are you holding up? I tried calling you all day," he says. He smells like peppermints. Ahh . . . I feel better already.

Oh wait. I forgot.

"I, I, um . . ."

This is the first time I've seen Austin in person since he *maybe* said he loves me. It's been over a week since we've been face-to-face due to all this craziness. We've talked, but asking him to clarify the love question over the phone seemed cheesy (well, to be honest, I was dying to, but Nadine said it was a bad idea). I've been rehearsing what I would say to Austin when I saw him, but now that I'm here, I'm at a loss. I search his face.

Does he look like someone who is in love? Am I supposed to say, "Hi. I love you too"? Am I ready to say it or do I want to say it because I *think* he's said it? This whole thing has left me feeling so awkward around the one person I truly trust. "I, um, I, um . . ."

"Burke, what's wrong?" Austin laughs. "Don't tell me you ran out of things to say after all that talking today?"

I grab a coconut shrimp from a waitress making rounds,

pop it in my mouth, and nod. Maybe if I just keep stuffing food in there, I won't have to talk to Austin about the L-word all night! Yippee!

There's definitely enough food here for me to do that. The great thing about Liz's parties is that no matter what the occasion, the scene is as hot as a celeb part-owned restaurant opening. Tonight she hired DJ Samantha Ronson to spin tunes, has a parade of waiters carrying everything from curry chicken to spinach quiches, a sushi chef making fresh Maki rolls, and even "SATs ARE OVER" gift bags done by celeb gift basket giant On3 Productions containing cucumber herbal eye wraps, Archipelago candles, and Origins Peace of Mind stress-relief cream. Liz's dad is a celebrity lawyer to the stars (including me) and makes up for his long hours at the office with a no-limit Amex for Liz. No wonder Liz's parties are the most coveted invite at her school.

"Laney booked me so tight I barely had time for a bathroom break," I explain to Austin. Laney forgot to leave a slot open for lunch too, so I am starving. "Your e-mails kept me going." I can't look Austin in the eye. What if he drops the L-bomb again, right here? What would I do?

HELP!

Austin smiles. "Listen, I wanted to talk to you about the dance."

OH NO. OH NO. OH NO. OH NO!

"Hey." My friend Allison walks over wearing a cute fitted ballet-neck tee and slim jeans. "How are you holding up? I hate that Alexis Holden. You poor thing."

SAVED! Oh wait. She's talking about Alexis. That's not an easy conversation to have either. Hmph. "I'm okay. How are you?" I ask instead.

Beth hugs me too. "We saw you on *Access Hollywood*." She pushes her tortoiseshell frames onto her nose as she stares at me with sad eyes. Beth's in a houndstooth mini and a cream-colored sweater. "Who would be stupid enough to circulate a bogus script? Seriously, are you okay?"

"It's good she's getting out," Liz says as Josh appears at her side. Besides Nadine and me, Josh is the only other non-Clark person at this party. Josh puts his arm around Liz's waist. "It will take your mind off what's going on."

"You're not being fired, are you?" Josh asks. Liz elbows him hard and he winces.

"Of course not!" Liz admonishes. "They'll find out who did this and fire them and then everything will be back to normal." Liz flashes me a big smile. "Besides, Daddy says you're still under contract through the end of the season. If they're axing any teens, it can't be you."

"Oh, because I keep reading that Kaitlin is a suspect and with all the fighting you're doing with Alexis, you and Sky might be the ones to go," Josh adds.

"You can't believe that stuff," Austin tells Josh. "Kaitlin isn't going anywhere." He squeezes my hand.

"I'm sorry," Josh apologizes as Liz gives him the evil eye. "I thought . . ." He trails off.

"It's okay, Josh." I try to sound light. That's how I was with Nancy O'Dell earlier. ("This whole mess has been blown way out of proportion. We just want to concentrate on fixing *FA* right now. I hope to be there for a very long time.")

Everyone stares at me sympathetically and it's beginning to make me feel worse. Like I've already been fired. "Guys, forget about me," I tell them, turning on my acting charm and thinking of the countless party scenes I've done as Sam over the years. Sam and Sara have always been the co-queens of the Summerville party scene. Well, at least they were until Colby arrived. "You guys should be celebrating, not worrying about me and some silly TV show." I laugh, trying not to sound fake.

"Let's change the subject," Austin suggests. I could kiss him. But then he says: "Let's talk about your birthday instead."

I groan. "That's not a good topic either. How about politics?"

Nadine laughs. "Austin, hasn't anyone told you? Kaitlin hates her birthday. Something goes wrong every year."

"I'm jinxed," I admit.

"You are not," Liz scolds. "You're just a victim of some bad party planning. Seriously, Austin, at the last party her mom and Laney threw, paid for by Neutrogena, I knew exactly *two* people. They didn't invite anyone Kaitlin knew."

"I've heard all the horror stories," Austin cuts them off. "But I'm not giving up. There's got to be something you'd like to do. Tell us, Burke. You've got witnesses."

"I can't think of anything," I say. "I'd rather hear about the SATs."

"Liar," Austin accuses.

"How do you all think you did?" I ignore him.

Everyone starts talking at once and I hear a few collective groans mixed in.

"The essay was tricky," Austin admits.

"I didn't mind that as much as I did the sentence completion section," Liz says. "The questions were much harder than the ones in last week's sample tests."

"The math multiple choice," Josh says. "I got tripped up on that student lottery question."

"Me too!" Liz says. "I answered 3/8."

Josh frowns. "I think I picked 2/9."

"The worst part is the waiting," Allison interrupts. "I can't believe we're not going to have the results for a month! I don't think I can take it."

"I took the test three times before I was happy with my score," Nadine says. I stare at her in disbelief. Nadine didn't ace it on the first shot?

"Let me guess — you scored a lowly five hundred in writing?" Liz jokes.

"The test was a little different when I took it," Nadine says brusquely. "But in answer to your question, on my third test I got a fourteen eighty out of a possible sixteen hundred."

"Show-off," Allison mumbles.

I laugh, but I'm distracted by a familiar voice coming from the TV.

"Hi, I'm Brian Bennett, and you're watching Celebrity Insider! First up, the question on everybody's

lips this weekend — Who's being axed from America's beloved nighttime soap, Family Affair?"

"Could somebody shut that off?" Liz yells. Instead of hitting the power button on the remote, the girls on the couch turn the volume up so loud it's drowning out Maroon 5.

"It's no big deal," I assure Liz, trying hard not to listen to the gossip show even though part of me wants to hear what they're saying. "Don't worry about it."

"Ever since last week's fiery walkout and bogus script caused more drama on the set of Family Affair, Celebrity Insider and fans have been wondering what would happen next. The show's executive producer and cocreator says otherwise, but sources close to the show say heads are going to roll."

"Nobody in our cast is going anywhere."

That's Tom talking. I still won't turn around and face the screen, even if everyone else I'm standing with can't help but watch. I hear Josh whisper to Liz: "I told you so."

"Sources tell Insider that whoever created that fake script will obviously be on the unemployment line alongside Peter Hennings, who plays Dr. Braden. But rumor has it that someone else will be getting the ax as well. Since it's the teens who've plagued the set with

delays and a Vegas PR nightmare, our sources hear that the network wants one of them to go to show that this kind of behavior won't be tolerated. They're just trying to decide who — their new shining star, Alexis Holden, who is rumored to be difficult to work with, or their longtime siblings act, Kaitlin Burke and Sky Mackenzie. But don't listen to me. Let's hear them speak for themselves."

"Brian, Brian, Brian, do you really think if I was being fired I would sit on your couch and deny it?"

That's Sky talking. She's always had a thing for Brian, even though she pretends she doesn't. I wait to hear if her charm works.

"Even if you're not going anywhere, Sky, you can't deny your feelings about your costars. It's no secret that you and Kaitlin Burke have never gotten along."

Sky taped an interview with him today, just like I did.

"Who says? Kaitlin and I may not spend every waking minute together, but I certainly respect her as an actress. I would work alongside her any day."

"Wow, what did you have to pay her to get her to say that?" Liz gives me a wink.

"Guess that deep frost between Sky Mackenzie and Kaitlin Burke is finally thawing, because Kaitlin, too, had nothing but kind words to say about her costar."

I slowly turn to face my on-screen self. At least a dozen partygoers are staring at me. There I am, larger than life, wearing the same dress I have on now. I'm sitting cross-legged, leaning my two elbows on the arm of *Insider*'s earth-tone-striped couch. My hands are resting under my chin and you can prominently see the Coach Gallery Breast Cancer watch that Mom insisted I wear ("Everyone knows proceeds from the watch go to charity," she said. My stomach turned as I realized what she was implying. "You'll look extra sympathetic.")

Brian looks at me with concern. He's wearing a blue pinstriped suit and his pompadour is unusually bushy.

"The rumor mill can't stop talking about the alleged script that basically wrote Sam and Sara off the show. Is it true? And what about the fight in Vegas? Did you really throw a punch at Alexis Holden? Tell us the truth: Are you okay?"
"I'm fine, Brian. Thank you for asking."

I give him my thousand-watt smile and laugh. Brian is giving me a tougher time than his darling Sky.

"As far as I know, Sky and I aren't leaving the show. But if you've heard differently, Brian, please reveal your sources. Inquiring minds want to know."

"You look great," Austin whispers in my ear as Brian proceeds to grill me about my feelings toward Alexis, the vibe on set, and the truth about the rumors behind Alexis's supposed behavior toward selected cast members (I deny, deny, deny, just as Sky and I were told to do). "And you sound even better," Austin adds.

"So there you have it, folks — right from my pals Sky and Kaitlin themselves. The only FA member not talking these days is Alexis Holden. Ever since the showdown in Vegas, FA's newest star has shut the door on the media, only increasing the speculation about her supposedly difficult set behavior. All flacks for the star would say is, "Alexis Holden has no comment at this time." Hmm . . . they've been saying that for weeks now. Could it be that Hollywood's newest golden girl has finally tarnished her halo? Stay tuned. After the break, Angelina Jolie tells us why she thinks she's ready to adopt again."

"Are you okay, Kaitlin?" Allison asks as *Insider* cuts to a Thanksgiving Hallmark commercial.

"Of course she's fine," Liz says defensively. "She squashed Brian Bennett. By the way, what was up with his hair?"

"Seriously, somebody needs to tell that guy to get a haircut once in a while," seconds Nadine. "He could be a stand-in for Donald Trump."

"Do you want to get some air?" Austin asks me while everyone continues to discuss celebrity manes. I nod.

Austin leads me past the offending TV, past the sushi chef who offers us a spicy tuna roll, past the Clark girls whispering about me on the couch, and onto the vast Mendes patio. I'm surprised there aren't more people out here. Aside from the couple dipping their feet in the water by the man-made waterfall that empties into the hot tub, we have the yard to ourselves. It may be November, but the night is still balmy in Los Angeles and the sky is so smog-free that you can actually see stars. I take a seat on a teakwood rocking love seat.

"Kates, I wanted to talk to you about . . ." Austin begins, but I interrupt him.

Oh God. Here it comes. The L-word! "It's okay! You don't have to say anything!" I say hurriedly. "You didn't mean it."

"I didn't mean it at all," Austin agrees.

"Oh." I try to hide my disappointment. "That's okay. It was kind of soon, I guess." I trail off.

Austin frowns. He takes a seat next to me and his long legs touch the etched stone pavers on the ground while my heeled toes dangle in the air. Pushing off the ground, Austin begins to swing us gently back and forth. "I don't know what you mean by soon, but I did want to say I was sorry. I hope you didn't think I was rude for refusing to let you give me an actual present."

OH.

OH! That's what this is about? He's not talking about the L-word! Maybe he does love me! "Not at all," I insist happily.

"Because I was telling Mom and Hayley and they thought I shouldn't have been so gruff about the whole thing." Austin looks nervous. "We were just having such a great time, and all I could think about was . . ."

NOW he's going to say it. He's going to apologize, even though he doesn't need to, and then he's going to toss in how he said he loves me. I just know it. And then we can get it out in the open!

". . . how I had the coolest girlfriend on the planet and I didn't care about a gift. I hope that didn't offend you."

Hmph. I so can't read guys' minds. "I wasn't offended at all," I tell him, but I must look upset because Austin seems really concerned and reaches for my hand.

"I feel like an idiot," he says. "Why am I talking about this when you have so much on your mind?"

"It feels good to take my mind off work," I say.

"Do you want to talk about it?" Austin asks, and I realize I kind of do. And then we don't have to talk about love, or not being in love either. Maybe that's easier right now.

I tell him exactly what happened when we walked off set. All about how Laney and Amanda sprang into action, working around the clock to get us as many interviews as possible that would let us tell our side of the story. They've also been leaking their own information about Alexis's attitude problem. I talk about how Sky and I have teamed up to present a united front and prove to the show, Tom, and the world what an asset we are to have around.

I have to admit, I was petrified about what would happen when Sky and I walked onto set the first day back. I thought everyone would be mad at us for delaying filming. But in reality, everyone from crafty to the crew was incredibly sympathetic about what happened, and Melli and Spencer welcomed us back with open arms. Alexis has actually steered clear of us and has been telling anyone who will listen that she's "mentally exhausted and worried for our job security."

Tom has still been so busy trying to find the script bandit (the crew's new nickname for the culprit) that he hasn't had time to meet with Sky and me yet. He's been totally professional, but he hasn't seemed like his usual self and that worries me. His assistant swears he'll talk to us any day now. God, I hope so. My stomach is in knots waiting to hear who is being canned. No matter how many times Laney says *FA* needs me and will renew my contract, I can't help but worry. Alexis has had people fooled pretty well for a while now. Laney's answer to that is to stay out of Alexis's way and pretend to be nice to avoid any more problems. I'm not sure that's enough.

"Laney and Mom keep telling me I shouldn't be upset about what happened last week. They say the whole thing will blow over and my job isn't in jeopardy. They've drilled it into my head that I should tell every reporter I'm fine, but the truth is, I'm not fine," I tell Austin. "Not in the least. And you want to know the worst part? It's not for the reason everyone thinks."

"What's the real reason?" Austin asks. The rocking motion of the swing is soothing. I lean my head on his shoulder.

"You promise you won't tell anybody?" I whisper hoarsely.

"I swear." He crosses his heart. "I'm having a hard time following everything that's happening. It's so weird seeing you and Sky doing interviews together and being on the same team."

"I know," I admit. "But Alexis is awful, Austin."

"It sounds like it," he agrees as he strokes my hair. He waits for me to speak. How does he know me this well already? It's only been six months since we started going out. My eyes fill with tears and the words start tumbling out.

"This whole thing is my fault!" I practically cry. "If I hadn't been so caught up with being jealous of 'Alexis, the new girl,' then I would have seen what she was about from day one," I say. "I would have been prepared to fight back, like I did with Sky in the past. We wouldn't have had a meltdown in Vegas and Sky and I wouldn't have been so angry that we walked off set last week. I'm more professional than that."

"Don't be insane," Austin says. "You couldn't have stopped what happened!"

"I've jeopardized my career again," I sob. "I feel like it was some cosmic force that sent all this trouble to punish me for being jealous of not just Alexis, but everyone around me."

Austin gives me a questioning look and I can tell he's confused.

"I'm jealous of you guys!" I feel so small even saying it. "Yes, I love hitting the red carpet and signing autographs and being a celebrity, but when Alexis started getting so much attention on the show, I freaked. I felt like I was being pushed aside. Then you guys started talking about college and moving across the country to go to school and I guess the little green monster inside me started to rear its ugly head about that too. All I could think about was being left behind — by Hollywood, by you and Liz. What if you guys go off to college, and I don't, and then we have nothing in common anymore?" I sniffle. "What if I do go to college and then my career dries up because Alexis becomes the star who takes my place?"

"I didn't know you felt like we were squeezing you out." Austin looks aghast. "I don't want you to feel that way."

"You didn't do anything wrong," I backpedal. "It's me. I feel like I'm losing everything I care about."

"You are *not* losing everything." He grabs me by the shoulders and looks deep into my eyes. I resist the urge to squirm away. "Even if I go three thousand miles away to college, you're not going to lose me, Burke. I'll be home on breaks, and by that time you'll probably be doing so well you'll have a private jet at your disposal and can come visit me anytime you want." We both laugh. "And you're forgetting something very important — we'll always have these." He holds up his cell phone and the Sidekick I gave him months ago. I smile.

"We're going to be fine," Austin assures me. "It's *you* you need to worry about. Don't freak out about what everyone around you is doing. Pick one project to focus on. If you want to learn how to drive, you will. If you want to ace the SATs and go to college, you'll do that too. You just can't do it all at once." He smiles. "Even Kaitlin Burke can't do that. But if you want my opinion?" I nod. "The first thing I'd do is deal with Alexis. Show her how a real *FA* star acts."

How can someone so amazing have so much confidence in me? "As usual, you know exactly what to say," I tell Austin and kiss him fiercely. "Thanks for helping me see the bigger picture."

If I want to keep my job, then that's what I should focus on first. Then I can figure out what I want to do next. On my own. I've spent so much time lately being jealous of Alexis's new fame, or Lizzie's freedom to move to New York, that I stopped seeing what was right in front of me. I have a great life, whether I go to college or not, and I have to stop worrying so much about what everyone around me is doing and start worrying more about what I want for myself.

Austin kisses me back. "You're welcome."

I look up at the starry sky. "I'm going to figure out a way to deal with this thing with Alexis once and for all. After that, the future is wide open."

SATURDAY, 11/9
NOTE TO SELF:

Call Sky. Discuss game plan 4 Monday.

FIFTEEN: *Truce and Consequences*

The large silver clock above the lighted mirrors in the *FA* makeup room may say 5:47 AM, but Sky and I are wide awake, have had breakfast (Special K for her, Froot Loops for me), and are in our makeup chairs being blown out by our hair stylists, Paul and Raphael. Shelly and Mallory, our makeup artists, are at the ready to do their part too.

"Paul, isn't it nice to see cheerful faces in the morning?" Raphael styles Sky's raven hair flat.

The two of us are humming along to the John Mayer CD I popped in the stereo. Since we usually have the same call times, we've always fought over makeup mood music. But ever since our karaoke session and career powwow with our publicists two weeks ago, our musical tastes have been in sync.

"I'm enjoying the positive energy around here," Paul agrees, curling my hair into tight ringlets that look remarkably like his own short bouncy brown mane. "Catfights before nine AM are so last year." I tickle his tight black

D&G T-shirt–clad arm as Paul reaches over me to grab the Bumble and Bumble hair spray.

I have to admit, it is nice to avoid the early-morning catfight. Our friendly strategy has not only made my life easier, it's made everyone's lives better on set too. We've been arriving early, staying late for wardrobe fittings, and making sure the only exchanges we have with Alexis are scripted ones. The best part is that our good behavior has made Alexis's increasingly obnoxious behavior stand out. The other day, she staged a foot-stomping, blood-boiling rant at our crafty guy because he ran out of mini M&Ms. Apparently Alexis was convinced Sky and I stole her stash just to upset her, but begged him not to tell anyone because we had "so many other problems already." Thankfully, crafty wasn't buying it and soon news of Alexis's tantrum was all over the set. HA!

Speaking of candy... I reach into my Dooney and Bourke purse and pull out a bag of Razzles. I pop two in my mouth and wordlessly offer some to Sky. She pours herself a handful and gives the remainder back to me.

"You know, K, calling a truce with you has done wonders for my body," Sky tells me as she stares at her reflection in the mirror. "I haven't had a blemish in a week, I started eating carbs again, and last night I actually had eight hours of sleep."

Paul tilts my head left to finish curling my hair. "Wait — if you had eight hours sleep that means you didn't go out last night. That has to be a first," I joke.

"You look more relaxed around me too, K," Sky points

out. "Your shoulders aren't as locked up as they used to be. You've always reminded me of the Hunchback of Notre Dame."

I purse my lips. "Okay, I admit it. Getting along with you is not the tortured hell I thought it would be. But let's not get ahead of ourselves."

Sky gives me a knowing smirk. "Touché. But since all this pathetic togetherness seems to work for us, we *might* want to consider extending our peace agreement beyond just getting rid of the shrew."

Nadine clears her throat at the mere mention of anything having to do with Alexis. Our camps have warned us to stay off the topic whenever we're within fifty feet of the sound-stage.

"Sky Mackenzie, are you suggesting what I think you're suggesting?" I ask.

"Well, I never thought I'd see the day," Shelly exclaims as she overhears the exchange. Unlike most people, Shelly can pull off six AM. Her round face looks thin with her hair pulled back in chopsticks and bronzer on her cheeks. And she's wearing a white corduroy blazer and jeans that shrink her size fourteen body to a size ten. I'm about to tell her how good she looks when Melli walks in.

"What are you two doing here so early again?" Melli yawns. She shuffles into the room wearing last night's pajamas and no makeup. All of us like to arrive wearing something casual. I'm in my favorite oversize worn green turtleneck sweater and khaki cargos and Sky is in black velour hip-huggers and a wrinkled pink baby tee. "I thought your call time wasn't until eight this morning," Melli says.

"We're trying to be on our best behavior," I tell her, giving her a kiss on the cheek before she settles into the chair to my left.

Melli puts her oversize Louis Vuitton on the floor and unzips the bag. "It's nice to see my girls back in fighting form. I think you're both handling yourselves beautifully under all this scrutiny and I hope you know I'm a hundred percent behind you."

I feel myself blush. A compliment from Melli means more to me than any Emmy nomination ever could.

Melli pulls out an envelope and hands it to me. "I know it's early, but these are the new pictures of the boys and the baby."

"I can't believe she's two, Melli," I marvel, looking at the super-chubby toddler in the Juicy Couture sweats.

"Neither can I." Melli sighs. "I feel like I've missed all her big moments."

"What do you mean?" Sky asks as I hand her the pictures. "Doesn't your nanny bring her by for lunch every day?"

Melli nods. Her eyes look sad. "It's not the same thing, girls. You'll see when you become mothers."

Sky moans. "Stop making me feel old, Melli," she complains. "I'm already older than Burke."

The dressing room door swings open and I tense up, thinking it is Alexis. That's another reason Sky and I have been getting here early — to avoid two hours of sitting next to her in a twelve-by-twelve room. I breathe a sigh of relief when I see it's Tom, but then I see the grave look on his face. Uh-oh.

"Hey, girls," he says.

He turns to Melli. "I need a moment alone with you when you're done. I spent two hours on the phone last night with you-know-who."

Sky and I exchange hurried glances.

"What did he say?" Melli asks breathlessly.

"He kept trying to talk me out of it, but I told him I was firm," Tom tells Melli. "I said we'd meet with him to discuss it over breakfast." Tom senses us staring and turns around. I quickly pretend I'm staring at the tacky vase filled with flowers on the makeup counter. "Girls, I'm glad you're both here. I was hoping we could finally sit down and talk this morning. I feel awful that I've been so busy."

Finally! Now we can tell Tom everything.

"No problem, boss," Sky says.

Nadine coughs. She's been getting a real kick out of Sky's attempts to be nice.

"Do you want Sky to go first or me?" I ask.

"Actually I wanted to meet with both of you together if you don't mind," Tom says frankly. His face is blank and I can't read him. Together? Why together? This doesn't sound good. "Does nine-thirty work for both of you? I've got a half-hour window before I have to be on set." We both nod wordlessly.

"What was that about?" Shelly asks when Tom leaves.

"I don't know," I admit and immediately feel my shoulders tense up.

"Relax, okay?" Sky tells me sternly. "Mel, tell her to relax. I'm sure it's just to hear us tell our side of the story together."

"Um hm," Melli says, but her mind is obviously elsewhere. Melli stares at her grande cup of Peet's coffee, letting the steam from the flap hit her in the face while her stylist combs out her long black hair.

Once we got through hair and makeup, we made an emergency run to crafty. (Pete hadn't unpacked the chocolate yet, but we told him the brownies were a matter of life and death.) Now we're on our way to see Tom. I feel like I need my trusty paper bag again. I'm so going to throw up.

"I'm afraid we're about to be ambushed," I whisper to Sky. "We should call Laney and Amanda beforehand, don't you think?"

"And tell them what?" Sky hisses. "That Tom wants to meet with us? We've been asking to meet with him. They'll think we're nuts."

Sky has a habit of making me feel like I'm borderline crazy (or is it playing the rational role to my paranoid hysteria? Whatever.), but I can tell she's worried too. She took *three* brownies while I only took one. The last time Sky tried to out-dessert me we were in kindergarten. She's been on a diet ever since.

"But he's met with everyone else alone," I say. "Hi, Luis," I wave to a crew member walking past us. "Why would he ask for us to go together? Do you think someone from the network will be there? They only come down during contract negotiations or if someone is being fired. We have to be prepared, Sky. I'm not leaving this set without a fight."

"Annmarie, that sweater looks amazing on you," Sky tells a passing crew person. "I hate this," she whines and stops short. "I can't do the Miss Goody Two-shoes act like you do. It's just not me. If Tom wants to fire me, then let him fire me."

"You don't mean that," I scold.

"I do," Sky says. "For the first time in my life, I'm *not* the one who's making everyone's life miserable and I'm getting punished for it just the same. What's the use? You are who you are, K. Why fight it?"

I think of Austin's pep talk. "That's not true, Sky. You just have to figure out what you want and make it happen."

Sky glares at me. "Who are you? Dr. Phil?"

I roll my eyes. "I'm trying to help."

"Well, try harder," Sky huffs.

I have an idea. "I know what will cheer you up. What if we play Pass the Carrot during this morning's scene?"

HOLLYWOOD SECRET NUMBER FIFTEEN: When stars are tied up filming one scene for hours, we can get creative with our ways to pass the time. One thing we like to do is play what I call Pass the Carrot. During taping, we try to find new ways to hide objects in our clothing without Tom noticing. Or we try to pass an item, like a cookie or a pen or a carrot (get it?), without disrupting anyone. The game helps when we're shooting our umpteenth camera angle for a hectic family dinner scene.

"You've never invited me to play that game before," Sky sniffs.

"That's because I never liked you enough to play it," I remind her. "But maybe this once, I'll let you play with me and Trevor." Sky grins. We head to the stairs in the back of the building that will lead us to the administrative wing of *FA*. Tom's office is a plush corner one with huge windows that overlook the lot. It's pretty quiet back there, which means no one will hear me begging for my job. As we reach the door to the stairs, we see Max, the show's cutest writer.

"Hi, Max!" Sky says, sounding flirty. At the mere mention of his name, Max jumps so high he practically hits his head on the high ceiling.

Max's dark brown hair is hanging in his face and when he pushes it away, I can see the beads of sweat dripping down his tan face. "Oh, hey, girls," he says with a small grin. "What are you two doing over here?"

"We have a meeting with Tom," I explain. Max nods. I wonder if he's sick. He's usually a big flirt and today he seems very quiet. "Are you okay? I'm sure the writers' room is pretty stressful right now, huh?"

"Yeah, yeah," Max says, absentmindedly tugging his hair. "It's awful. We can't wait for the interrogations to be over, you know?"

"Do they have any leads?" Sky asks hopefully. "They must suspect someone at this point. Does anyone have a motive?"

Max shakes his head. "I don't know...I don't think so...this whole thing was probably someone's idea of a practical joke and now their career is going to be ruined because of it."

"Joke?" The hairs on my arm stand up. "Some joke," I snap. "Whoever wrote it canned our characters. I'd hardly call that funny."

"You're right," Max says quickly. "I'm sorry, Kaitlin. I'm sorry the whole thing happened to you two. Listen, you guys better get going. Don't want to keep the boss waiting." He smiles. "I've got to get back to the writers' room myself."

The writers' room is clear across the building. What's he's doing over here? Maybe he just had his own tête-à-tête with Tom and doesn't want to talk about it.

"Maybe we can chat about all this later, say, over coffee?" Max adds.

My cheeks flush. Now I feel silly. I can't believe I snapped at Max. He's always been so nice to me. Like two weeks ago when he brought me an iced coffee because I looked tired. I'm about to apologize when I hear *her*.

"MAXIE POO, WHERE ARE YOU?" Alexis comes from the opposite corner and I see Max's face pale.

Maxie Poo?

"What are you two doing up here?" Alexis demands. She is wearing a pink cashmere turtleneck and barely visible jeans that are tucked into thigh-high black boots. Her red hair is smoothed under a black velvet headband. She doesn't look happy to see us, but what else is new?

"We're talking to Max." I point out the obvious.

"Why would you two need to talk to Max?" Alexis seems anxious.

"None of your business," Sky says. "Why do *you* need to talk to Maxie Poo?"

"She doesn't," Max says at the same time Alexis says, "I don't." They look at each other.

"I just mean, don't worry, girls," Max says, cracking a lop-sided grin. "There's enough of me to go around. Now, listen, I've got a lot of work to do this morning so I'll catch you all later, okay?" I could swear he gives Alexis a look before he walks away, but I'm not sure. "Have a good meeting."

"Meeting?" Alexis asks, looking nervous. "What meeting? Who's having a meeting?"

"It's one that doesn't involve you," I tell her. I grab Sky's arm and lead her to the staircase before Alexis can say anything else. I start ascending it quickly and Sky pulls me back.

"What are you doing?" I whisper.

"I just thought of something," she says. She takes off her shoes, tiptoes down the steps, and peeks around the corner.

"What are you looking at?" I whisper. "Is Alexis still there?"

Sky ignores me. Then suddenly she starts waving her arms frantically. "Come quick! I knew it!" she whispers. "I knew Max was acting weird."

I quickly slip out of my boots and down the stairs too. Sky makes room for me to look and I peek around the door frame.

What the . . . ?

Halfway down the hall, Alexis and Max are clearly in the middle of a heated argument. Alexis keeps trying to grab his hand and Max keeps pushing her away. Alexis keeps touching him. She grabs his hand again, caresses his shoulder, tries to hug him, and then she KISSES HIM! ON THE MOUTH! AND HE KISSES HER BACK!

EEEEEWWWWWWWWWWWWW!

It doesn't last long though. Max pushes her away and storms off. Alexis quickly races after him.

UGH. What does Max see in her? I mean, yeah, she's kinda beautiful, I guess, and has a great body, but she's catty and backstabbing. Max seems like such a weird choice for Alexis. She seems like the type to be jockeying for lip time with Zac Efron or Ryan Gosling. What would she see in Max, who is just a TV writer?

A TV writer.

MAX IS A TV WRITER!

I gasp. "Oh my God! Max must have had something to do with that script!" I blurt out. I think I might faint. Or throw up. I'm not sure which would be more inconvenient.

"You think?" Sky mocks me. She grabs our shoes and throws me my boots. "Quick. Let's follow them."

sixteen: *You Can Run, but You Can't Hide*

"Could you slow down?" I beg. Sky is moving swiftly down the hallway, peeking in doorways and opening doors in her frantic search for Alexis and Max. "They're not here. They're probably in Alexis's dressing room or the writers' room."

"Let's go there then," Sky begs. "If we can catch them talking about being the script bandit, then we can tell Tom. We could be rid of Alexis and save our jobs by noon."

It's a tempting idea. I look down at my Coach watch and frown. It's 9:10. "Sky, we've got to be in Tom's office in twenty minutes," I remind her. "We'll never make it to Alexis's dressing room and back in time and we can't be late for this meeting."

"If we don't find Alexis and get some dirt then there's no point in even going to the meeting," Sky counters. "Tom adores Alexis! The network loves her! She's got a much smaller salary than we do. Who do you think they're going to choose? Her."

"If you really believe that, then why are you even showing

up at work?" I argue. "Why did you agree to team up with me to take down Alexis? Why are you meeting with Tom?"

"Because. I didn't say that's what I *want* to happen, I said that's what I think *will* happen." Sky is still on the move. We pass empty writers' offices and an abandoned wardrobe room. Everyone must be on set setting up for the first scene.

"Sky, Tom said he had a half hour for us." I grab her arm and pull her in the direction of Tom's office. "Don't you think it's more important that we see him first and then find Alexis? How will it look to Tom if we're late?" I drag her down the corridor.

"Let go!" Sky complains. "Get your man hands off me!" I don't budge. "Geez. You have some grip."

"Stop yelling," I say, turning around to yell at her. OOOF! I'm not looking where I'm going and I bang into someone. It's my brother.

"Matty, what are you doing down here?" I demand. Matt and I had a *huge* fight after I walked off set with Sky a few weeks ago. When I finally made it home after karaoke and the publicist powwow, Matt was waiting. He started yelling at me about not answering my cell, leaving him on set without telling him what was going on, and then he said I was jeopardizing both our jobs by being so unprofessional. Yowza. So then I started yelling about how he was still hanging around Alexis after he said he wasn't going to. I told him he had clearly chosen her over his own sister, which was a shame because it was clear that Alexis was totally using him. It was a pretty ugly spat and I've felt awful about what I said but have had too much pride to say I'm sorry — he could apologize too, you know. Now we're kind of not speaking. The most we've said to each other is "Pass the rosemary and garlic potatoes" during our chef-prepared dinners (Mom can't even make Jell-O).

"I, uh, had an appointment," Matt says cryptically. He shifts in his red-and-black customized Nike IDs. His honey-colored hair looks like it hasn't been combed in days and his long-sleeved Gap logo tee and cargo pants are wrinkled, which is weird because Matt has everything ironed for him. Even his underwear.

"What kind of appointment?" Sky demands, wriggling free from my grasp. "Were you just with your girlfriend? Did she come this way?"

"She's not my girlfriend," Matt says stiffly.

"Whatev." Sky shrugs. "Have you seen her this morning?"

"No," Matt says. He glances at me out of the corner of his eye. I don't say anything.

Sky studies Matty closely. "Has she ever said anything about the script bandit?" Sky asks. "Did she mention Max? Or revenge or anything? You must know something! You're her lackey!"

"Sky, lay off," I demand. I can't stand watching Matty squirm even if I am mad at him. He may like Alexis, but he'd never withhold info about the script bandit from me. "He doesn't know anything."

Matt looks like he wants to say something, but he doesn't. "I have to get to wardrobe," he says and then he walks away without saying goodbye. Hmph. A simple "thank you" would have sufficed!

Sky takes off, in the opposite direction of Tom's office again, and practically knocks down Matt as she whizzes past him.

"Wait!" I scream as I run after her. "SKY! Don't do this! We've got a meeting! What am I supposed to say to Tom about where you are?"

I'm out of breath and wheezing by the time I catch Sky. She's made it all the way to Alexis's dressing room. Seriously, who knew Sky was so fast? I've never seen her run a day in her life, unless it was after a reporter. Or Orlando Bloom on the red carpet.

"I can't believe you!" I reprimand, but Sky shushes me. She points at Alexis's door. I can hear mumbling and it sounds heated. Yep, that's definitely Alexis and Max in there.

"I can read lips. Always did the trick for spying on you," Sky says as the muffled voices grow louder. "Let me try to find out what they're saying." She peeks through the door's small window above my head.

"Be careful," I remind her.

"You should see this." Sky is standing on her tippy toes. "Alexis is sobbing about how sorry she is. You should see her face, K. Mascara running everywhere. She looks awful." Sky laughs wickedly.

"Are they saying anything important?" I need Sky to focus. We don't have much time. It's 9:22.

Sky squints hard. "It's hard for me to understand with all

her whining. WAIT. WAIT. What did she just say? I think she said script!" Sky looks at me with eyes as wide as the Four Seasons's teacups. "K, she's crying about a script!"

I feel nauseated. "Are you sure?"

"Hey, girls!" someone interrupts. Sky and I whip around. Trevor is walking toward us. He has a cute new buzz cut and he's wearing loose-fit jeans with a thermal tee over a long-sleeved white one. How did I miss him sneaking up on us?

"Everything okay?" Trevor asks. "What are you guys doing here? Everyone's on set. We're getting ready for Tom. He has some sort of important meeting." Sky and I can't move. What if Alexis and Max hear him? What if Sky misses them talking about the important stuff? I'm sweating. I can't think of a single thing to say that could explain what we're doing, and if we don't get him out of here quick, we're ruined.

Trevor's smile fades. "Do you guys hear someone crying?" he asks.

"Nope," we say in unison.

"It sounds like it's coming from Alexis's room." Trevor puts his hand on the doorknob and peeks in the window. "Hey, why is Alexis kissing . . . ?"

NOOOO! I begin to hyperventilate. I look at Sky. I feel like the moment is happening in slo-mo. Sky throws herself at Trevor, knocking him backward across the hall, and passionately kisses him on the lips. He looks as surprised as I am, but then he starts enjoying it. I don't know what to do.

"Listen, I've been meaning to talk to you," Sky murmurs

in Trevor's ear. "I'm just finishing something up with K, but can you meet me in my dressing room at one for lunch?" Trevor says something incoherent. He must still be in shock. "Great." Sky turns him around and sends him away. "See you then!"

I look at her sternly and try raising my right eyebrow like Mom does.

"What?" Sky shrugs. "He looked hot. Man, I forgot what a good kisser Trevor is. And those arms . . ." She sighs.

"What about Cody?" I ask.

"I'm keeping my options open." She winks and then takes her place back at the small window again. It's so quiet in the hallway you can hear the central air unit whizzing. "Okay, so Alexis is still groveling. She's definitely talking about the script," Sky reports. "She's crying. Blah, blah, blah. Wait. She's apologizing now and saying no one has to know. Max is yelling back that he's going to get fired because of her. I don't understand what he's saying. "This is all part of some big use." That doesn't make sense. A muse?"

"A ruse?" I suggest.

Sky looks at me. "What's a ruse?"

"Just keep reading lips," I tell her. Sky could seriously benefit from some SAT prep work herself.

"Alexis was his *muse* and she took advantage of that," Sky repeats. "She made him do it. Do what? Lay it on the table, Max! Come on!"

Sky gasps.

"What?" I hiss.

268

"We've got them, K," Sky says, sounding hoarse.

"What? What did they say?" I can feel my heart beating out of my chest in anticipation. "Tell me!"

"Alexis just said, 'But you wrote the script! You can't pin this on me!'" Sky relays. "And now Alexis is crying again."

A wave of nausea comes over me as I realize our suspicions about Alexis were dead-on the whole time. Alexis isn't just a major heap of cow dung. She's a scheming, vindictive piece of cow dung.

Okay, a person can't be cow dung, so that doesn't really make sense, but I'm angry! I want her to pay. "I knew she hated us, but I never thought she'd do anything as stupid as this," I say. "It's career suicide! But Max . . . what have we ever done to Max?"

"Shhh," Sky hushes, still listening intently. "Max is saying something. 'I wanted to write you the *FA* ending you would have wanted. I told you this was for our eyes only. You swore you wouldn't show anyone. And this is how you repay me? Distributing copies to the whole cast and crew? Trying to get the show filmed behind Tom's back? What were you thinking? You've successfully destroyed any chance either of us have of keeping our careers!'"

"Oh my God." The story begins to make sense. "Alexis thought that by charming the writers she could get better material, so she came on to Max to try to get him to help her."

"The girl is brilliant," Sky says. "I only wish I had thought of that move when you were driving me up a wall."

"Thanks," I say drily.

Sky turns back to the window and gasps again. "What a . . . K, get this. Alexis just told Max, 'If you think I'm taking the fall for this, you're mistaken. You wrote the script because you're obsessed with me. I'll tell Tom I had nothing to do with it. Who do you think he'll believe?' Max looks furious. He said, 'You wouldn't! How could you do that to me?'" Sky turns around. "We have to tell Tom."

I look at my watch. "Sky, it's 9:55! We've missed most of our meeting and we only have five minutes left!"

We take off running. All I've done today is run. I must be burning off a ton of calories. I could probably eat another brownie.

We run past Tom's assistant outside his office. "WAIT!" She hollers, but we don't stop. We keep going and bust through Tom's office door without knocking.

"Tom! Tom!" We're both talking at once, completely out of breath. "Tom, you have to give us five minutes!"

I finally look around and realize Tom isn't alone. Melli is sitting on his dark brown leather couch, dabbing her eyes with a tissue. Wait? What's happened now?

"You two are late." His voice is gravelly. "Where have you been?"

We start talking over each other, tripping over the words, trying to get out what we heard and saw. And Tom actually listens. Every few minutes he looks wordlessly over at Melli.

"Girls," Tom says in a warning tone I recognize from set. He usually uses that tone when we're fighting with each other.

"We can prove it!" Sky blurts out. "Call them down here! We'll interrogate them ourselves. Please, Tom, you have to believe us."

"Sky, calm down," Tom says evenly. "I believe you. I already know."

"You do? But how?" I want to know.

Tom looks at Melli then back at us. "Your brother came and told me on Friday," Tom says.

I nearly fall over.

"WHAT?" Sky shrieks.

"Matty knew? Why didn't he tell me?" I ask.

"That's why I wanted to speak to both of you this morning," Tom says. "I wanted to tell you what happened and apologize for my behavior during all of this. I should have seen what was going on with Alexis. Instead, I was so busy being wowed by our new ratings and the network's praises that I forgot about the two young ladies who have been my stars all along." He smiles. "When all those stories started coming out about someone being fired, I should have assured you that you two weren't going to be let go. The network wanted someone to take the fall for all the bad press and what happened in Vegas, but I never for one moment thought of getting rid of either of you."

"Thank you, Tom," I say. It feels good to hear our boss say that. "But I still don't understand how Matty knew about Alexis."

"Alexis slipped up in front of Matt after you two stormed off the set," Tom explains. "She apparently tried to pay Matt to keep quiet and when that didn't work, she even told him she'd date him for a few weeks to up his profile. He told her he'd think about it. Last Friday he came to me and told me what happened. He was really torn up about the whole thing and afraid to make matters worse for you and Sky. He thought Alexis would deny the whole story anyway and I would believe her over him. But I know the Burkes — they don't lie. Matty's story added up." Tom smiles at me gratefully. "I'm sorry we kept you in the dark for a few days, but I begged Matt not to tell you, Kaitlin, till I spoke to our lawyers. I am so proud of Matt for coming forward. I don't have to tell you that Matty has a thing for Alexis and it took a lot for him to confess. But he said he cared more about you, Kaitlin, and you being fired."

So Matty defended me and I've been ignoring him.

He's never going to let me live this down.

"Since we don't need any more bad press around this place, the network is going to say publicly that the script bandit has still not been found. Alexis will be let go, per her storyline, and Max will be fired due to budget cuts," Tom says.

"So that's it, then. Alexis is out of here," Sky says with glee.

It's over. My job is safe! I've got my work family back! Alexis is leaving! I feel like celebrating. Maybe I will have that big birthday party after all. The past few months of hell are finally over! Wait till I tell Austin and Liz, Rodney and Nadine, and . . .

"Sit down, girls, there's more," Melli says, and judging by the look on her face, whatever it is, isn't good. "Tom, tell them."

A lump forms in my throat and my voice is shaky. "Tell us what?" I ask. Suddenly I'm very afraid.

Melli takes our hands in hers and clasps them tightly. "I've been thinking about this day for a very long time, girls, and it's finally here. I'm leaving the show," she says hoarsely. Tom takes a seat next to Melli and puts his arm around her shoulder. Sky and I sit down. I think my knees might buckle.

"When the show started I was in my twenties," Melli explains. "I figured a nighttime soap about a dysfunctional family would last five years at the most." She laughs. "But it didn't, and I got older, got married, got divorced, had babies, remarried, and I was still here." She takes a breath. "This place has been wonderful, but it isn't how I expected to spend almost two decades of my life."

"I thought you loved this show," Sky says.

"I do," Melli assures us. "Even when the tabloids were writing about my failed first marriage or when they were complaining about set squabbles, this place has always been home." She hesitates. "But maybe it's time for a new home. After what I've seen go on here this year . . ." She shakes her head. "Well, I just think it's time. There's so much more I want to do with my career."

"You can't leave us," Sky says with a quiver of her pointy chin. Melli's eyes fill with tears again. I see Tom's eyes begin to tear up too. Sky sobs and I begin to hiccup.

I can't imagine this place without Melli. I don't know if I can handle it. Melli is my work mom. She's the backbone of this show. What will *FA* be like without her?

"There's more," Tom says delicately. "Actually, girls, we're both leaving."

"WHAT?" Sky and I shriek.

"Melli and I have been together since the beginning and we had a pact that when one of us was done with the show, we would leave together," Tom says. "I love you all, but I can't do this show without her. Melli told me at the beginning of the season that this might be her last one and we've been talking about it for months. This thing with Alexis and the script has only driven the point home further. It's time to move on. This season will be *Family Affair*'s last."

Sky lets out an audible sob, but I'm in shock. *Family Affair* going off the air? It can't be! This show is my home. What am I going to do? Where am I going to live?

Oh wait. I do have a home. But still . . . this is my other home!

"Fifteen seasons is an unbelievable run, you know," Tom is saying. "The network would like *FA* to go out in style and we've given them enough notice to do that. We have the whole second half of the season to wrap up loose ends and give the fans closure."

Sky is inconsolable. She's sobbing so hard that she can barely breathe. Tom gets her a glass of water. I, on the other hand, am suddenly a dam. I just can't deal with the finality of it all. This has got to be a bad dream. *FA* can't be over!

"Girls, I know this is hard," Melli says, "but you're both young and extremely talented. As soon as this is announced, the offers will start pouring in."

"My life is over," Sky says. "I'll never get another TV show like this one. Never!"

"I can't imagine working on another show," I agree. "Nothing will ever compare to the experience I've had on this one."

"The network would kill to work with you two again, despite everything," Tom tells us. "They told me personally. You'll probably get a call from them next week asking to take a meeting about creating your own series or about shooting a pilot."

Sky stops crying. "You think so?" She wipes her face and I notice her expression change.

Tom laughs. "I know so. You girls have the world at your feet right now. And Melli and I finally have the freedom to do what we want. This is a good thing, girls. You'll thank us someday."

"I can't think of someday," I say quietly. "All I can think about is now and how this is almost over."

He smiles. "Well, someday soon you'll think about what you want to do next," Tom says. "Pilot season is coming up. Maybe you'll want to do another TV show. Or concentrate on films," he says. "Wait and see how you feel after the official announcement is made in a few weeks."

"Please don't tell anyone till then," Melli says.

"Your family, your agent, your manager, your friends, Matty," Tom adds. "Nobody. I'll tell the rest of the cast and crew beforehand, but for now, you three are the only ones who know. We don't want this getting out to the press before we're ready. We want *FA* to go out looking like the fine show it is. No more bad publicity."

My legs feel like they're ready to collapse. My head is spinning and my mouth is dry. "I guess congratulations are in order," I say shakily, and then I grab Melli, never wanting to let go.

"We're sorry you two have been having such a rough season," Melli says as she hugs me. "But I can promise you the last half of this one will be a picnic."

"Alexis will film her final episode in a quickly wrapped up storyline next week," Tom tells us. "And then we can get to the fun stuff. The studio wants to do it all."

HOLLYWOOD SECRET NUMBER SIXTEEN: I guess I can take heart in the fact that a beloved TV show never really ends. Networks love to milk every last drop out of hot commodities. We have retrospective programs to plan, last goodbye videos to tape, favorite cast episodes to run. There will be last-season Emmy nods, possible spin-offs with popular characters (even though those shows usually bomb), and rumors about reunion specials. I won't be saying goodbye to these people for a long time to come.

"I'll help you, Tom," Sky says. "I've always thought the episode where Sara gets hit by a drunk driver should have won an Emmy. That should be rerun for sure. I want the executives to think of me as a versatile actress who could headline any series. Anything but one with twins. I deserve my own series. No offense, K."

I stop myself from rolling my eyes. I sense the old Sky returning.

"I'll keep that in mind," Tom says. "What about you, Kates? How do you want to be remembered?"

"Can I get back to you on that?" I ask as I head to the door. I think I need to go back to my dressing room and be alone for a while. "I have a lot to think about."

MONDAY, 11/11
NOTE TO SELF:

Figure out what to do with the rest of my life.

15 EXT. SUMMERVILLE BUS DEPOT — INT. SAM'S VOLKSWAGEN
CABRIOLET CONVERTIBLE

COLBY

You didn't have to drive me here, you know.

SAM

I know I didn't. I wanted to.

COLBY

Even after all I've done to you? To your family?

SAM

(smiles) I'm trying to be the bigger person here. (Sam
pulls a wad of fifties out of her wallet). Here. This
should be enough to get you started wherever you go.

COLBY

You're crazy, you know that? Why are you so desperate
to fix me?

SAM

Because even if you aren't my sister, for a short time
you were my friend. And I know, despite how you tried
to play my family, how you tampered with our blood
work and everything you put my mother through with
the maternity tests, the bottom line is you saved her

life. Don't you think that's worth paying your bus
fare?

COLBY

(opens the car door and slings her tattered green army
bag over her shoulder) For what it's worth, I'm sorry.

SAM

(grabs Colby) Wait. Before you go, please just tell me.
What made you do it?

COLBY

You. Your sister. Your family. I thought, There is a
family that has it all. I wanted to be part of that.
To feel that loved for just a fraction of a second. I
didn't think about what that would cost everyone else.

BUS DEPOT LOUD SPEAKER

Final boarding call for bus 1104 to Las Vegas. This is
the last call.

COLBY

Well, that's me. I better go.

SAM

(lets go of Colby's arm) Yeah, you'd better go.

Sam steps out of her idling convertible and watches Colby walk away. As Colby hands the bus driver her bag and steps onto the bus, she takes a last look back at Sam. Sam waves as the doors close. The CAMERA PANS IN on Colby's face as the bus pulls away. We hear tires screeching and the sound of feet running across the concrete pavement.

                    SARA
     I knew I'd find you here! What are you doing?

                    SAM
Saying goodbye.

                    SARA
     To her? Sammie, after all she's done to us?

                    SAM
I know. I know. You don't have to remind me.

                    SARA
     She's just lucky I wasn't here to tell her what I really
     think of her!

                    SAM
Everyone at this bus station is lucky they didn't have
to hear that.

                    SARA
     Ha-ha. Hey, how'd you find this filthy place? I didn't

even know Summerville had a bus station.

                    SAM

Sara! Of course we have a bus station. Colby came into
town this way and wanted to go out the same way.

                    SARA

Did she say anything to you? I mean, did she say
why she made our lives a living hell these past few
months?

                    SAM

She said she wanted a family. Our family.

                    SARA

I guess you can't blame her for that one. The
Buchanans do rock.

                    SAM

(smiles) Rock? The Buchanans rock? Who are you?

                    SARA

According to Summerville Hospital's finest, I'm your
twin, darling.

                    SAM

I guess I'm stuck with you then.

                                  SARA

I guess so. Let's get out of here and go home.

                                  SAM

Home sounds really great right now.

Sam and Sara link arms and the CAMERA FADES OUT as the two
walk to their cars. CUE MUSIC.

seventeen: *The Last Supper*

This has never happened to me before. I'm out to dinner at Wolfgang Puck's Cut, a swanky steakhouse in the Beverly Wilshire hotel, and the Burke brigade — Laney, Mom, Dad, Matty, and Nadine, in case anyone forgot who they are — have zilch to say.

Not a single snide comment about a famous actress sitting at the next table who looks like she put on a few pounds, no critiques of my outfit (a green fitted corduroy blazer over a cream-colored sweater with Seven jeans and brown suede Pumas), and not a single thought on what my next career move should be.

That's because an hour into our "Ding-dong, Colby's Dead, Thanks to Matt" lunch celebration (which Laney, Mom, and I gleefully organized), the studio released an exclusive statement to *People* online that sent my team into a tailspin: *Family Affair* will end its run in May. Of course I already knew. I had been dreading the release for weeks. I had no clue how to break the news to Mom and Dad or Matty or Laney, especially when we're in the middle of toasting Matty's bravado. Sigh. Sometimes it's really hard being the only one in on a big secret.

As soon as the *People* online link (titled "The *Affair* Is Officially Over") was sent to my Sidekick by Tom, I knew I had three minutes to tell everyone myself before they heard the news via cell phone, BlackBerry, or pager. I shut off my Sidekick and mobile so that I wouldn't be interrupted and delicately broke the news.

"Guys, it's going to be okay," I say for the umpteenth time. They haven't said a single word in, like, ten minutes.

"That's easy for you to say," Matt complains, stirring his Coke with a long straw. "Your career is set. You've been on that show practically since birth!" His arms are waving in a crisp white Polo that really brings out his tan. "I've only been on for half a season. No one will remember me when it comes time to film the show retrospective."

"I just can't believe you've known for weeks and didn't tell us." Mom looks hurt. "Or at least tell your own mother." She stares at the restaurant's pristine high white ceiling (this place was designed by Getty Center architect Richard Meier) and fights back tears.

"Mom, Tom and Melli told me I couldn't tell anyone before the announcement," I try. "I didn't have a choice." She doesn't look at me. "We still have reason to celebrate," I remind her. "Alexis is off the show and we still have half a season to shoot." I turn to my brother, hunched in his chair and looking glum. "And Matty, Tom told me your character is in all of the remaining episodes." He perks up. "Tom says we're going to go out with a bang. People are going to re-member *Family Affair* for a long time."

"And there's always the DVD sales," Dad points out. "Katie-Kat will make a killing when they release the final season on DVD. We should suggest to Tom that they also do a final episode DVD and a top-of-the-line box set of all fifteen sea-sons. The more DVDs, the more cash in our — I mean Kate-Kate's — pockets."

"I would see some dough, wouldn't I, Dad?" Matty looks up. "I am on the final season." He pauses. "Can we get dessert after this?"

"How can you think about food?" Mom groans.

Cut's menu has great high-priced food to drown your sorrows in, including tasty Kobe-style beef, lobster-and-crab Louis cocktail, and rare Wagyu beef. I ordered the grilled Sonoma lamb chops.

"Well, I don't know about the rest of you, but I'm really proud of how you're handling this, Kates." Nadine is beam-ing. "No tears, no freak-outs. You're acting very grown-up."

"Thanks." I blush. "I've been thinking things over and try-ing to concentrate on my future." Okay, that's a lie. I'm in to-tal denial. That's the only reason I haven't flipped out yet.

"Yes, the future," Laney repeats, staring into the other din-ing room that leads to the brick-lined patio. "Let's talk about your next move so I can release a statement."

Mom perks up. "We should call Seth and set up a meet-ing to take a look at prospective offers," Mom says, more to

Laney than me. "I'm sure they'll be pouring in this afternoon. Movies, TV shows, she'll have a lot to pick from."

Whoa. She's moving too fast.

Laney pulls out her BlackBerry and begins typing herself a note. "We can say Kaitlin is mulling over offers and will announce her next project soon. What do you think about another TV show?" she asks my mom.

Wait! I can't decide right now. "Well, I was thinking . . ." I start to say, but Mom interrupts, so I turn to the waiter and ask for a soda refill.

"No," Mom says, shaking her head so that her honey-colored hair flaps in her face. "How many stars transition from one hit TV show to the next?"

"*Frasier*," Dad says. "That was a spin-off of *Cheers*."

"*Joey*," Nadine groans. "Even the popularity of *Friends* couldn't launch that show."

"Good point," Laney observes. "Movies it is. Should we go for action? A big-name director again and huge stars? Or maybe the independent route? Get Kaitlin involved in the festival circuit for a while. Beef up her art appeal?"

I feel around in my leopard-print Louis Vuitton satchel for my Sidekick and turn it on to see if Austin's around. The gadget buzzes to life and I see I already have sixty-three messages. Yikes. Word travels fast in this town. I scan the list and see WOOKIESRULE. Austin. I open it up and quickly reply. He gets back to me right away, allowing me to tune out the ongoing discussion about my career taking place without me.

WOOKIESRULE: Hey. How R U holding up? Liz just got the news from her dad.

PRINCESSLEIA25: OK. Sorry U didn't hear it from me first. I was sworn 2 secrecy. That was rough. W/ Laney & Mom now. They're not taking it so well.

WOOKIESRULE: Shocker. :)

WOOKIESRULE: They'll get used 2 it. You will 2. Maybe it's the change U need 2 shake things up, U know?

PRINCESSLEIA25: U R right.

WOOKIESRULE: Remember: change w/ work. Change w/ school. Not w/ boyfriend.

PRINCESSLEIA25: Never! :)

WOOKIESRULE: I think U need cheering up anyway. Let's celebrate UR b-day. Plz?

PRINCESSLEIA25: NO! No b-day plans! U promised!

WOOKIESRULE: I said I'd *think* about it. I've got 2 do something! Especially now. U need a party.

PRINCESSLEIA25: No parties!

WOOKIESRULE: How many people do U consider a party? :)

PRINCESSLEIA25: Noooooooooo parties!

WOOKIESRULE: Under 25 OK?

PRINCESSLEIA25: Aargh! If U want 2 do some-thing, make it small. U, me, and a slice of pizza, OK?

WOOKIESRULE: Hmm . . . good idea. Got 2 go. Mr. Hammond is staring. Hang in there. Chin up & remem-ber: don't let them decide UR next move w/o U!

Good point.

"I think that's a great plan, don't you, Kaitlin?" Mom is asking.

I slide my Sidekick off my lap into my purse. Nadine gives me a look. "Hmm?"

"Peter Jackhorn," Mom says in exasperation.

I'm confused. "Oh, he's great. *Ring Keeper* had a real *Star Wars* vibe to it with all the good versus evil mumbo jumbo. Why?"

"He's contemplating a new trilogy that will film in New Zealand," Laney says.

"He's shooting the films back-to-back so the whole thing will take roughly eighteen months," Nadine adds with a "they're nuts" look.

"EIGHTEEN MONTHS?" I shriek, startling our waiter as he brings me my lunch. I have a habit of doing that. No Austin for eighteen months? Eighteen months abroad? I want a change, but not one this big. "I think that's more time away than I can handle," I say.

Mom sighs and stares at the see-through view of Cut's kitchen. "Laney, what else do you have?"

Laney reads from her BlackBerry. "Seth says he has a new script with Clooney that will film in Romania. Sounds delish. And a musical with Angelina that shoots in L.A. next summer. He's also got a new script from Quentin that has hit written all over it. Pretty gory though. Do we want Kaitlin to do a horror film?"

"Hmm, I'm not sure," Dad says to Mom. "I think that

would be a step backward. Most girls do horror to get noticed and Kaitlin is already noticed."

"I don't want to do horror," I say, but no one listens.

"It could give her visibility in an area she's never been seen in before," Mom argues. "It could throw the public for a real loop and open a bunch of new doors."

"So would working with Neil LaBute, but I'm not sure we want her getting naked for her next role," Laney argues.

"A musical sounds like a good idea. Could we find something like *Hairspray*?" Matty asks. "They could cast me at the same time. I've heard Kaitlin sing in the shower. She's not that bad."

"She was pretty good that day at karaoke," Laney agrees. "I'm sure if we got her a voice coach and started working with her right away she would be ready if they ever decide to turn *Wicked* into a movie."

I can't say it's a bad idea, now that I'm over my fear of singing in public, but still. I feel my head begin to spin. This is déjà vu all over again. I feel faint. They're going too fast for me. *FA*'s demise was only announced minutes ago!

"*Wicked* is all about vocals," Nadine counters. "I don't know if Kaitlin could pull off Galinda. Maybe we should think of something else."

"I don't want to do a . . ." I start.

"Maybe you're right." Mom drowns me out. "What did you say Neil LaBute is doing next?"

I think I'm going to explode. They're going to pick my next move without asking me if I don't stop them. I need time to think. I want to tackle things one at a time, just like Austin said, so that I don't make any more mistakes.

"But the nudity!" Laney is saying.

I am so not doing a nude scene. "Guys?" I say.

Mom shrugs. "That never hurt Scarlett Johansson. If it's done tastefully, I wouldn't be opposed."

"Ewww," Matty says. "I don't want to see my sister naked!"

"Guys?" I try again.

"I'm not sure I would want to sit through that either." Dad frowns. "I think we should go back to discussing another TV show. Fine-tuning an engine never hurt anyone. Maybe all Kaitlin needs is a TV show with more grease. You know what I'm saying?"

"Doesn't anyone want to hear what I think?" I ask, but no one is listening.

"Let me say this again: *Joey!*" Nadine says.

"STOP!" I yell. Everyone freezes, including our waiter. Mom drops her fork, which makes a loud *clink!* as it hits her steak salad, which looks pretty yummy, by the way. Everyone stares at me in stunned silence.

"Kaitlin," Mom stutters. "What's wrong with you? You can't yell in Cut, for God's sake."

"I'm sorry, Mom, but I'm not having another conversation about my career unless *I'm* part of it," I say firmly. "This is *my* career we're talking about and no one has asked *me* what I want to do."

"What do you want to do?" Mom says in what I consider a mocking tone.

I pause. "Well, I'm not sure yet," I admit. Matty groans. "But I want a little time to figure it out without you guys coming up with a game plan first."

"How much time do you need? Would a week from Monday be enough time?" Laney asks, punching what I assume is her calendar up on her BlackBerry. Mom and Dad do the same and I see Matty whip out his Sidekick. Nadine shakes her head.

I pull out my Sidekick so that I look just as efficient. "No, I don't think that will be enough time," I say firmly. Laney looks at me in surprise. "I agree with you guys that the next decision I make is a big one, but I've been on *Family Affair* so long I don't even know what I'd like to do next. I need a few weeks to figure that out on my own. I have a problem with being too impulsive." I think of my stint at Clark High, my driving class debacle. "I don't want to rush into anything this time around. I want some time to really think about my options."

"But Katie-Kate, you spend every summer hiatus shooting something, whether it's a TV movie or a film. How can you not know what you like?" Mom asks.

"Usually you guys pick my summer movie by committee," I remind her. "I know I pushed for the Adams flick, but most of the time, you show me the roles you think I would like. I want a chance to make my own decision for a change." I look at Mom. "You can have Seth send me all the scripts you want." And I look at Dad. "And you can suggest TV shows." I look at Matt. "Ones that might be right for both of us." I glance at Laney. "And ones that have the most potential to give my career a grown-up makeover. But in the end, *I* want to make the decision and it has to be one I'm excited about." I look at Nadine, who is smiling. "I want to weigh all my options. Not just film or TV. I want to explore the same things other teens do." I pause. "Like going to college."

"Not the speech about college again, Kaitlin," Mom moans. She begins nervously pulling on her hair extensions. "I thought you were over the school thing! Look what happened when you went to Clark."

"That was a disaster," Matty seconds. "You're crazy to want to try that again. Why would you want to take time off when your career is hot?"

"Most stars' careers tank when they take time off for college," Laney reminds me for the umpteenth time.

"That's not true." Nadine defends me. "Natalie Portman has done quite well."

"Name five girls who have actually gotten their degree. They all seem to drop out. And if they don't, how many of them actually come back to the same career?" Laney challenges.

"I'm not saying I'm going," I interrupt. "I just said I need time to think. Anyway, this is my decision. I'm turning seventeen in a few weeks . . ."

"That's right!" Matt is excited. "Can I plan Kaitlin's party this year, Dad? The press would love me for being such a cool brother. You would foot the bill, of course."

"I'm not having a party," I say. "I'm not having any big parties, because I hate them. I hate a crowd of people I don't know."

"I always liked your parties." Dad looks disappointed. "They were great for networking."

"My point is, I'll be seventeen soon and eighteen in a year and then you won't be able to tell me what to do anyway." Mom and Laney gasp.

"That's nonsense," Mom scoffs. "You *always* listen to us."

"I just mean that when I'm eighteen, I'll be an adult and won't have to make all my choices by committee," I add, softening a bit after Mom practically chokes on a hunk of steak. "It's still my life and my career and I think the end of *Family Affair* is a great time for me to think about shaking things up. I like the idea of doing some festival flicks or doing a TV show with a character that is the complete opposite of Sam, but I also want to look into taking classes about art and history. I don't want to look back ten years from now and realize I missed out on something I really wanted to do."

Mom looks pale. I think my speech may have been too much for her.

"Would you consider cutting a CD? Mom and Laney said you sounded great that day they heard you. I could call Clive Davis right now and set up a meeting," Dad says. Mom looks at me hopefully.

"I wouldn't call him just yet," I say. "We still have months left on *FA* before I can do anything else." Thank God. I'm really not ready for the show to be over.

"Don't take too much time," Laney warns. "Pilot season is coming up and if you wait, all the good ones will be gone. If you have an inkling that you'd like to do another TV show, you should decide after the holidays. The town shuts down in December anyway so we can wait till early January."

"January sounds fair," I agree. "I want to look at the end of *FA* as a beginning and you guys can help me work out my options by giving me some space to figure out what that new beginning should be."

"I think that's a really mature decision, Kates," Nadine says. "And one that your work will benefit from."

My mom looks from my dad to Laney and then to Matty. She avoids Nadine's penetrating stare. "Okay," Mom says simply. "We'll give you till January."

"Thanks." I immediately feel relieved. I wave over our waiter. "Bring us over one of each of your desserts," I tell him. "We're celebrating."

"Are we still celebrating Alexis's departure?" Dad looks confused. "Or your slightly bossy independent streak?"

I grin. "Both. Just as soon as I get back from the loo."

"I'll join you," Nadine says.

I walk confidently through the crowded restaurant. Who knew it could feel this good to be assertive? Sure, Mom and Laney will probably forget my speech by the time they reach Mulholland Drive. I'll probably have to give it to them again and again, but eventually I'll drive the point home. Especially now that I know for certain what the point is.

"You were great," Nadine whispers as I push open the

bathroom door. "You should have seen your mom's face! I thought she was going to need a face-lift on the spot."

I laugh, but stop when I see who's standing at the bathroom mirror reapplying her Lip Venom. It's Alexis Holden. I should have known that chill wasn't from an overworked central air unit.

Even though it's only been a few weeks since I've seen Alexis, she already looks different. She's got a short bob and is wearing a sleek but conservative black pantsuit. She must be on a lunch meeting. Before I can decide whether to slip back out the door or march right past her, she sees me.

"Well, if it isn't America's sweetheart." Alexis's voice is like syrup. "Guess you're feeling pretty stupid about getting me canned now that your own show is going off the air. Who's the loser now?"

"It's still you," I counter. "You're out of our hair, which was the most important thing, and now our show can get back to being the class act it always was."

"You're an idiot," Alexis declares. A gray-haired older woman, who looks vaguely familiar, skips the hand washing and hurries out the door, leaving us alone.

"Kaitlin, let's go," Nadine says. "You don't need to listen to her garbage."

"No, I'm going to finish this," I say. "I'm the idiot?" I ask. "I'm not the one who hit on one of our writers and distributed a mock script. You screwed up. You cost yourself your job and probably your career. I had nothing to do with it."

"My career is hotter than ever," Alexis counters. "I'm actually here taking a meeting with Fox about a film, *Paris Is Burning.*"

"She's lying," Nadine tells me. "*Paris Is Burning* was shot last winter."

Alexis snickers. "They hated Ciara Covington's performance and are reshooting most of the movie, including all of Ciara's scenes. Fox thinks I have what it takes to make the film a shoo-in for the Oscars." Her eyes are blazing. "You see, Kaitlin? There are people in this town who love a bit of scandal and I'm going to ride that wave into the sunset while you and Sky watch your careers die this May. You actually did me a favor. You got me off that show before it completely fell apart. I hope you enjoy your fall." Alexis pushes past Nadine and me and I grab her forearm.

"Good luck out there, Alexis," I say simply.

Alexis rolls her eyes at me as she pulls open the door. I walk over to the mirror and splash some water on my face.

"Why did you let her talk to you like that?" Nadine asks.

"Karma." I grin.

I tell Nadine HOLLYWOOD SECRET NUMBER SEVENTEEN. Extensive reshoots can mean the kiss of death on a movie. While the studio responsible for the flick will probably say the film just needed a little adjusting, many reshoots stem from bad test screenings. If an audience hates the ending, then something better be done quick or it's straight to DVD for that release! To be fair, sometimes the studio requests reshoots, or a director decides he needs additional footage to ensure that his masterpiece in no way resembles another director's masterpiece. But changing the lead in a movie after the movie's already been shot? Yikes. Alexis is going to be back in Vancouver begging the Canadian Broadcasting Network for a bad movie of the week in no time. Getting a DVD of that to watch with a tub of gooey popcorn and Raisinettes will be my best revenge.

"Come on," I say to Nadine. "I think I hear a slice of walnut crumb cake calling our names."

SAT. 11/30
NOTE TO SELF:

Get party dress 4 my birthday date w/ A. U Never Know.

In The Know

The *Affair* is Over

by **AnnMarie Pallo**

The show that made careers for Melli Ralton, Kaitlin Burke, and Sky Mackenzie — and taught us the art of brawling in a pool wearing an evening gown — is going off the air this May.

Can we officially start crying yet?

After weeks of rumors, brawls among the teen cast, and countless In the Know polls, the network has announced that *Family Affair* will be a family no more. With ratings still in the top ten, and the top five this season alone, fans everywhere want to know why the show is ending its run. This reporter's guess? Fighting amongst the teen queens and newcomer Alexis Holden sent queen bee Ralton over the edge.

Not true, *FA* executive producer Tom Pullman told me. "Alexis was never a factor in ending the show," Pullman said. "After weeks of determination, we decided to take the Colby storyline in a new direction. By wrapping up the Colby storyline, it allows FA to concentrate on what it does best — focusing on family matters that involve the original cast. We want time to tie up loose ends before the series finale and releasing Alexis from her contract gives us more airtime to do that." Holden's final appearance on the show aired on December 2.

Hmm, my pretties. Does anyone actually believe this storyline hogwash? Not this In the Know crony. That's why we went to our sources to find out the real deal. Turns out her exit was anything but a story wrap. "Alexis has been a problem since day one," says this intimate connection to the *FA* cast. "She's never gotten along with any of them, especially Kaitlin and Sky." Even with the firing, the show's big gun, Ralton, couldn't be persuaded to stay with the *Family*. "Melli started thinking about how long she's been on the show and how many other things she wants to do," says our source. "She wants more time with her kids. She decided to leave the show and Tom took it as a sign to end *FA* altogether rather than go on without his biggest star."

So now we're all In the Know, m pretties. Make sure you tel everyone where you heard it first And get your tissues ready for the last-ever episodes of *Family Affair* Sob. ●

> "Alexis has been a problem since day one . . . She's never gotten along with any of them, especially Kaitlin and Sky."

eIGHTeeN: *Happy Birthday to Me*

When I open my front door, I'm so busy looking at Austin's gorgeous smile that I don't notice what he's waving in his left hand. It's a familiar-looking Pucci print scarf with pink and purple diamonds on it.

"Is that Liz's scarf?" I ask.

"No questions." Austin walks past me into the foyer and grazes my lips, making my spine tingle. Then he walks behind me and pulls Liz's scarf over my eyes. He ties it snugly.

"What are you doing?" The world goes semiblack. I say semi, because the Pucci scarf is pretty thin and I can see shadows. Austin must be trying to surprise me. That is so romantic! "Does my family know you're kidnapping me?" I ask. "I promised them I'd be home before midnight to share a piece of birthday cake."

"Shh," Austin says. "No peeking. Rodney, the birthday girl is ready." Heavy footsteps clomp down what I assume is our main staircase.

"Where are we going?" I ask even though I know Austin won't tell me. With my eyes covered, my other senses are heightened like a superhero's. I can hear every click of Austin's shoes as he walks around our marble tile entrance. I can pick up scents, like Rodney's Eternity cologne. Austin smells like a mix of the peppermint he was sucking on and the lavender hand soap the Meyerses have in their guest bathroom.

Do I remember what Austin's wearing? Yep. I really do have superpowers! He has on a blue silk button-down shirt and dark brown cords. I know because when I opened my front door, I purposely checked out his outfit to see if I was overdressed.

It's hard to dress for your birthday when you're not sure where you're going!

After much debating, I decided to go cocktail chic in a brown silk halter-style Valentino dress that skims my knees and is gathered at the waist with a matching wide brown belt. On my feet, I've got open-toed cheetah-print heels. The look should work anywhere but Carl's Jr.

I feel Austin place an arm behind my back and take my right hand. We begin to move. "Follow my lead," Austin says. We start walking. "Step down. Step down again." The front door closes behind us.

"Make sure she doesn't trip on the potted geraniums," Rodney says.

"I know you won't tell me where we're going, but can I ask you something else?" I question.

"Rodney, for someone who didn't want a birthday celebration of any kind, she's awfully inquisitive about our plans, isn't she?" Austin points out.

Rodney chuckles. "I'm not surprised. We're seeing a more assertive side of our Kates these days."

I take that as a compliment. "Just one question, Meyers," I beg. "We're obviously doing something cool if you're going through the trouble of blindfolding me."

Austin laughs. I hear a car alarm beep and a door open. We're driving somewhere! "Let me just get you into the car and then I'll answer your question." He helps me duck my head and I slide across the seat. I feel his breath on my shoulder as he reaches across me for something. I hear a clicking sound and realize that Austin's just buckled my seat belt. "Fire away," he says.

"I really appreciate this cloak-and-dagger thing you've got going on," I tell him, "but promise me, just promise me, you're not a pawn in my mother's or Laney's clutches." Austin laughs again. "Swear you're not in on some elaborate bash Mom and Laney cooked up at the eleventh hour to keep their minds off the fact that *FA* is ending and they want to keep me in the spotlight."

"I won't lie to you," Austin says as the car begins to move toward points unknown. "They begged me to help them throw a big party with a monstrous guest list that included everyone from Jennifer Aniston to Fergie, but I told them you were dead set against it."

I exhale. "Thank you."

"Does she know about the offer from *Hollywood Nation?*" Rodney chuckles.

"Your mom said the *Nation* called and asked to throw you a party," Austin explains. "They apparently felt bad about all the garbage they printed about you and Sky versus Alexis and wanted to throw you a party at Hyde sponsored by Juicy Fruit gum."

I groan.

"And Tom and Melli told Nadine they wanted to do something major for your birthday on set to make up for the rough time you've had, but we told them you banned organized birthday parties this year."

"You're the best," I say, beginning to relax. "I've never had a birthday where I didn't have to spend the whole evening greeting everyone from Prince William to Chris Brown." I smile. "It's nice to know we're spending the night alone."

"Who said alone?" Austin teases. At least I think he's teasing, but it's hard to tell when I can't see his face. "We may not be the only people where we're going, but I promise you're not having a Tom and Katie–type affair. No fireworks, no camera crews. Now stop worrying and just wait. We'll be there in a few minutes."

"The place must be close to the house," I say. "Hmm . . ."

"You're going to ruin the surprise," Austin scolds. "Just relax and talk about something else. How's work? You've been so busy these past few days I've barely spoken to you."

"Work is good," I admit. "Quiet but good. We're all a little melancholy, I guess. Every time we shot a scene this week someone would be, like, 'This could be the last time we film at the Summerville Diner.' But at least no one's crying yet, or fighting over who's going to get the brass candlesticks on the Buchanans' dining room table."

"Huh?" Austin and Rodney say in unison.

I explain HOLLYWOOD SECRET NUMBER EIGHTEEN. When a TV show goes off the air, most objects from the set get locked in storage until they're recycled by another show or, if the show was big (like *FA*), get donated to a Planet Hollywood or a museum. But before any of that happens, the cast and crew get to pick a few souvenirs. If the memento is more sentimental than valuable — like the portrait of my TV family that was painted in 1996 and hangs in the Buchanans' living room — then the network will probably let you have it for free. But if it's something expensive, like the Beamer Sara drives that Sky has been eyeing forever, then you have to cough up dough. Sky won't mind. When you think about it, a tile from the Summerville Diner, a vase from Paige's bedroom, or a portrait of Sara and Sam from season ten is just the TV show version of a graduating class's high school yearbook. Okay, I'm going to cry now.

"Do you think they'll let me take a souvenir too?" Rodney asks. He sounds choked up. I can tell with my new supersensitive hearing ability.

"I'm sure Tom will let you take something." I can't believe how many people are as sentimental about this as I am! Now I'm really going to cry.

"Both of you stop," Austin warns. "It's Kaitlin's birthday! Your only job tonight is to be happy."

"I know," I reply. "But my emotions are all out of whack. I'm happy, then I start thinking about the show and I get sad." My lip quivers and I blindly reach for Austin's hand. Instead, I smash my wrist on the seat console. Ouch!

Austin massages my aching fingers. "Everything's just changing," I say. "It's terrifying."

"Change is always scary," Austin agrees. "But exciting."

"Speaking of change, did you get your SAT results yet?" I ask.

"No." Austin sounds disappointed. He's been racing to his mailbox all week. "I'm sure I'll have them by next week though. Then I can really start thinking about colleges."

"Yeah," I say. I can't even begin to think about Austin leaving for college or where I'll be when he goes. Maybe we'll be in the same city and maybe we won't. I can't expect him to make his decision based on my plans, even if I secretly, selfishly wish he would. It's too overwhelming and upsetting to even begin to guess. Austin's right — I can't think about the future tonight. I'll start crying again and then my makeup will be ruined. We can do the big life changes conversation another time. Tonight is my birthday and even though I didn't initially want to celebrate, I'm getting really excited.

The car stops and Rodney shuts off the engine.

"We're here, kids," Rodney exclaims.

A lump forms in my throat, my palms begin to sweat, and my pulse speeds up. I wonder where Austin's taking me. It's like I'm stepping out at the Oscars and all eyes are on me, but I can't see them. The feeling is a bit overwhelming even with my new superpowers.

I feel Austin unbuckle my seat belt and I drink in the smell of his aftershave as he leans over me again. I giggle nervously, knowing he's close by, and feel my pulse quicken as he takes my hand and begins to lead me to points unknown. I'd trust Austin to take me anywhere, but I can't help being turned on by his take-charge approach.

Now the question is: Where are we? Okay, the air doesn't smell salty so we're not in Malibu having a candlelit dinner on the beach. (That's a fantasy date of mine.) It would have taken longer to get there too, not that I know how long we've been driving since I can't see my watch. I hear traffic so we must be somewhere in central Los Angeles. Hmm ... Austin's house? No, there wouldn't be so much street noise. Liz's? I would be able to hear music pumping from the curb. Carl's Jr.? I sniff the air. No fried meat aroma.

"Are you ready, Burke?" Austin asks and my pulse races again. I stop short.

"Why are you doing all this for me?" I ask.

"When you love someone, you want to do things for them," Austin says.

OH. MY. GOD.

He DID mean it! He said the L-word again and he actually said "When you love someone," which must mean me because I'm the only one here!

I think.

My mouth is dry. My hands are clammy. I want to say "I love you" back.

I think.

But I can't say it blindfolded, can I? That would be cheesy. Besides, I can't see Austin's face. Whenever anyone says "I love you" on *FA*, or in a Reese Witherspoon movie, they can always see each other's faces so that they can immediately have a passionate kiss. I won't even be able to find Austin's lips if I'm blindfolded!

I reach up to pull off my blindfold. "Austin, I . . ."

"Don't touch the blindfold, Burke," he says. "Give me one more second."

"But Austin, I have something to tell you." But Austin obviously doesn't hear me because I feel myself pushed from behind. I hear a heavy door open and then my blindfold is pulled off my face.

"HAPPY BIRTHDAY!" A chorus of familiar voices shouts as confetti is thrown at me like I'm a bride. I'm still in shock from Austin's very clear "love you" admission, but my eyes focus in time for me to see Liz throw herself at me. Squished behind her are Mom, Dad, Laney, Matty, Nadine, Rodney, Paul, Shelly, and Josh. While Nadine hugs me, I glance over her shoulder and spot Tom, Melli, Trevor, Hallie, and some of the other *FA* folks. Beth and Allison are next in line along with Austin's sister, Hayley. Everyone I care about, and just the people I care about, are here. It's overwhelming.

"Happy birthday, Kaitlin!" Antonio, A Slice of Heaven's owner, muscles his way through the crowd toward me. He's a large man with a thick Italian accent, and he smells like meatballs.

I should have known! I did tell Austin to take me for a slice of pizza. I look around and recognize the old booths with vinyl seats and checkerboard tablecloths, smell the mozzarella cheese in the air, and see the flashing "Your Slice of Italian Heaven Is Ready!" neon sign in the window. The tables in the middle of the small restaurant have been cleared to make a dance floor. In the corner, I notice my pal Samantha Ronson has set up a DJ booth and is spinning dance tunes. She blows me a kiss.

"You did all this?" I ask Austin.

"You said you didn't want a big party with tons of people you barely knew," Austin explains. "But you didn't say anything about celebrating with the people you love. Liz, Nadine, and I came up with this instead."

I don't care who's looking. I grab my boyfriend and kiss him firmly on the lips. "Thank you," I whisper. "I can't believe you did all this for me."

"It was nothing." Austin blushes.

"Well, it means a lot to me," I say and then I know what I have to say next. I feel my brain willing me to say it. I feel flush with happy thoughts. I feel super emotional. This must be what it's like when you want to say what I'm about to say. I don't even feel nervous anymore. I take a deep breath and the three little words I've never said to a boy before come flying out. "I love you, Austin," I say.

"I . . ." Austin starts to say something back.

"Hey, so no one else is coming?" Matty interrupts.

NOOOOOOOOOOO!

"I'll let you two talk." Austin winks at me. "I'll be back."

NOOOOOOOOOOO!

"Where's Vanessa Hudgens, Miley Cyrus, and Ashley Tisdale?" Matty asks. "Where's Zac Efron? No one's here."

"Sorry," I say, trying not to sound irritated as Austin disappears into the crowd. "I don't think they were invited." I like the people Matty mentioned a ton, but I'm glad my birthday isn't a media circus this year.

"I was going to say, I'm glad they're not here." Matt takes a bite of gooey pizza and I notice he's eating my favorite kind — Sicilian with extra cheese, peppers, and broccoli. "Tonight should be all about you. You deserve it, even if Mom is freaking out that Nadine lied to her about where she was taking us." Matty chuckles. "We told her A Slice of Heaven was this hot new club run by Justin Timberlake."

We both laugh. Mom, Dad, Nadine, and Laney surround us.

"Happy birthday, sweetie," Mom says. I notice she's wiping her soda glass with a napkin. "This is an interesting place Nadine, Liz, and Austin picked."

"It's Kaitlin's favorite hangout," Nadine says with a sly smile.

Mom looks around. "It's so . . . so . . . what's the word I'm looking for, Laney?" Mom asks.

"Pedestrian?" Laney says with a frown.

"We were just thinking, Kate-Kate," Mom says. "Maybe next week Laney and I can throw you a party too, since you've had your little fun with this one. Nothing major. Just seventy-five of your closest friends."

"Maybe at that *real* club that just opened in West Hollywood," Laney says with an annoyed glance at Matt. She pulls out her BlackBerry.

"And no paparazzi. Just an exclusive with one or two key magazines," Mom suggests.

"Ladies." Dad's voice has a warning tone I recognize from my days of playing basketball in the living room with Matty. "This is Katie-Kate's party and this is what she wanted. Let her be. You don't get every sale, you know." He winks at me. I throw my arms around him and give him a bear hug.

Nadine moves next to me. "Austin is amazing," Nadine whispers. "You should have seen him hold his own with your mom. He wasn't intimidated by her or her Rolodex! He wanted to have your party here and he stuck to it. With Liz's and my help, of course."

"Thanks," I tell her as Mom and Dad start to bicker over Dad siding with me instead of her. Laney is shaking her head and Matty has already walked off. "This is the best thing you guys could have ever done for me, and wait till I tell you what just happened."

"I bet I know," Nadine says with a smile. "But we won't talk about it here. Tonight is about celebrating. There's only one thing I would have done differently," she says. "I don't know why Austin insisted on inviting her." Nadine points to the *FA* table where I see the gang is chomping down on Antonio's specialty, fried capellini. He takes capellini and ricotta and fries it like a mozzarella stick. It's so yummy.

"Who?" I ask, not seeing anyone I don't like.

"She means me," someone says. Nadine and I turn around and practically knock over Sky, who is standing behind us holding a beautifully wrapped small silver present.

"I can't stay," she says stiffly. She looks ready for a rave in a short blue mini I recognize from J'Aime's spring line, and black fishnet stockings. Her usually long raven hair is styled in a bob, which I assume means she's wearing a wig. Sky would never cut her hair or shave her head like some people we know. "But I didn't want to be rude and not at least make an appearance."

"I think I'll go get a drink," Nadine says, leaving me alone with Sky.

"Thanks for coming." I feel awkward.

After a few weeks of being joined at the hip to save *Family Affair* from Alexis's evil clutches, Sky and I are back to being, well, ourselves. A new and improved version of ourselves, I should say. Now instead of fighting or shooting daggers, we just quietly do our work, exchange small pleasantries on set, and when cameras aren't rolling we basically ignore each other. I guess we'll never have enough in common to be close friends, but now that we know so much about each other, we can't really be enemies either. We're frenemies, as Nadine calls it, and that's okay.

"This is for you," Sky says. "You don't have to open it. It's just a spa certificate to Sonya Dakar. You look like you could use a facial."

"Thanks," I say, ignoring the dig.

"I have another party to get to," Sky says, "and I have to be up early tomorrow for a meeting with Paramount."

"Good luck," I tell her. "They asked me to come in next week." I know I said I wouldn't make any decisions about work yet, but how could I say no to Paramount?

I see a flash of annoyance flicker on Sky's face and I realize I just put my foot in my mouth. "I'm sure they have a project for you to consider," Sky says, "but they've already chosen several for me. No one's talked to you about that remake of *Blue Lagoon*, have they?" Sky asks suspiciously.

"No, but I'll make sure no one does," I say with a smile.

Sky actually smiles too and without another word, disappears into the sea of dancers squashed onto Antonio's tiny dance floor.

Sky's going to be okay in Hollywood.

And so am I.

I'm a year older, and hopefully a year wiser, and I can't wait to see what happens to my life next.

"This next request goes out to our birthday girl from her number one guy," I hear our DJ, Samantha, say. Stevie Wonder's "Isn't She Lovely" begins to play and I grin. My dad grabs my mom and spins her out onto the floor while Matty takes Laney's arm. Even Nadine pulls Rodney out there. I laugh, watching them all.

"Birthday girl, can I have this dance?" Austin appears at my side and holds out his hand.

"With pleasure," I say.

Then I take his hand and join the party with my favorite people in the world.

HOLLYWOOD SECRET NUMBER NINETEEN: Never ever take anything for granted in this town. Just when you think you have your career figured out, your entourage well in place and a handle on the fame game, that's when it all gets ripped out from under you. Guess that means my life is in for a major shake-up. Stay tuned . . .

SECRETS OF MY HOLLYWOOD LIFE: PAPARAZZI PRINCESS

coming in March 2009

Acknowledgments:

And the Oscars go to . . .

Cindy Eagan and Kate Sullivan, my uber-talented editors. Thank you for loving Kaitlin's zany world as much as I do. Laura Dail, for being the best agent a writer could have. Elizabeth Eulberg, I will miss you, but remember you promised to still hit Tortilla Flats with us! Ames O'Neil, the best travel partner there is. Tracy Shaw for her brilliant covers. Andrew Smith, Lisa Laginestra, Melanie Sanders, and the rest of the Little, Brown Books for Young Readers gang for pushing *Secrets* to even brighter heights.

Mara Reinstein, you're still my go-to girl for all matters Hollywood.

Lisa, AnnMarie, Joanie, Christi, Elena, Joyce, Miana, Erin, and the rest of my wonderful friends — thanks for supporting me and lending a hand with Ty when I need it.

Grandpa Nick Calonita, for giving me a strong last name.

My parents, Nick and Lynn Calonita, my mother-in-law, Gail Smith, my sister and brothers-in-law, Nicole and John Neary, and Brian Smith — thanks for being my cheering section.

And last, but certainly first on my acceptance speech list: my family. Tyler, for being an awesome little guy, Jack, for his continued lap warming, and my husband, Mike, for being my leading man and number-one fan.

Want a chance to get the *real* Hollywood star treatment?

go to
www.pickapoppy.com
for details.